T0123356

WHEN TWO WORLDS COLLIDE

A Love Story That Transcends
Space and Time

From Best Selling Author
CAESAR RONDINA

authorHOUSE®

AuthorHouse™
1663 Liberty Drive
Bloomington, IN 47403
www.authorhouse.com
Phone: 1 (800) 839-8640

Published by AuthorHouse 05/31/2019

ISBN: 978-1-5462-7163-5 (sc)
ISBN: 978-1-5462-7161-1 (hc)
ISBN: 978-1-5462-7162-8 (e)

Library of Congress Control Number: 2018914420

Print information available on the last page.

*All names and events in this book are fictional
and do not relate to any people or events.*

ALSO BY CAESAR RONDINA

Life Through A Mirror-When Murder Calls (Book 3 - trilogy)

Life Through A Mirror-The Battle Rages On (Book 2 - trilogy)

A Woman's Fear

The Warrior Within

Life Through A Mirror (Book 1 trilogy)

Making Partnership Choices

Balancing The Scale

Who Are The Heroes

The Soul In Our Hearts

Best-Selling Author of

Management and Employee Relations

(available as a tutorial on udemy.com)

Leadership Skills for Success

www.caesarrondinaauthor.com Twitter - @
caesarrondina Facebook - Caesar Rondina Author

TABLE OF CONTENTS

DEDICATION

This book is dedicated to every individual that has a love story. A story of how their love together began and grew. How they overcame obstacles that every love story has. Yours may be similar to the ones you will read about, or different. That doesn't matter because you are special.

PREFACE

Can love to transcend space and time? What is space, time, distance, and energy? Time is the measured or measurable period during which an action, process, or condition exists or continues. It is a duration. A nonspatial continuum that is measured in terms of events, which succeed one another from the past, present, and future. Space is an area of dimension. A measurement in height, width, and depth to which all things occupy. Distance is the measurement of one fixed point to another fixed point. Energy, on the other hand, has varying degrees of meaning depending on what you believe.

In theory, it is the strength and vitality required for the sustained physical or mental activity or the power derived from the utilization of physical or chemical resources. The interesting and questionable part is, many believe energy never dies. It lives on. Since our bodies are made of electrical impulses, otherwise known as energy, many believe when the body dies, it's energy lives on. Some refer to this as their soul or spirit. A concept from which many believe there is life after death. What do you believe? Energy can break the boundaries of time, distance, and space. The real question is, while we are alive, can love, which is an emotional response derived from chemical changes due to hormones which in turn is energy, transcend time, distance and space?

This is not a book about science. This book is about an emotion we call love. A love story. One in the truest sense. A love story of two people that will find out if their love can transcend those obstacles. A love story about Anthony and Jill. Two different people from two different worlds. They will face many obstacles. Is their love that strong? Can and will it survive? It will be put to the test. Through happiness and sadness, two young lovers face it all. At times, a happy story. At other times, one that can only be described as a heartbreaking tale of love as you've never read before.

As you follow this love story, see if Anthony and Jill experienced anything similar to your own love story. Then ask yourself. If you were Anthony and Jill, would you have survived? Love is a mixture of many things. Many of which I have discussed in detail in my book *"Making Partnership Choices."* Love is more than just an emotion. It's a concept. You either believe in the concept, or you don't. You're all in, or you're not. There is no half-way. Let's see how Anthony and Jill's love story develops. A love story that will undoubtedly touch your heart.

CHAPTER ONE

HOW IT BEGAN

TONY

Anthony came from New Jersey. Everyone called him Tony. He was Italian by descent and had two brothers and two sisters. They grew up in a three-family house. His grandparents lived on the first floor. His family lived on the second floor, and they rented the third floor. His mom, Carmela, and dad, Vincent, had their bedroom. All the boys shared another bedroom, and his sisters shared another. When they were young, this arrangement was fine. As they got older, privacy became important. Eventually, the girls moved downstairs with their grandparents. Tony was the oldest. His family did not come from the rich side of town. They came from "the other side of the tracks." Tony's father was a hard worker, he worked overtime almost every week. He did not want his wife to work. Tony's father worked in a union shop and made good money. They made ends meet. Tony's father walked to and from work each day regardless of the weather. Taking time off from work was not an option. Even when he was ill, he went to work.

There were no fancy vacations each year. When it was hot, the kids sprayed themselves with a garden hose to cool off. Tony started working at the local grocery store delivering groceries at a young age. He was the eldest son and needed to help his family. As they all got older, one of his brothers got involved with the wrong crowd and started using drugs. Those were very difficult times for Tony's family. They needed his help. Tony's mother was a strict Italian woman. She taught Tony self-respect and how important it was to respect others. Their father didn't buy their first car until Tony was thirteen years old. It was used but in good shape. He bought what they could afford. In the old neighborhood, the fish man came by once a week. People could buy fresh fish right off the truck. Groceries were delivered by the local market, and the milkman delivered milk daily. Garbage was kept in a container dug into the ground. Each week the garbage collector would pull the container from the ground, carry it over his shoulder to the garbage truck, empty it, and return it to the back to the yard. Not a glorious job. Many did not want to do it.

Tony did exceptionally well in high school. He graduated first in his class. There was no money for college. Tony received a small scholarship, and the remainder was financed through student loans. He was attending college for Architectural Engineering. He was in his junior year of college and made the dean's list every semester since he was a freshman. Tony was not a flashy dresser. There was no money for that. Tony didn't date much in high school. He was always working and studying. He was considered a "nerd," or a "geek." Mostly because his classmates never took the time to get to know him. He was an average looking man. Reserved and shy. Once someone got to know Tony, it was clear that he had a great personality as was not as he appeared. Looks can be deceiving. Tony's had very little self-confidence. He could approach a girl, but when it came to asking her out, he simply froze and walked away. If he met them prior, and the ice was broken, it was no longer a problem. Tony feared rejection, and never learned how to approach a girl. He was halfway through his junior year at college. He noticed Jill at the end of his freshman year. He was spellbound. When he started his sophomore year, he roamed the campus looking to see if she had returned. They were in different academic programs and were the same age and graduating class. Because they had different majors, they never shared any classes together. He never had the opportunity to casually meet her. The first time he noticed Jill she was in the library, and then again in the student center. His heart pounded every time he saw her. He could not get the courage to approach her. A sad situation since this had now been going on for almost two years. Tony would go out of his way to find out what classes she was taking and always tried to be where Jill was with the hopes of gaining the courage to approach her. Sadly, he could only admire her from a distance.

JILL

Jill was a Physiology major. Her background was completely different. She came from California. Her father, Frank, was a prominent attorney. She came from money. She lived in a beautifully landscaped home. Jill had a twin sister Callie. They each had their own bedroom that had a bathroom. There was a large built-in swimming pool in the yard. Her parents entertained and hosted many parties at their home. They were members of the golf club, lake Club, and other social organizations. Jill was raised learning respect. Unlike her sister Callie, she never acted like a rich snob or a spoiled brat. Many of her friends displayed those traits, but not Jill. She was a down-to-earth good-hearted person. Regular vacations and all the other amenities were their way of life. Jill was an excellent student and always worn nice clothes.

Tony was intimidated by Jill because he could tell they came from two different backgrounds. Jill was a member of a sorority and served on many student committees. Jill's twin sister was attending a different university to study law. Their educations were completely paid for. Jill was outgoing and social. Tony always wondered why he never saw her with boys on a date. What Tony did not know was Jill did not trust men any longer. In high school, Jill dated a young man whom she met the summer before their freshman year of high school. They spend much of their time together. Jill was madly in love with him. His name was Carl. He also came from a wealthy family. Jill's parents liked him. Jill's mother, Julia, told her many times not to get serious. When they both left for college, they would be meeting other people, and they should have that opportunity. Jill would have no part of it. She and Carl claimed their love for one another. For Jill, that was all she needed.

Carl was studying literature at a different university. They wanted to attend the same college, but the programs they were majoring in were not offered at the same universities. They agreed they would be fine. They would talk every day, spend the holiday and school breaks together, and have the entire summer as well. Their plan seemed perfect. Carl was also very social. He was the captain of the football team at their high school, and Jill was a cheerleader. About three months after the start their freshman year of college, Jill noticed she didn't hear from Carl as much. Her attempts at calling him mostly went to his voicemail. On numerous occasions, he did not return her calls. When they spoke, he used the same excuse.

"I'm sorry. These classes are much harder than I expected."

At the beginning of the school year, they exchanged schedule's so they would know one another's availability. Shortly after, Carl told Jill he had moved some classes around, but would always change the subject when she asked for his new schedule. Jill had asthma as a child. For the most part, she grew out of it. Occasionally it would act up if she got very upset, or was under a great deal of stress. As a child, she was always catching a cold or sinus infection. Nothing serious. When Christmas break came, they would both be home. Jill thought they would work out the kinks at that time. You could be miles away from someone and sense when something is wrong.

When they returned for holiday break, Jill asked Carl what is going on. They rarely spoke anymore, and he rarely returned her calls.

Carl told her he was just very busy with all his classes.

Jill said, "Don't bullshit me, Carl, we've been together for almost five years. I know you. Studying has never been a problem for you. Let's start over again, and this time, tell me the truth."

Carl was reluctant to respond. He knew it was not right to deceive her. Jill didn't deserve that.

Carl said, "I met someone. I should have told you sooner, but I couldn't bring myself to tell you while we were apart. I am sorry that I hurt you."

At first, Jill was angry. It did not take long for her anger to turn into feelings of devastation, deception, and feeling used. She wanted no part of Carl and asked him to leave the house.

She ran to her room crying. Her mother, not trying to listen, couldn't help but overhear their conversation. She went up to Jill's room to speak to her. Jill was a mess. She was crying hysterically. This brought about an asthma attack. Her inhaler was not helping. Her father called 911, and Jill was taken to the emergency room by ambulance. They prescribed something mild to calm her down after they got her asthma attack under control. She wasn't admitted and was released when she was stable. They gave her a prescription to take to help keep her calm which her parents filled at the hospital pharmacy before they left. It kept her calm. However, it didn't help the hurt she was feeling. Her holiday was ruined. From that day on, Jill decided that love and men were not worth the pain and suffering. She wanted to drop out of school. Her twin sister was the one who convinced her to go back. They were home for just under a month. That was enough time for Jill to accept what had happened, but she was not over it. Almost two years later, she still carried that hurt with her. Tony could have been the best-looking man on campus, the nicest dresser with the fanciest car, and Jill would not have noticed him. Her focus was solely on her studies and activities.

The Story Begins

Each time Tony came home from a school break, he would talk with his brothers about his inability to approach Jill. He also talked with his parents about it. No matter how hard they tried, even when they believed he was ready to approach her, he always got cold feet. He was not aware of her past relationship history with Carl.

It was a little before mid-year into their Junior year. Tony was starting to panic. It would not be long until the school year would be over. He would not see Jill all summer. His mind started wandering. He asked himself many questions. What if she transfers to another school? He would never see her again. This was Tony's nature. This was who he was. Something would have to happen to break the ice between them. Tony was working part-time while he was in school and also doing tutoring for other students. Every penny he made he saved. At the rate he was going, he would have saved a good sum of money before the end of his junior year. This was an ideal situation for a twenty-year-old junior in college. However, he was lonely. He had a few friends, and some had girlfriends. His roommate Rob was his closest friend. They were roommates since freshman year. Rob was a playboy. Many nights Rob would want to use their dorm room for a while when a girl came over. Tony would go to the library or the student center and sit by himself. The student center had a pool table. Being in school for Architectural Engineering, he was great at numbers and angles. He was an excellent pool player. Most of the committees that Jill was a member of met in the student center. There was a meeting room in the center for students to use. It also had a small cafeteria and vending machines. Students could buy coffee, soda, or some snacks.

Tony was not a stalker. He was infatuated by Jill. He wasn't the type of guy who could easily go up to a girl he didn't know, introduce himself, and start a conversation. That was his curse. Tony was not the most experienced man. Tony had kissed girls before but had only slept with one girl. That was only one time. His lack of experience did not make it an enjoyable experience for either of them. It ended quickly. He was also insecure in that area as well. He felt all these things were stacked up against him. Most of them were in his own mind, which is where insecurity usually originates. He kept thinking; in *two and a half years, he couldn't get the courage to even say hi.* He was a wreck and running out of time. Whenever he was around Jill, he kept his distance. Appearing as if he was doing something else, but his eyes were mostly on her. Tony was his own worst enemy. Many times he thought to himself, *what would a girl like Jill see in me?* Tony had no confidence. Something would have to happen that would cause this to change, if only for an instant. Tony was not aware of Jill's Asthma condition since it rarely flared up. She knew exactly what she needed to do to avoid an episode. Jill was never alone. She was always with four or five other girls. How could he approach her without looking like a complete fool?

It was a cloudy day, humid and drizzling. Jill was walking from one class to another. Tony was quite a few steps back. This was a free period for him, so he was in no rush. Jill's phone rang. She answered it without looking at the caller ID. After two years, it was Carl. She stopped and sat on a bench. Tony stood behind a tree but was close enough to her part of the conversation. He would have to fill in the blanks.

Jill said in quite the angry tone, "What do you want?" She got up and started walking again and hung up the phone. A minute later, it rang again. She didn't answer. This happened two or three times. She stopped and sat on another bench. Tony was looking for a place to hide. There was no tree to duck behind. He could see she was anxious and upset. He took his phone out and pretended he was on a call as he stood by a trash container looking through papers as if he was trying to figure out what to keep, and what to discard. Her phone rang again. This time Jill answered it.

Jill said, "If you keep calling …. (she paused) …. I'll block your number. What you did to me after five years of being together was terrible. Now, after two years of not talking to me, you call? Give me one reason why I should talk to you?"

Tony noticed she was leaning over as she pushed her light brown hair back while she was listening.

Jill responded, "What happened, did your new girl dump you, and now you think you can come back to me as your backup? That will not happen." She kept listening then responded, "It took me months to get over us. I almost dropped out of school. If it weren't for my sister, I wouldn't be here today. You would have ruined my life if not for her. Just leave me alone. I have no feelings for you. I hate you."

Tony could see how upset Jill was getting as she started to cry. Jill and Carl started to argue. He could tell by what Jill was saying that Carl thought he was God's gift to women and appeared as if he wasn't taking no for an answer.

Hysterically crying and speaking in broken sentences, Jill said, "I'm hanging up and blocking your number. If you keep trying to call, I will tell my father."

Tony felt funny listening, but his curiosity got the better of him. After Jill hung up, he wanted to walk over to her. Tony was raised to care about people and wanted to help. He couldn't bring himself to move; thinking that *maybe this wasn't the right time.* Tony always made an excuse not to approach Jill. Would this time be different? He noticed Jill was breathing heavily and fumbling around in her pocketbook as if she were looking for something. Her phone was right there by her side. He thought; what could she be looking for? He watched her try to reach for her phone, which had fallen on the ground behind the bench. By this time, Jill did not look good and was gasping for air. Tony took an EMT class over the summer before he started college. He recognized these signs. Jill was having an asthma attack. He had to do something, and no one else was around. He ran over to her and offered to help. In between breaths, she kept repeating, "Inhaler, Inhaler."

Tony quickly looked through her pocketbook and told her it wasn't there. Jill kept saying, "Dorm, Dorm." Tony knew he did not have time to get to her dorm, get the room opened, and get back with her inhaler. He knew he had to calm her down and get help. Using his phone, he dialed 911. He held one of Jill's hand while rubbing her back with his other hand. He talked to her to help her control her breathing and calm her down until help arrived. Within minutes, an EMT and the school nurse arrived in a golf cart. The EMT administered oxygen to Jill while the nurse prepared a breathing treatment to help control her attack.

The combination of Tony calming her and the medication, Jill's Asthma attack passed. She left her inhaler in her dorm room. She rarely if ever had an attack. Her conversation with Carl was so upsetting, it brought one on. Soon after, the ambulance arrived. Jill did not want to go to the hospital. The nurse insisted. It was school policy.

As they put Jill in the ambulance, Tony said to the attendant, "I'm an EMT, may I ride in the back with her?"

The paramedic allowed him in the back thinking he could help to keep Jill calm. Jill and Tony did not speak in the ambulance.

The paramedic was busy taking care of Jill. Her lings were not completely clear, so he administered another breathing treatment. These treatments were geared to reduce inflammation and open up the airway so more air could flow into her lungs. When they arrived at the emergency room, Tony sat in the waiting room while they moved Jill into the patent care area. Meanwhile, in Jill's room, they took a chest x-ray and gave her some additional medication through her IV to reduce the risk of another asthma attack, and reduce the inflammation appeared on her x-ray.

The nurse said to Jill, "You can have a visitor now, do you want your friend to come and sit with you?"

Jill replied, "What friend? No one knows I'm here."

The nurse replied, "Oh yes, there is a nice young man who has been patiently waiting in the waiting area."

Jill, thinking that it might be someone who heard about her attack replied, "Yes. Please ask him to come in." She had no idea who this could be. Maybe it was a school administrator.

The nurse went out to Tony and informed him he could go in to see Jill now. Tony replied, "No, that's okay. I just didn't want to leave before I knew she was alright."

The nurse replied, "Don't be silly. You have been sitting here for almost two hours, and you won't go in? Come with me. She can use the company. She's fine."

Tony had no choice. He had to go with the nurse. What would he say? What would he do? His heart felt like it was pounding out of his chest.

When he walked through the curtain, Jill asked politely, "Who are you?" Tony introduced himself and explained who he was.

Jill asked, "What happened, I don't remember you?"

Caesar Rondina

Tony replied, "Do you really want to know? You probably have stress-induced asthma. We don't need to talk about it now. I noticed you needed help, and stopped to help you."

Jill asked, "How do you know that?"

Tony replied, "I took an EMT course the summer before I started college."

Jill said, "Yes, I remember now. I've seen you around campus. I remember you holding my hand and rubbing my back. You saved my life and calmed me down. I remember you talking to me. Thank you so much."

Tony laughed and said, "Well I wouldn't call it saving your life, but yes, I did help you."

Jill said, "OH MY GOD!" You were so sweet." Tony just blushed as Jill said, "Look at me, I'm a mess."

Tony looked at her and said, "No you're not. You look beautiful." All it took was for someone to get Tony to talk. Once he started, his personality did the rest.

Jill asked, "Why did you ride in the ambulance? The nurse told me you've had been sitting in the waiting room for over two hours. I don't even know you?"

Tony replied, "I wanted to be sure you were alright and help you get back to your dorm. I didn't want you to feel you were alone. They called security and told them they could pick you up because they were releasing you."

The nurse came in and handed Jill the phone. It was her mother. Jill took the phone. Her mother asked her what happened. Jill started to tell her the story. Carl called, and they fought. As she was getting telling her story, Tony got up and whispered, "I'll wait outside."

Jill nodded her head no and pointed to Tony to sit down. He sat and listened as Jill explained everything to her mother. He felt a bit embarrassed since he already knew most of the story. He never led that he knew. Jill spoke to her mother for about twenty minutes. Jill's mother told her she was going to have her father call Carl. He wouldn't bother her again. Her mother vividly remembered how Carl spoiled the holiday for Jill and how hurt she was. When Jill hung up, the nurse came in with two trays that had dinner on them.

She explained, "Security called and had an issue on campus. They will be here in about an hour. I thought you both might be hungry." She looked at Jill and said, "You have one heck of a friend there. Is he your boyfriend?"

Jill replied, "No. We just met today, but there are always possibilities." The nurse left.

Jill laughed and said, "I'm sorry. I'm so bad. I hope I didn't embarrass you. You probably have a girlfriend who is wondering where you are."

Tony said, "You didn't embarrass me. I don't have a girlfriend wondering where I am. However, there are possibilities."

They both laughed and ate. As they were talking, the time passed quickly. Security arrived and drove them both back to campus. When they dropped Jill off at her dorm, Tony also got out. The security guard asked, "Don't you want a ride?"

Tony replied, "No thank you. I will walk. Thank you for picking us up." The guard drove off.

Jill said, "Thank you so much for everything. I would ask you in, but honestly, I'm tired and want to take a nap." She pulled out some papers from her pocketbook and gave Tony her number. He also gave her his. Jill said, "Please, call me."

Tony replied, "I will. If you ever need to talk, you can always call me."

He asked what her class schedule was so he wouldn't disturb her during a class. This blew Jill away and caught her by surprise. She thought, "Who was this great caring guy and why didn't they ever meet?"

They exchanged email addresses and said they would exchange schedules. Jill gave him a hug and thanked him again. As they both started to walk away, Jill stopped and turned. Tony was still walking. She yelled out, "Did you think you were going to get off that easy?" If you're not busy tonight, let me take a nap. When I get up, I'll call you. Maybe we can meet in the student center and talk more."

Tony replied, "I'm not busy, but you don't owe me anything. I was only trying to help."

Jill said, "I know, maybe I just want to. Did you ever think of that?"

Tony replied, "Okay, under one condition."

Jill said, "Name it."

Tony replied, "Call me when you get up. I'll walk over and meet you here. We can walk over together."

Jill replied, "Deal."

Jill was feeling those butterflies in her stomach. Was it gratitude, or did she like Tony? Either way, she hadn't felt that way in two years and wasn't going to try to figure out why. She would just go with the flow.

While Tony was walking back, he was excited. He called his brother to tell him what had happened. This particular brother was a lady's man. He inherited the family charm. He was happy for Tony and said, "I'm not going to tell you what to do. You are doing fine on your own. Let me know how it goes."

Tony was on cloud nine all the way back to his dorm. What would he wear? What would they talk about? Then it hit him. Was this out of gratitude, obligation, appreciation, or was it genuine? If Jill liked him, it had to be because of him. Not what he was wearing or what he did for her. He decided to be himself. If that wasn't good enough, then so be it. Regardless of the reason, relationships started for a variety of reasons. He would go with it and be cautious. He couldn't remember the last time he felt this happy. When he returned to his dorm, he took a shower and got dressed. He turned on the TV and waited or Jill to call.

CHAPTER TWO

TRUTH IS LIKE GOLD

Over two hours had passed, and it was almost eight o'clock. Tony thought Jill probably changed her mind. He wasn't going to call her. If she was still sleeping, he did not want to disturb her. If she had a change of heart, he didn't want her to feel uncomfortable. Many possible scenarios went through his mind. He thought of them over and over in his mind, until he decided to get undressed. As he was unbuttoning his shirt, his cell phone rang. It was Jill.

She said, "OH MY GOD TONY, I'm so sorry.
I didn't expect to sleep this long."

Tony replied, "That's alright. You had a rough day. We can get together at another time if you still want to."

Jill answered, "Want to? Of course, I want to. Do you think I give my number to anyone I meet for the first time?"

Tony replied, "This is a little different, don't you think? Maybe you felt like you should. It's not impossible you know."

Jill answered, "One thing you need to know about me. I don't do what I think I should do. I do what I want to do."

Tony replied, "Fair enough."

Jill asked, "I'm wide awake, but you might be tired. Do you still want to go to the student center? It is open until midnight."

Tony replied, "I'm fine. I would like that. I'll walk over to your dorm, and we can walk over together."

Jill replied, "That's so considerate of you. I'll meet you outside in fifteen minutes."

Tony said, "See you then."

Short of running, Tony couldn't walk fast enough. Jill's dorm room window had a view of the front of her building. When she saw Tony approaching, she came out. He thought she looked beautiful. She was 5'7" and was slender. You could see she was athletic. Jill had brown eyes with long wavy light brown hair, almost a dark blonde. She had a fair complexion and did not require much makeup. Actually, she wore very little. Tony stood six-foot tall. He was also slender, but not muscular. He also had brown eyes with light brown hair. He had average looks. Not the type that would make twenty women's head turn when he walked across a room. He had an Italian olive complexion. You know the type, the one that never needs to wear tanning lotion to tan. He was a casual dresser, nothing flashy or outstanding. Certainly not the type that Jill had in Carl. Tony and Carl were the complete opposite. They walked slowly to the student center. It wasn't a long walk.

On the way, Jill asked, "Aren't you going to ask me what today was all about?"

Tony replied, "No. I think if you want to tell me you will. I don't want to see you get upset again."

Jill said, "I wasn't upset. I was angry. I was crying because I couldn't believe how stupid I was."

Tony said, "If you want to tell me, I'll listen."

It was like the dam broke, and the flood waters came rushing in. Jill told him everything. All about her five years with Carl. How much she loved him, as well as their plans. She also told Tony about the events that led to their breakup. She didn't leave anything out. Tony didn't say a word. He just listened. Jill told him she didn't want anything to do with men. She was not dating anymore. She would never want to experience that kind of hurt again. Tony laughed. She asked him what was so funny. Tony said, "Well, I hope you know I'm a man and not a girl."

Jill gave him a shove and laughed. "I can tell the difference silly. Why, is this a date?" Tony just smiled. Once Tony started talking, and the ice was broken, he was fine. He had a fantastic personality. He had to ask, "Jill, if you want nothing to do with men and dating, what the hell are we doing here?"

Jill replied, "I don't know. I know you seem different than other guys who have tried to ask me out. Maybe it's time."

Tony said, "Don't take this the wrong way, but I don't want to be someone's experiment; just so they can move on."

Jill responded. "Is that what you think?"

Tony replied, "Hey, don't shoot the messenger. You're the one who said you wanted nothing to do with men."

Jill laughed, "You're right. Forget I said it. Sometimes...she paused, something happens that makes a person look at things differently."

Tony replied, "Yes, you're right."

Jill told Tony she liked talking to him. He was honest and sincere. She could sense that. They arrived in the student center, got some nachos and bottled water. They found some empty seats on a three seater couch and sat down.

She added, "Anyone could have called 911 for me, but how many people would have come to the hospital with me and stayed until I was released? So tell me, what was up with that?"

"Since you were so honest, I guess I could be as well. Understand, I'm not some crazy lunatic who follows someone around."

Jill replied, "I know that."

Tony explained, "I first saw you in my sophomore year. I'm shy. I always have been. I was never the type to approach girls. I didn't date much in high school. Once I meet them, I'm fine. I have been told I have a great personality. When I dated, it was a result of someone introducing us. It made it easier. I think I became this way because being the oldest, I worked because my family needed the income, and studied. I didn't have much time for dances and socializing. I guess I never learned how. Anyway, when I saw you, I thought you were beautiful. You seemed like you had a great personality, but I always wondered why I never saw you with any guys out on dates. I understand now. It wasn't hard to find out your class schedule, so I planned on being around when I could with the hopes I would get the courage to introduce myself to you. I never did. I've been interested in you for two years. There is it, the truth is out, and the truth is like gold. It's precious. Please understand, it's not easy for me to tell you this. Actually, it's a little embarrassing."

Jill didn't laugh or tease Tony. She knew he was sincere. She smiled and said, "Did you really think I didn't notice that everywhere I was, you were also there? Just so you know I'm telling you the truth, you are quite a good pool player." Tony was shocked.

Tony replied, "Now I'm really embarrassed. I'm probably blushing. Why didn't you ever say anything, or talk to me?"

Jill replied, "Because I wasn't raised that way. Who knew, maybe it was just coincidence, and I was wrong? At least now, I know I was right."

Tony said, "I understand." Really, what does it matter? We are sitting here today. That is what matters." Jill agreed.

They both started exchanging questions and answers. Tony explained about his childhood and Italian upbringing. He explained where and how he lived, and how he was raised. Tony was Catholic. His mother insisted he attend church every week. He told Jill how he got a small scholarship, and the rest of his education was in the form of student loans. He told her that he didn't really have time to date or play sports in high school. He loved baseball and was quite a good pitcher. Because he worked every day after school, he never tried out for teams, although when he was younger, he played little league, and pitched for the church baseball team. He told Jill he had only dated one girl in high school, and he thought that was for, well (he paused) …. you know."

Jill laughed and replied, "Yes. I know." Jill explained she was half Swedish and half German. She got her looks from her mother. She was also Catholic but rarely went to church. There was always some type of event on Sundays that their family needed to attend. She explained she had a twin sister, but her sister had short hair. I only dated Carl throughout high school. I had many girlfriends. They were well off as my family, but many were snobs. She told him she was not like those girls, probably because most of her time was spent with Carl. My parents really liked him until he hurt me. His family was more well off than mine. We met at a country club dance. We went out a lot because our families attended the same events.

She said, "You know, like Allie and Johnny in the Karate Kid movie. That's what people called us. The Karate kid socialites. That used to piss me off."

They talked until the student center was closing, and all the way back to Jill's dorm. When they got back to Jill's building, Tony said, "I had a great time. I was so comfortable with you. We have to do this again sometime if you'd like."

Jill replied, "Yes we do. I was comfortable with you as well, but remember; you have to call me. I don't do that until I'm more involved. Sorry, it's just me, or should I say, my mother in me?"

Laughing Tony said, "Don't worry, I get it. I will call you. I promise."

They didn't shake hands, no kiss on the cheek, or hugs. They both said goodnight, turned and walked away. After a couple of steps, Jill turned and said, "Wow, you really are shy. I don't bite you know."

Tony took two steps towards her and leaned over. He kissed her on the cheek and said goodnight. As he was walking back to his dorm, he picked up his phone and called Jill. It only was five minutes since he left her. When she answered, she asked, "Is everything alright?"

Tony replied, "Yes. Everything is fine. I promised I would call you. Besides, I miss you already."

Jill replied, "I can't get over how sweet you are. I almost broke my own rule and dialed you first. I miss you too. I had such a great time, can we talk while you walk back to your dorm?"

It was only a ten-minute walk. Tony and Jill agreed to exchange their class schedules. It was late. Tony was so wound up he couldn't sleep. His roommate was also up and teased him.

"Don't tell me you finally had a date?"

Tony told him all about Jill. He was happy for him, and they went to sleep. Over the next couple of weeks, Tony and Jill spent a great deal of time together. Almost all their free time. They studied in the library, went to the student center, out to a movie, or get a bite to eat. They were great friends, and it was starting to turn into more. Tony was developing strong feelings for Jill and wondered if she was as well. They held hands, kissed more often, and sat around cuddling each other. They did not sleep together. Tony didn't want to be pushy and wasn't that experienced in that department. One night they were hanging out in Tony's dorm room. His roommate had a date and would not be back for some time. They were cuddled on his bed watching a movie. It wasn't that good. As they talked about changing it, Tony thought this might be a good time to have a discussion. By this time, they were very comfortable with each other. It was much easier for Tony to be more open. He joked a lot. That always made Jill laugh.

He said, "I want to talk about something if you're up to it."

Jill replied, "Sure."

Tony told her he had many things on his mind. It was only a couple of months before summer break. He was wondering what

that meant for them. He told her he really cared for her and wasn't
sure if she felt the same way. He added that he wanted to make
love to her, but he needed to be honest about something first.

Jill replied, "Wow, that is quite a lot. Do you think we can talk
about all of that in one night?" Laughing, she said, "I'm only
kidding. Before you start, I want you to know that I care a great
deal about you as well. I never thought I could do that again,
but here I am. I've been thinking about summer break as well.
I know we can talk often, but I don't want to go all summer
without seeing you. Maybe we can each take a turn and visit
each other for a week at a time. Honestly, as for making love,
I have thought about that as well. It scares me. I have only
been with one person in my life. Maybe you won't like me
after that? It's not like I have a great deal of experience."

Tony laughed and said, "That was going to be my
confession. I have only been with one girl. We can
help each other along the way." Laughing, he added,
"You know, it's not like we don't how it's done."

Jill said, "I'm sure we do. I just don't know if I'm ready. I mean, I'm
ready; I care for you that much, but I don't want to be hurt again."

Tony held her tightly and said, "I've been watching you
for two years. I've never dated anyone during that time. I
always wanted you, even when my friends and family told
me I was crazy. I couldn't hurt you if I wanted to."

Jill said, "I believe you. Can we give it a little more time?
Will I lose you? It's just that when I do that, it means
so much to me. It means I am totally committed. Right
now, I only see you, but you know what I mean."

Tony said, "We can give it as much time as it takes. I
waited for you so long, you won't lose me unless you
don't want me. I'm in no rush. I understand. I just
thought it was time to get it out in the open."

Jill kissed him, and it started. They kissed and held each other very close. Tony was very excited and trying to respect her wishes as he held back. As she pressed her bottom against him, not only could she feel how excited he was, he could feel her excitement as well. *He wondered, what should I do?* They were rubbing each other's backs as they kissed with great passion. They were both breathing heavily. Tony kept starting to slide his hand up Jill's blouse and would stop. Jill never stopped him. He was wondering why. Occasionally they would both place their hand on each other's bottom and press themselves against each other. When Jill did this, Tony would move below his hips to tease her. Pressing himself all around her. Finally, their excitement had peaked. Tony said, "We need to stop."

Jill asked, "Why, aren't you enjoying me?"

Tony replied, "I am. That's the problem. I want you so bad, how can I respect your wishes if we keep this up? I am only human you know."

Jill replied, "Well. I want you to respect me, but maybe not my wishes." Jill reached down and put her hands between his legs and started to rub him. Tony started to move and pulsate. This was driving him crazy. He slipped his hand under her blouse and under her bar. He started to caress her breasts. Tony asked, "Are you sure you are ready?"

Jill replied, "Yes. I'm ready. The way you responded to my concerns and feelings, made me realize I was ready to commit to you. I'm falling in love with you."

Tony said, "Don't be frightened by it. I feel the same way."

Jill said, "I know you do. I can sense it. Do you want to do this?"

Tony replied, "Yes. I want you to be mine forever, in every way."

At that moment, there was a knock at the door. Tony's roommate was back and laughingly said, "Are you guys dressed before we come in?"

"Yes, come in."

His roommate Rob walked in with a six-pack of beer and pizza, along with a girl of course. Rob said, "I figured if you two weren't screwing each other's brains out, you might be hungry and thirsty. Maybe I should have called first?"

Tony replied, "No problem."

They all sat around drinking beer, eating pizza, and laughing. It was getting late, so Tony walked Jill back to her dorm. It was their regular routine. Two minutes after Jill was in her room; she would call Tony and talk to him on his walk back to his dorm. When she called, she was telling him how good he made her feel, and she couldn't wait to make love to him. Tony explained that he was ready for this and a commitment for some time. He explained how happy she made him feel. He said, "Can I ask you one more question?" Jill replied, "You can ask me anything."

Tony asked, "Don't get me wrong, I like myself and am happy with whom I am. However, after hearing you describe Carl, I don't have his looks, cars, clothes, and certainly not his money. Does that bother you?"

Jill replied, "Babe. That's why I never hung around with the girls back home. Sure, we were friends, but I was different. Look at who I hang out with here at school. That shit doesn't mean anything to me. It's what's inside that counts. You have that special quality. You always think of me first, and I think of you first. We are so much alike. If we want those other things, we can work together to get them. As for me, I want to be loved. Money can't buy that. That is the only thing I learned from Carl. Does that answer your question?"

Tony said, "I wish I could kiss you right now. Yes, it does."

Tony had arrived at his dorm, and they said goodnight. Tomorrow was Friday. He was thinking of getting a room for the weekend off campus in town. He would ask Jill tomorrow. They could enjoy the town and have the nights together so as not to be bothered by roommates. When he got into bed, he couldn't wait. He called Jill and mentioned his idea. He asked her what she thought. He said, "I could go into town on my two-hour break between classes and get a room for Friday and Saturday night." Jill loved the idea under one condition. She wanted to split the cost. At first, he did not want to do that. He wanted it to be his treat. Jill explained, if they are going to be a couple, neither one should pay that type of total expense. This wasn't like going to the movies. Something like this was far more than a date and was for both of them. After some discussion, Tony agreed. The next day he went into town and got a room for the weekend. It wasn't as expensive as he thought it would be. Jill sent him a text during his next class asking him if he picked up the room key. He replied yes, and added a smiley face. She responded with the same. They were planning on meeting at three pm. Their classes would be over by then. They would have an overnight bag ready and head into the town. The town was only a half-hour to forty-five-minute walk from school. Many of the students went into town on the weekends. They received a college student discount at the hotel.

It was a cute town in the Midwest that catered to the college students. This was their main income during the school year. Although the school ran summer courses, the main population was during the normal school year. There were many things to do, and much to see during the day. It had a safe nightlife. Police presence was high. The college ran buses back and forth into and out of town on Friday and Saturday nights so the students would not have to drive. Tony and Jill decided they wanted to walk. They could jump on the shuttle anywhere along the way if they wanted to. All they had to do was show their school ids. The rest of the day they were both excited and couldn't wait for three pm. Their classes seemed like it would never end. They each had their bag packed. All they had to do was meet. Tony would meet Jill at her dorm at three-thirty, and they would start into town, get settled, and have a bite to eat and go from there. Everything went as scheduled. On the walk into town, they were both excited. Jill said, "This will be like playing house over the weekend. It will definitely tell us if we are good together." Tony agreed. Tony was very laid back, as was Jill. They both accommodated each other. They were good together. Neither one was selfish. When they settled into their room, Jill asked, "Are you hungry?"

Tony replied, "Yes and no. If you are I can
eat, if you want to wait, I can wait."

Jill responded, "Me too. Why don't you relax for a minute?
I have to use the bathroom. We can decide after."

Tony said, "Take your time." He just chilled on the bed.

A few minutes later, the bathroom door opened and out
walked Jill wearing a completely see-through negligee.
She said, "I lied. I am hungry, but I'm hungry for you."

Tony stood up and walked over to her. His kissed
her so passionately. While he was kissing her,
she was unbuttoning and taking off his shirt, and
undoing his pants. They both got on the bed.

Jill asked, "Are you as nervous as I am?"

Tony said, "More, I'm sure."

Jill said, "I think in about five minutes or so, we won't be."

As they lay on the bed, they were both so gentle. Taking their time, and lightly touching each other. Exploring one another's body. Tony slowly untied her top, and her breasts were completely exposed. In his eyes, they were perfect. As he caressed them and placed his mouth upon them, he could feel her excitement growing. She was far more passionate then he had imagined. Maybe because she always seemed so cold when he would follow her. He was now seeing and learning the real Jill. Her true personality, one without fear. As he caressed her breasts, she reached down and was gently stroking him. His other hand was feeling how wet she was while paying close attention to her most sensitive spot. She was squirming on the bed. She moved downward and placed him in her mouth. He laid back and just relaxed enjoying every minute of her advancements. Trying not to have an orgasm, he switched positions and did the same to her. She was outstanding. Talking to him, letting him know what she liked. They both went on their sides at opposite ends as she wrapped her leg around his head as they enjoyed each other at the same time. Both talking, comforting each other, letting each other know how much they were enjoying one another. Suddenly, Tony stopped. He took out a condom and Jill helped him put it on. He penetrated her so gently that they both gasped to catch a breath when he first placed himself inside her.

Jill said, "I'm sorry babe, but this isn't going to last long. I am so ready."

Tony replied, "No need for that. I can't hold it that long either. It's been a while for both of us."

Within two minutes, they both exploded. Tony was in so deep and moving just right that Jill was going crazy. She was moving with him. They moved as one. They could feel every part of one another as they experienced an orgasm together. They rolled over and held each other. There was no getting them apart. Tony explained how great it was. He felt so emotionally close to her. Jill felt the same way, and asked, "Do you think badly of me?" Tony looked at her and kissed her. He asked, "Does that answer your question?" Jill smiled. They got up, took a shower together and got dressed. They decided to get a bite to eat and would decide what they would do. They both knew they had until eleven o'clock on Sunday morning when they would have to check out of the room. They had a bite to eat. Nothing expensive, and decided they would walk around a bit. There was a local club all the college kids went to. They decided they would check it out later. There was no cover charge for college students. Little did they know they would see many of their friends there. Rob would also be there with his girl.

They didn't want to get back to the room too late. The purpose of this weekend was to spend time alone. During the school week, they were always around people. This weekend was for them to have some quality time together. It was about nine o'clock. The shops were closing. They decided to go to the club. Everyone was twenty-one, so getting in was not a problem. As it turned out, Jill and Tony's birthday were less than a month apart. They had both recently turned twenty-one before they met. Many of the kids from school they knew were arriving on the shuttle. They hung out with Rob and his girl. They had a drink or two and danced. About eleven, Jill leaned over to Tony and said, "Let's leave." Tony replied, "I was just thinking the same thing." Rob knew Tony had a room for the weekend. He said to Tony, "Why don't you let us crash with you guys this weekend." Immediately he laughed and said, "Just kidding, get the hell out of here." Tony and Jill left. They walked back to their hotel. On the way back they were talking about the great time they had today. Tony was teasing Jill how she caught him completely by surprise, and how much loved that.

Jill said, "Get used to it. I like surprises." At that moment, Tony stopped and turned to Jill.

Jill asked, "What's wrong?"

Tony kissed her and said, "I love you. I fell in love with you."

Jill hugged him and replied, "I love you too. Can this be possible so soon?"

Tony said, "When two worlds collide, anything is possible." They finished their walk back.

When they got to the door of their room, Tony unlocked it, picked up Jill and kicked the door closed with his foot. He carried her to the bed and said, "I like surprises too." He took a candle out of his overnight bag, lit it, turned out the lamp next to the bed, and made love to Jill. Skipping most of the foreplay this time, most of their nervousness was gone. He penetrated her ever so slowly, and they just took their time enjoying every moment. Every word, every touch, and feeling. They moved as if they were one being. This sensual moment lasted much longer. They fell asleep in each other's arms. It was a long day for them. They experienced many new experiences together. They slept in, and Jill awoke before Tony. She was lying in bed next to Tony thinking that she had no regrets. Although she would never say this to Tony, for fear he might think she was comparing, she thought in all the years with Carl, she never felt this loved, wanted, and desired. She wanted to tell him. She viewed this as being a good thing, not a comparison. Tony awoke and gave her a hug and a kiss.

Jill asked, "Can we agree on something?"

Tony said, "Of course."

Jill said, "I never want us to have secrets. I want us to be able to tell each other anything. If either of us has a question when we're talking, we should stop, and get it clarified. I don't want either of us to get mad, and I hate arguing."

Tony replied, "I like that. I think that's a good idea. So tell me, for you to bring this up, there must be something you want to say."

Jill gave Tony a shove, "I hate you, but you are right."

Tony said, "I'm shy, but not stupid. What is it you want to say that you are so afraid I will get mad?"

Jill replied, "How can you know me so well this soon."

Tony replied, "Because I love you. I make it my business to know you. However, that's not what you wanted to tell me, is it?"

Jill said, "No. It's not. Understand I was not comparing. I was only thinking, and it was in a good way. I woke up a few minutes before you. I was watching you sleep. I thought about last night and how far we had come in such a short time. We have made love twice, and spend all our free time together. I thought to myself; I spent a long time with Carl. He never made me feel as loved, wanted, and desired as you do. I wanted to cry. Not because I was sad about Carl, because of how happy I am now that I found you."

Tony said, "Honestly, I was never with anyone for that long. I understand that when two people spend that length of time together, I guess they don't know anything else. Maybe we think we have it good. I can't say. You're the psychology major, you tell me. I will say this. I am not mad. In one sense you are comparing. Not Carl and I, but what you and I have compared to what you and Carl had. That doesn't get me mad unless you think what you and Carl had was better."

Jill laughed, "Not even close. You have to admit it, it's funny. For the past two years, you have been following me. Trying to meet me, and it took me having an asthma attack to meet you. Look how far we have come in a few weeks. Just think of where we might be if you had some balls two years ago?"

Tony laughed and said, "Maybe if I did, the timing wouldn't have been right. Everything happens for a reason."

They had a great Saturday. They laughed, did things, and had fun. No talk about the past. They just enjoyed the present. They agreed that the past needed to stay where it belonged and move forward. In one sense, they met due to their past, but in a real sense, they meant because of the present. Something that was possibly their destiny. They had pizza in a local restaurant. They both loved pizza and popcorn. Neither of them wanted to go out that night. Tomorrow they would have to go back to campus. They wanted tonight to be quality time. Just for themselves. They decided to get some snacks, hang out in their room and enjoy a movie and each other's company. While they were relaxing on the bed, Jill asked Tony if he had told his family about her yet.

Tony replied, "They've known about you for two years, but yes, I did tell them we were now dating. They were very happy about that. Besides telling them all about you, I sent them a picture of you by text. They thought you were beautiful, intelligent, and good for me." Jill was happy about that.

Jill asked, "Why do they think I'm good for you?"

Tony explained, "Remember I told you I had to work a lot in high school because my family needed the financial help? Don't forget, there were five children. I was the oldest. My mother didn't work. I think they always felt guilty that I never actually had a normal social life like my friends. I guess they feel that what we have is making up for that time."

Jill said, "Well at least, I know they will like me."

Tony asked, "What about you? Have you told your family yet?"

Jill replied, "Yes and no. I told my sister everything. She is very happy for me. She never liked Carl anyway. She never trusted him. She told me she has never seen me this way. I talk to her at least every other day about you. My parents know I met someone. That don't know everything. I don't have any brothers. My father has only had two girls, so he is very protective of us. I really don't know if they liked Carl or the fact that his family was well off. I mean, we were well off as well, but I think it's more in the sense of knowing I would be taken care of."

Tony said, "I can understand that. However, that could mean they won't like me. Once I graduate and get a job, I will make good money, but for now, all I have is what I've saved, and my parents aren't well off. They just make ends meet. We don't belong to Country Clubs, but we have love in our family. That's where our wealth is."

Jill replied, "That's the best type of wealth to have. We all love one another, but it is a lifestyle. One I never really liked. I'm a big girl and make my own choices. Choices they will have to live with. I plan on taking to my mother about us this week. I have to ask you one thing though."

Tony said, "You can ask me anything. I will never lie to you. You may not always like my answer, and we can work on that together, but I will always tell you the truth."

Jill asked, "Are we committed? I mean, this isn't a challenge or a fling is it? Are we together?

Tony replied laughing, "Fling? I wouldn't know how to have one. We are together and committed. I am completely committed to you. Now, the rest is up to you."

Jill kissed Tony, cuddled up close to him, and told him she loved him. They watched a bit more of the movie and turned it off. They made love so passionately. They were getting very comfortable together and learning so much about one another. Tomorrow was Sunday. It would be back to reality. Tony was a bit concerned about Jill's parents. He did not want to be the cause of any problems for her. He also knew these things had to be her decision. As much as neither of them wanted to talk about it, summer break was only six weeks away. A conversation they would need to have.

CHAPTER THREE
WHEN THE STORM COMES

Jill and Tony returned to campus the following afternoon. Finals would be coming soon. They both had a lot to catch up on Sunday night. They decided not to spend it together so they could get themselves caught up. Jill told her roommate all about the weekend. Jill and Jodie, her roommate, were like Rob and Tony. They got along great and had been roommates since freshman year. Jodie really helped Jill get over Carl, and also liked Tony. Jodie was a tough cookie. She didn't take shit from anyone, especially men. She was very happy for Jill. She was telling Jill she has never seen her this happy.

Jodie said, "Girl, let's talk reality. You know your parents aren't going to accept Tony. Not because he's not nice, but let's call it what it is. You're their little girl, and he doesn't come from money."

"I know. I guess I've been trying to avoid that part. That will hurt Tony. He is proud of his family. He is the kindest man I have ever known. I told Tony I needed to stay in tonight to get caught up on some things and would call him later. I'm going to call my mother and talk to her."

Jodie said, "If you want some privacy, I can go out."

Jill replied, "Hell no. I need your moral support."

Jodie said, "I'll stay. Have you and Tony talked about the summer yet? Y two live on opposite sides of the planet."

"We said we would talk a lot, and spend a week at each other's house. He needs to work, and I have a part-time job as well."

Jodie asked, "And if your mother won't go for that?"

"I'm a big girl. I can make my own decisions. This isn't a stupid or irresponsible decision. They allowed Carl and I go away for a weekend together before I was twenty-one. If we can't figure it out, I'll see if I can stay with Tony for the summer. What can they do, cut me off? I'll take a student loan out for my last year of school."

Jodie replied, "Okay, get off your high horse. It shouldn't come to that, but I'm sure it will be a battle at first."

Jill said, "I guess we'll know in a couple of hours."

Jill got unpacked and started to do some laundry. All the time thinking about how she would start the conversation. Her parents knew of Tony. They only knew that he was the boy who called 911 when she had her asthma attack. Jill and her mom spoke a couple of times a week. Since Jill and her sister were away at school, her parents were always going to an event somewhere. Jill did not want to start having to do that over the summer. She knew she would be required to attend certain ones, that was expected. She had no desire to go to as many as she and Carl used to attend. Jill did not want to see or have anything to do with Carl. She was thinking of working more hours and trying to get some of her internship done over the summer. Hopefully, that would take up much of her time. She wasn't worried about Carl. Her mother told her that her father spoke with Carl, and Carl's dad. He made it very clear that Carl was to leave Jill alone.

Both their fathers had business dealings together. They were not going to allow something such as this to interfere with that. Jill called Tony around six-thirty to see what he was doing. They laughed because they both were doing their laundry first. A chore neither of them liked. Jill expressed how much she missed him. Tony also missed her. Neither of them wanted this weekend to end. They agreed before summer break, they would do that again. Tony had a great class schedule. Most days he was done by one o'clock and could work from two to six. This gave him the evening to spend with Jill.

Jill said, "Well I might as well tell you."

"Tell me what?"

Jill replied, "I'm pregnant."

Tony did not hesitate and said, "That's great. Wait …. (he paused), how could that be? This was the first weekend we had sex, and I wore a condom every time?"

Jill laughed, "Gotcha. I'm not pregnant silly. I just wanted to see what you would say."

Tony replied, "If you were, that's fine. I'm not going anywhere."

That made Jill smile. "That's why I love you. Seriously, I am going to tell my mother all about us tonight. In six weeks we are both going to opposite sides of the country. She needs to know, and we need to know what we are going to do."

Tony replied, "I know. I try not to think about it. We talked about coming to see each other for a week at a time. Wouldn't it be great if we could find jobs for half the summer and split the rest between California and Jersey? I was also thinking in our senior year, I could use the housing allowance of my school loan. Maybe you can use yours, and we could rent a small apartment off campus together."

Jill was shocked that Tony was thinking that way. "Your serious aren't you?"

"Of course I'm serious. Am I moving too fast?"

Jill replied, "Not at all. I love the idea. First, I have let my parents know how far this has gone."

Tony did not want Jill to sense his sadness and replied, "I know. We have time. Let's take it one step at a time."

Jill sensed his sadness. She had gotten to know Tony and replied, "Keep those thoughts. I love them. I'm going to call home now. I'll call you after I get off the phone with my mother."

Tony replied, "I hope it goes well, and don't
get upset. I'll wait to hear from you."

This was it. Jill had to do this and be strong. She had to
show her parents how sure she was about this. She did not want
to get mad, but she knew her parents would only care about his
background and money. Jill was sitting on her bed staring at
her phone. Jodie cracked two beers and sat down next to her.

She said, "Hey, I'm right here. Let's get this done."

Jill dialed her house, and her mother answered. They chatted for
a moment about general things. How school was going, and how
Jill was feeling. Jill told her everything was great, and she was
feeling fine. She explained that one of the reasons she called was
she wanted to talk to her about something. Jill's mother was easy
to talk to. However, she could be a little opinionated at times,
especially when it came to Jill and her sister. Jill asked her if she
remembered Tony, the student that helped her by calling 911. Her
mother remembered the name. Jill never told her the details.

Jill went on to say, I have to tell you the full story, which
I didn't know at the time. At first, I thought meeting Tony
would not develop into anything, but it has. With summer
break coming, we need to talk. Jill's mother listened. Jill told
her everything, except for them spending the past weekend
in town, and told her everything about Tony, including his
background. At first, Jill's mother was very understanding.

She said, "Honey, that's so cute. Some men
are shy. They need that extra push."

Jill went on to add that they have been spending a great deal
of time together, actually, every day. She explained he was
studying architectural design and was on the dean's list every
semester. Tony was the kindest man she had ever met.

Jill's mother asked, "Is this serious?"

Jill hesitated, "Very serious. Mom, you know I haven't even been on a date since Carl. Tony just blew me away."

Jill's mother responded, "You're not a baby any more honey, but you can't rush into things either."

Jill explained this is why this was special. They started as friends, and it happened on its own. She said, "I'm not stupid. After Carl, I know what to look for."

Jill mother started to ask questions. Where is he from? Jill told her he was from New Jersey. He had two brothers and two sisters. He was the oldest. Her mother said there are some very nice areas in New Jersey. With a family that size, his father must be in business and make good money. Jill explained that he wasn't from the higher financial area of New Jersey. His father worked hard, they made ends meet, and his mother didn't work. Tony was paying for his own college tuition. Jill thought she would just get it out there. Jill wanted her to know the truth about Tony. Jill knew her parents would eventually need to know. Her mother's voice changed slightly as she replied, "Jill, he may be the nicest boy you ever met, but this is not what your father and I had planned for you."

Jill's tone changed. "Mom. He's not a boy. He's a man. He has helped his family and takes care of himself. That's more Carl ever did. Would you and dad rather have me be with someone like Carl just because he comes from money, or with someone who treats me with respect, listens to me, my opinions, and loves me? Since when do I have to live my life by what you and dad have planned for me? Aren't my life choice's my own? Doesn't what I want matter?"

Jill's mother could hear how upset and angry Jill was getting. She did not want this to turn into an argument. "Honey, calm down. We can discuss this when you come home for the summer."

Jill responded, "No. We have to discuss this before the summer. I want you to meet Tony before you judge him. Do you honestly think we are going to go all summer without seeing each other?

Mom, I wasted two years of my life without anyone because of Carl. I finally found someone who accepts me for what I am. Not the money my family has. Tony never knew about your money until I told him I was going to call you. I will not risk losing that. His mother and father were very happy for him. They didn't even ask about our background. If, and I say if, this is meant to turn into something long term, it has to be what Tony and I want. Not what our parents want it to be. If we can't agree on this, I will find a job locally and stay here for the summer. If I have to, I will get a student loan for my last year at school. I love you and dad for all you have done for me, but that doesn't give anyone the right to run my life. You need to talk to dad and decide. My God, can't you at least give him a chance before you judge him?" Jill hung up.

Her mother tried calling back two or three times. Jill would not answer. She left to walk over to Tony's dorm with Jodie. She was angry. Jodie did not want her walking alone, and made sure she took her inhaler. When they arrived at Tony's dorm, Jill called Tony. They decided to sit outside and talk. Jill, Jodie, and Tony sat on a bench beneath a tree across from the dorm. This provided them with privacy. Jill told Tony the whole story. Tony explained he did not want her arguing with her parents over him. However, he was not going to give her up. He explained they had to find another way.

Tony asked, "Can I call your mother?"

Jill replied, "No way."

"I know you're angry. Anger never solves anything. Your mother is probably worried sick about you right now. Please, let me talk to her." Jill paused and looked at Jodie. Jodie gave her a nod and said, "Roommate, they're going to have to talk at some point. Let him call."

Jill hit her speed dial and called her mother. The first question her mother asked was if she was alright? Jill replied, "Mom. I'm with Tony. I told him everything. We don't keep secrets. He wants to speak with you." Her mother asked her to put him on. Jill looked at him and said, "You better have a set of balls now."

Tony took the phone. Tony said hello and introduced himself. He said, "Mrs. Muller, this is Anthony Ricci. It is a pleasure to speak with you."

Jill's mother replied, "How can I help you?"

Tony started to explain that he wasn't going to waste time explaining everything since Jill had informed him that she knew the whole story. He explained he didn't care. He didn't know Jill came from a strong financial background. Honestly, that didn't interest him. He explained that he did not want to be the cause of any family arguments. He was not raised that way. His mother was very strict, and their house was always filled with hard work and love. That's what kept them together as a family. He added, "However, I am not going to give Jill up. I do believe that our life choices are up to us to make. The best part of family love is when together, as a family, those choices can be supported. I am going into a profession that provides quite well, as is Jill. If we are meant to be, no one is asking for money, nor will we. All we are asking for is a chance. An opportunity to see where this may go. You have never met me, but yet you judge me. I have never met you, and I have not judged you. Honestly, I understand you. When and if the day comes that I have children, I will want the best for them as well. I must realize there will come a time in their life and they will reach an age, where their circle of life continues. They will need to make their own choices. That is all I wanted to say. I will always take care of Jill because I love her. That is something you and Mr. Muller will never need to worry about. I will listen to whatever you have to say."

Jill's mother said, Thank you, please put Jill on the phone."

Tony handed Jill the phone. Her mother said, "We will talk. I need to speak to your father. By the way. He does seem very nice. " They ended their call.

Jill was impressed with the way Tony handled the conversation. He was firm, but also very respectful. Something she thought her mother would appreciate. Now it would be a waiting game. At times, Jill's father could be more reasonable than her mother. They would have to wait and see.

Jill asked Tony, "If this doesn't work out, how do you feel about visiting your family? We can find an apartment here. We can both work, and stay in that apartment during our senior year. You did mention finding a small apartment together during our senior year?"

Tony replied, "Yes I did. However, I think we both know that is not the right way to start this off. We need to try everything we can to fix this first. If all avenues fail, I told you. I won't lose you. We will do whatever we need to do to be together. My only concern is we haven't been together that long. Are you strong enough for this?"

"What did I ask you over the weekend? Didn't I ask you if you were committed?"

Tony replied, "Yes."

"Then please don't ever ask me that question again. You should know the answer."

Tony said, "Agreed. I just needed to be sure. That's all."

Jodie, Jill, and Tony walked back to Jill's dorm. Tony needed to work off some stress. The walk to and from Jill's dorm would do him good. Jodie was the type that gave her opinion, whether you asked for it or not. Jodie told them she heard all the conversations. She felt they were trying to do things the right way, and shouldn't be hard on themselves. These things are never easy. If this is what they wanted for each other, they would have to be strong, and not start arguing with each other. That could only make things harder and possibly tear them apart. Jill and Tony agreed it would come to that. Everyone had the right to their opinion, but the final decision was up to them.

On the walk back, Tony called his mother. He explained what had taken place. He wanted her opinion. He had the phone on speaker so Jill could hear the conversation. Tony introduced Jill to his mother. She told them they should not disrespect Jill's parents. However, she agreed that the decision they made had to be their own. Before things got that bad and if Jill agreed, she would call Jill's parents. She added, if all that fails, it's crazy for them to waste money on an apartment all summer. If that's what they wanted to do, they should at least come and visit. If not, they could stay in Jersey for the summer. However, that should be the last resort. Tony took the phone off speaker. Jill and Tony's mom talked for a few minutes before she gave the phone back to Tony.

Tony's mother said, "Don't forget how you were raised. You are my son. I will support whatever decision you both make as long as it is done properly and for the right reasons." Tony thanked his mom, and they hung up.

Jill said, "I really like your mother. She is so nice."

"She is, but she is big on respect. She will honor everything she says unless we screw it up. We both know we won't do that."

Jill replied, "No we won't. I love my parents. I don't want to hurt them. They have to understand that I'm old enough to make my own choices. Growing up, I did everything I was supposed to do. I went to every event I was expected to. I showed them respect. Now, they need to respect my wishes. Respect is a two-way street."

Tony kissed Jill goodnight and started to walk back. Like clockwork, two minutes later, Jill called to keep him company on his walk back.

Tony and Jill had time. Tony was thinking, if it came to staying in New Jersey, where would they sleep? Jill would have to bunk in with the girls in his grandparent's apartment, and he would be back in his room with his brothers. Certainly, they would not have their own bedroom. He and Jill were discussing this on his walk back. They really did not want to use that option. They were hoping everything would work out. On the other hand, they both didn't want to see each other only two times over the summer. They had almost eleven weeks off between school years. To see each other two out of those eleven weeks would be terrible. They could possibly stretch it to three; however, Tony needed to work. He was fortunate that the summer job he had was flexible. He could probably work something out. He could also work double shifts for a week to get the next week off. There were options. Before they hung up, they decided they would not let this ruin their last six weeks together. They could spend every minute together playing *"what if."* It was an emotionally draining night for them both. Before they hung up, they agreed. They needed to make love to each other to calm them down. Since that wasn't going to happen, a kiss goodnight on the phone would have to do.

*****

The next few days passed. Jill did not hear from her mother. They both followed their regular routine. They studied together, went to the student center, and did the things as normal. It was now Thursday. This was an early class day for both Jill and Tony. Jill's parents had her class schedule. Her mother sent her a text message that she and her father wanted to talk to her tonight, and asked if she could call around seven o'clock. Jill sent her a text saying, yes I can. She also asked if Tony could be a part of this conversation. Her mother sent a text back saying this was a family matter. Jill responded, "Tony is family. In the end, it is our decision." She explained how polite and understanding Tony was. Wouldn't this be a good way to get to know him? Reluctantly, her parents agreed. It was a beautiful night. Tony and Jill had been together since three o'clock. They wanted to think about a place that would be private to have this conversation. Rob would be in his room. Jodie had an evening class. They decided they would speak to them from Jill's room. They had a quick bite to eat at five-thirty and got back to Jill's room at six-forty-five. They really didn't discuss what the subject of the call would be, but agreed they would stand strong, and not be disrespectful or argue. That alone would surprise Jill's parents. Jill was always the one who spoke her mind. Callie, Jill's sister, was the rebel. She didn't speak her mind; she just did it.

It was seven o'clock when Jill placed the call. Her father answered and told Jill her mother was there. He asked if they were on speaker phone and if Tony was there. Jill told him, yes, and they were also on speaker phone. Tony introduced himself to Jill's father and said hello to her mother. Jill's father started the conversation by thanking Tony for being respectful and understanding when he spoke to Jill's mother. He asked that they listen before they commented. Everyone agreed. Jill's father explained to Jill and Tony that this was not personal against Tony. They appreciated what Tony did for Jill. This was about with they envisioned for their daughter. Although Carl was not the right choice, he was local. He had a better chance of success after college because of the backing of his family. Jill was their daughter. They did not want to see her have to struggle. He asked Tony if he could understand that. Tony explained he fully understood. No parent wants to see their child struggle. However, Tony stated, in our professions, we don't see where there would be a struggle. In life, no one starts off with a great deal of money, unless it was left to them. Everyone has to work to achieve it. That what makes a family strong.

Tony asked, "Sir, although I understand what you are trying to say, may I ask a question?"

Her father said, "Of course."

"Did you achieve your financial goals through hard work and sacrifice, or did your family have money?"

Jill's father replied, "You should be an attorney. I know where this is going. We had to work hard for it. No one handed it to us."

Tony replied, "Exactly my point. Although Jill and I will have to work hard for it, we will achieve it. You are the perfect example of that sir. I am not judging you for loving Jill the way you do. That is not my place. What I can say is, if the day comes, and we are well off, it will be because together, we worked for it. I will continue to help our children, even if their choice is not what I envisioned for them. If they are working hard to achieve their goals, struggling is not an obstacle. It builds character. It should not such as it rules their life."

Her father replied, "You make some very good points young man. Truthful ones. I know my wife is not going to like this idea, but let me make a proposal. You say you will not give up on my daughter, and you won't lose her correct?"

"That is correct sir. I will not give her up or lose her. I have waited my entire life to meet someone like Jill."

Her father replied, "We have time. Hasty decisions don't always have a positive outcome. I suggest my wife and I drive into town this weekend. I have plans we can change. We can spend the weekend together and get to know one another. We can see where that takes us. How do you both feel about that?"

Jill and Tony thought that was an excellent idea. Tony replied, "I would love to meet you both. It is a wonderful opportunity for us to get to know one another. However, I only have one request."

Jill's father asked, "And what might that be."

"We agree that no one tries to sway anyone. I would like us to spend time together. I would like you to see how Jill and I interact. How we think alike, and share the same goals and desires."

Jill's parents agreed. They thought it was a good idea. Jill's father added, "I want you both to understand something. There is no way I will condone Jill living in New Jersey all summer, or Tony living with us all summer. You both speak of sacrifice, that is part of the sacrifice. You both have to finish school. That must come first. If it's meant to be, you will both survive the summer with visiting each other whenever possible."

Jill spoke up and said, "Dad. I know I am speaking for Tony when I say I totally agree. It will be difficult, but we love each other and can do it. However, you both need to

be open-minded. As long as you don't try to back me into
a corner, and force a choice upon me that I don't want,
we should be able to meet somewhere in the middle."

They made their weekend plans and hung up. Jill and Tony
seemed happy with the way the conversation went. I would be
hard for them to settle on just seeing each other two or three
weeks over the summer. However, Jill's father was right. They
knew that. They had to finish school, work over the summer,
and if this were real, they would survive it. If they could afford
it, they could always come back a little early, find an apartment
that rents to college students, and live together in their senior
year. They thought this was a small sacrifice to make considering
the overall picture. They both wanted to go to graduate school.
They could do that online, but that would take longer. Jill would
also have to do an internship next year and take her boards to
become a certified psychologist. This was all well over a year
away, but Jill and Tony talked about everything together. Tony
was deeply in love with Jill. He hoped to work a great deal over
the summer. For graduation, he wanted to ask her to marry him
and get engaged. He wondered, was he thinking too far ahead? He
wanted to feel Jill out. He would say, let me ask you a question.
If I wanted to marry you one day, would you marry me?

Jill would sit back for a moment, look at him, and ask,
"Are you serious, or just breaking them off?"

"Breaking what off? That's a pretty serious question,
why the hell would I ask it if I wasn't serious?"

Jill replied, "Yes. I would say yes today. I can't explain it. It's
the way I feel. Nothing in my life has ever felt so right."

"Good answer. I just needed to know. I guess I
knew, but sometimes you just need to hear it."

Jill replied, "I know."

It was only seven-thirty. Jill wanted to talk about the weekend. Where would they take her parents, and what would they do? Tony explained that he wanted it to be a run and relaxing weekend. He did not want Jill's father to pay for everything. He wanted to buy lunch one day, and maybe dinner the next day. He asked Jill how she felt about that.

Jill agreed. They weren't children anymore. The only way her parents would see how serious they were, and can take care of themselves, would be to act like adults, and take responsibility. She asked Tony if they could afford that?

Tony thought they could. He had saved money working over the school year. More so before they were together and he cut back on his hours. Jill told him she had some money saved as well from tutoring she had been doing throughout the school year. She told him she could give him one hundred dollars if that would help.

Tony said, "I'm good. I can do this."

Jill replied, "Babe. This is my family. I have to feel as though I am contributing. We've talked about this, remember?"

Tony replied, "Yes honey. I remember. You're right. I'll pay as we go, and we can square up after your parents leave." They agreed. Tony said, "Tell me what you think of this. They are coming on Friday. We can bring them around the campus, get a bite to eat, and relax in the student center and talk. On Saturday, there is so much to see. I'm sure they will enjoy themselves. We can spend the day showing them some of the sights, take them to the ranch, have lunch, then go into town and shop. Have dinner and talk. They are leaving late Sunday morning. We can meet and have breakfast together before they start their drive back."

Jill said, "I think those are wonderful ideas. It's relaxing, fun, and it gives us time to talk. Everyone will get to know each other better. They are very nice people, just a bit overprotective."

Tony replied, "I understand. We'll probably
be the same way with our kids."

"Oh. I see. You have this all planned out. We are having kids now?"

Tony said, "You know what I mean." Jill just
laughed but replied. "You're right."

It was obvious they were both thinking the same way and had
long-term plans for their future. They never talked about it
until Tony made this statement. He found out what he needed
to know. Tony did that. He would make a comment to see
what Jill's response would be. After a while, she figured
out what he was doing, but never let on that she knew.

CHAPTER FOUR
WHEN TWO WORLDS COLLIDE

When Friday arrived, Jill and Tony were a little nervous about Jill's parents arriving. They wanted everything to go well. They met for lunch between classes. They each had one more class to attend, and shortly after, her parents would arrive. Tony had a nice weekend planned which included time to chat and get to know one another, as well as shopping and sightseeing. He could only hope that Jill's parents would enjoy themselves. Everything was flexible and could easily be adjusted. They were somewhat calmer by lunchtime. Jill was excited since she hadn't seen her parents in a few months. When their class was over, they each went to their dorm rooms to shower and change. Shortly after, Tony arrived at Jill's. When she saw him from her window, she walked outside. It was a beautiful sunny day. Her parents called to let her know they left the house and would call her after they checked into their hotel. Right next to Jill's dorm was a student parking area with room for visitor parking. Jill told them she was excited to see them, and she picked up their visitor parking pass from the student center. Tony and Jill hung out and waited to hear from them. When Jill's mother called to let her know they were on the way to her dorm, Jill explained that she and Tony were sitting on the bench under the tree directly across the entrance to her building. They had a perfect view of the entrance of the lot and would watch for them. After they hung up, Jill said to Tony, "They sounded like they were in good spirits." Since Jill's father was an attorney, she had a hard time figuring out his moods, but today, he sounded normal. Tony said, "I'm not worried. Things should go fine. If it's all about money for them, no matter what I do, it might not be good enough. There is no point in worrying."

Jill agreed and asked, "I just have one question."

"What is it?"

Jill asked, "I need to be sure that no matter how this goes, or what the outcome is, it will not affect us or our plans."

"Babe. I don't want to see you argue with your parents. I told you, I won't give you up. The only way that will happen is if you end this. It won't be me that does that. After this weekend, the choice is yours. You have to promise me one thing."

Jill asked, "What?"

"If this turns out to be a problem for your parents, at first, it will be easy for us to take a stand. After a time, any battle can wear on a person. I know. When my brother went through something like this with a girl he was dating, he had some issues which he corrected. It took time. After a while, his girl couldn't take the constant grief from her parents and ended the relationship. If that happens to you, don't ever lie to me. If it is getting too hard, and you want to throw in the towel, just say so. Please don't lead me on. That would really hurt me. Losing you would hurt enough, I wouldn't want to know you had a change of heart months earlier and couldn't tell me."

Jill replied, "Let's get something straight right now. I will not make that promise. I don't need to. I love my parents dearly. I have always done what I needed to do to support my father's career, but I always had a mind of my own. If I were doing something wrong or illegal, that would be different. What we have is neither of those two. What we have is good, and it's real. I will not have a change of heart. They will have to live with the choices they make. Do you believe that?"

Tony smiled. "Yes, I do. Let's hope that's a road we don't have to travel." Jill agreed.

Ten minutes later, Jill saw her parents entering the parking area. She told Tony they should walk over to greet them. As they both approached the car, Jill's parents got out. Jill gave them both a hug and kiss while Tony stood a few steps back. Jill gave her dad the visitor pass for the car. Jill took Tony's hand and brought him closer.

"Tony, this is my mom Julia, and my dad Frank." Tony put out his hand to shake her father's hand and said, "Mr. and Mrs. Muller; it is a pleasure to meet you. Jill has told me so much about you."

Frank laughed, "Oh really? You'll have to tell us what she said. I can only imagine."

Tony laughed and replied, "It was all good. Would you like to relax for a bit, or walk to the student center? You must be tired after your drive. We can get a snack and have coffee if you'd like. Later, we can go to dinner. I had some thoughts for the weekend we can talk about."

Julia replied, "Honey. I think Tony has a good idea. I could use a cup of coffee." They started to walk to the student center. Jill walked next to Tony. They took a path through a small park. The park was in the center of the campus. Tony chose this route because it gave him the opportunity to explain what some of the new construction was for and point out some other changes that had been made around campus. He thought that would help to break the ice. Tony was very smart. As a junior, and first in his class for architectural design, this gave him an opportunity to brag. He explained to Frank that part of the design of the new construction he was looking at was his design. He worked on the project while doing an internship with the company that was contracted to design the building. As he was explaining this to Frank, Jill looked at him quite confused and whispered, "You never told me that. Now I know why you went this way." Tony just smiled. Frank was interested and asked Tony what his input was on the project. Tony explained during his internship, he had to work on every aspect of the project.

He worked on the outside design, the interior design, and had to create the model that the school would see in the presentation. Once the company had the approval for the design, he worked on the costing aspect of the project. Once the company submitted the bid and won the contract, he continued on with some of the smaller details. Tony added, "I didn't get paid for this work because it was an internship program. The reason I was chosen was during my three years in this school, I have been first in my class and made the dean's list every semester. To have this on my resume from a company this large, would almost guarantee me an entry-level architectural design position at any company. They were so impressed by me and my input to the project; they asked me to apply when I received my degree. I was very proud of that.

Frank replied, "As you should be. That is quite impressive. How much does a job such as this pay?"

Tony replied, "Entry level starts at around 65,000 yearly. Once you obtain your masters, it increases to around 85,000. Once you're established and proven, it's over six figures. That timeframe is dependant on the size projects you get assigned to, and if your designs land a signed contract. Many designers are in great demand. They receive a smaller salary and receive a percentage of the project. That is my goal. You can make as much as six or seven hundred dollars a year when you reach that plateau, depending on the size of the projects."

Frank asked, "Do you think you are that good?"

Tony replied, "I don't want to sound like I am bragging, but I am better than that good. I will do it."

Frank said, "Well, I will say this. You certainly have spunk and confidence. I believe you will."

Jill was impressed. She had never seen this side of Tony before. He handled her father like Carl never could. However, Carl came from money. He never had to work for what he wanted. Therefore, he lacked that hunger. The drive someone would need to reach their goal. Tony had all of that. Jill's mother was listening to this conversation. Jill whispered into her ear, "Isn't he everything I told you he was?"

Julia replied, "He certainly is more mature for his age."

Jill asked, "Do you know why?"

"How would I know that smart ass. Tell me."

Jill explained Tony doesn't come from money, he has had to work hard for everything he has achieved. Don't you remember? I do. When Callie and I were very young, daddy was never home. He was always working to build his practice. You were always taking us to the office so you could help him with paperwork until he could afford to hire more people. Is Tony any different than dad?"

Julia looked at Jill and said, "You make a good case, and you're not wrong. Don't be mad at your father and me because we want the best for you. You will understand one day when you have kids. Let's just enjoy the weekend and see how it goes. You know that your father and I are reasonable people. Don't worry, let's have some fun together."

They arrived at the student center. They were all a little hungry, but not quite ready for dinner. They ordered nachos, and Julia got her coffee. They found a nice spot that had a table and two love seats around the table. The girls sat down so they wouldn't lose the spot. Frank and Tony picked up the food. While snacking, Julia asked Tony what he had planned for the weekend.

Tony replied, "I know at some point we all may want to discuss this, but I wanted to make it a fun weekend. Jill and I thought if you agree of course, that tomorrow we would go into town and have breakfast. You could do some shopping. They have added some very nice shops in town. We could have lunch, then show you some of the sites in the area. I do have one surprise that I know you will love. That is my secret. Even Jill doesn't know about it. After graduation, I was considering staying here if I was offered an entry-level position at the company I interned at. The town is growing so fast, there are always positions open for psychologists. If everything worked out, Jill might want to stay as well while she is studying for her Masters. We plan to keep all options open. When we get back, I would like to take us all out for dinner. Later, we could relax in a very nice café in town. They have four or five imitation fireplaces with seating. The atmosphere is comfortable, and they have a piano player. This would give us time to talk and get to know one another better. While I'm on that topic, I just want to add, please feel free to ask me anything you would like to know. I don't come from money, and I am not ashamed of that. I'm not afraid to work. I love my family, and I am proud of them. They raised five of us. My father always worked hard. I will answer any question you ask honestly."

Julia replied, "Frank. I think this young man has a nice plan for tomorrow. What do you think?"

Frank replied, "Sounds good to me, but I'll pay for dinner."

Tony said, "I'll tell you what. You buy lunch, and I'll buy dinner."

Frank said, "You drive a hard bargain son. I'll agree with one stipulation. I buy breakfast both mornings."

Tony said, "You have a deal." They shook hands.

Julia asked Tony to explain the two-year thing and how he and Jill finally got to meet. Tony explained everything. His shyness, why he was that way, and how he tried to gather up the courage to approach Jill and just couldn't. He explained when he saw Jill was having trouble breathing after arguing with Carl on the phone, he had to help. Tony said, "I cared about Jill before I even met her. I wasn't going to let her go to the hospital alone. I went in the ambulance with her and waited until I could see her. No one should be in the hospital alone. That is how we finally met."

Julia said, "That's surprising. You certainly don't seem shy."

Tony replied, "I'm only that way with women if I don't know them first. I guess I worked so much, I never went to the school dances and didn't date much. My brother, on the other hand, he's the Cassanova in the family, not me."

Julia replied, "I think that's cute, and we appreciated everything you did for our daughter and your honesty. Thank you."
Julia added, "Frank, it's ten o'clock. I'm exhausted from

all the traveling. Jill, why don't you come back to the hotel, and stay will us tonight? It will give us some girl time."

Jill replied, "I would like that."

They left and walked back to Jill's dorm. Jill took a minute to run in and grab some things. When she came down, Frank said to Tony, "Hop in the car, I'll give you a ride to your dorm."

Tony replied, "Thank you Mr. Muller, but I'll walk. I always walk Jill back to her dorm when we go out. This is a safe campus and security is always around. It's only a ten-minute walk. I feel better knowing Jill got home safe, but thank you for the offer."

Jill gave Tony a kiss goodnight and told him she would call him later. As much as Tony wanted to spend more time with Jill, he thought it was good that Jill would be spending the night with her parents. It would give them time to talk. Although, he wondered what that would lead to. Jill called to talk to him on his walk back. He was happy about that. He felt it showed her parents they cared about one another. Jill called him around midnight. Her mom and dad had gone to bed. She told him they would pick him up at nine-thirty for breakfast. He couldn't help but ask what they had talked about. Jill told him they talked about what was new in the family and her sister. They did talk about him as well, but not as much. She told him they seemed to like him and thought he was very nice. Jill added that her father mentioned he was impressed with your accomplishments at school, and my mother liked your honesty. Tony told her that is a good start.

They chatted for a short time and went to sleep. Rob, Tony's roommate, told him it sounded like the night went well. Tony explained it seemed as if it did, but he had a feeling they still had concerns. What can I say, I don't come from money. I understand the way they feel, but they should understand. They started with nothing and built it into what they have today. We'll see after the weekend is over. It was late, and Tony's mother called. She apologized for calling so late. She knew tomorrow would be a busy day and wanted to know how the night went.

Tony explained he thought it went well, and her parents were very nice. He didn't express any other concerns. He didn't want his mother to worry. He was the oldest. He had to help his family when they needed it. He always knew his mother felt guilty that he did not have a normal high school experience. He didn't want her to feel that way. He did it out of his love for his family. She felt better after talking to him. He told her he would call her Sunday night. She was happy for him, which made him feel good, although, the weekend had only just begun.

Jill called Tony in the morning to let him know they were on the way. He told her he would meet them outside. When they arrived, he got in the car. Everyone exchanged morning greetings. Jill gave Tony a kiss good morning.

Jill's mother turned and said, "Are you two going to do that all weekend?"

Jill replied, "Mom. I thought we talked about this last night. This is what we do, get used to it."

Tony knew there was more to last nights conversation than Jill led him to believe. Now was certainly not the time to discuss it. When they got to the diner, it was almost full, Jill and Tony got out to get a table while her parent's parked the car. That was Tony's opportunity to ask Jill.

He asked, "What was that comment about, and you didn't tell me about any other conversation you had with your parents?"

Jill replied, "We really didn't. My mother just said she felt uncomfortable watching us kiss each other every time we met each other or said good-bye. I told her that's was what we do. That's what people in a relationship do. She needed to get used to it. Babe, I'm not going to change, and I don't want you to. We need to act like we always do. They are going to have to accept it. Okay?" Tony agreed.

They had a nice breakfast. Julia apologized to Tony for her comment. Tony explained he understood their concerns. However, he thought it might be easier for everyone if they all were able to be themselves. No one wants to walk on thin ice all weekend. They left the car at the lot and started to walk around town. It had grown since the last time her parents were there three years ago when they were visiting the school. Julia loved to shop.

In jest, Tony asked Frank, "Does she ever miss a store." Frank said, "Never. That's why I don't go shopping with her. It's good that Jill and her mother are spending this time together."

Tony explained that he wasn't big on shopping. He explained when he needed something, he knew was it was. He was a directed shopper. He went in, found what he needed, and bought it. Jill could make a day out of it but was a thrifty shopper. Frank told him he if did that, he was a better man than he was. Don't start something you don't want to do for the rest of your life. Tony told him he really didn't mind. It was a break from studying and working. Frank looked confused and asked Tony about working. Tony explained he had a part-time working for a firm that reviewed insurance claims. He explained to Frank it was an excellent opportunity. He was learning a great deal about building construction and codes. It was helping him with school, and it would also look good on his resume. He loved the work and the hours were flexible. He could work while Jill was tutoring are doing something for one of the many committees she was on. Frank asked him when he and Jill had time for each other. Tony explained that was the easy part. We make time. We study together and keep up with our work during the week. This usually gives us the entire weekend to do things together. Frank seemed interested, replying, "You both certainly seem to have a well-planned schedule." Tony explained, they tired. Sometimes it would get messed up, but we work around it.

Franks said, "Tony, when Carl and Jill were dating, you must understand they were young. In high school. We liked Carl, but we knew once they both went away to school; it wouldn't last. We never expected him to do what he did, but it didn't come as a complete surprise. I'm only telling you this because I don't want you to think we are comparing you to Carl. They were just kids. You said something last night that made perfect sense. Jill's mother and I worked very hard. We started with nothing and built what we have together. My concern is not that you don't come from money. You both are adults now. If you really love each other, you will build your life. Jill is our daughter. We want what is best for her. Her mother and I are different. I want the best man for her. One that will work hard to build a future for his family. On the other hand, Jill's mother wants the same, but doesn't want to see Jill work like we had to so she could achieve it."

Tony said, Mr. Muller, I understand. My mother is no different. We made ends meet, but my father had to work hard and many hours. I started working at a young age so I could take care of myself. I think every person reaches an age when their parents shouldn't have to foot the whole bill. There were four other younger children in my house. I didn't want my father to have to worry about me as well. When I was old enough, I went to work. It's that simple. We weren't poor, but we didn't come from a fancy neighborhood either. We lived where we could afford to live. However, our house was always filled with love. Money was certainly important, but family love came first. I believe this has made me the person that I am today. I can only hope that is good enough for you and Mrs. Muller. I can't change where I came from, but I can push for where I want to be. Isn't that more important?"

Frank replied, "It is. You are right. Please. Don't think we are judging you. You aren't on trial. You have done nothing wrong. Actually, I think you have done it right from the start. You will be successful. However, Jill's mother doesn't think as practical as I do. Most mothers don't. That's her daughter. As her husband, I have to support her and allow her to see that for herself. It may take time. Are you up for that challenge?"

Tony replied, "I am. You know... Jill and I are not planning a wedding here. We are only planning how to see each other through the summer until fall when school starts. We thought we might get a place together off campus. We both still have

our masters programs to get through. We haven't discussed
anything past graduation. Yes, we talk about it, but that's it.
We have both decided we will take it as it comes. One step at
a time. We are not trying to play house, but if we love each
other, we can save a great deal of money living off campus. We
would take that money and save it. There is much ahead of us,
and much to get done. We know that. All we are trying to do is
not lose what we have in the process. Does that make sense?"

Frank replied, "It makes perfect sense. I don't know how keen I am
on the living together part, but next year you will both turn twenty-
two. That is your decision. Don't tell Jill's mother I told you, but
we didn't meet until after college and lived together for a year
before we got married. Remember, that's Jill's mother. She will not
compare what she did to what she wants Jill to do. A mother never
does. They are much more emotional. Men are different. We have
a tendency to be more practical. Let's take it as it comes. How do
your parents feel about this? Have you discussed it with them?

Tony replied, "Yes I have. They have expressed that they will
support any decision we make, and will help us as much as
they can. Like you, they told me I was a grown man now and
can make my own choices. I need to live my life, not them."

Frank said, "Maybe over the summer we
can all meet. Let's wait and see."

Tony and Frank were talking outside of each store, as Jill
and her mother went from store to store. When they came out
of the last store, Frank said he was hungry and suggested lunch.
Tony agreed. He added that their dinner reservations were at
seven, and he still had a surprise for them. They went to a nice
Bistro and had lunch. During lunch, Jill asked what they had
been talking about all this time. Frank and Tony looked at each
other, and they both knew, there was no way either of them was
going to answer that question. Tony stepped up and explained
they talked about school, law, work and how we managed to
make time for everything. Nothing more. He was holding Jill's
hand by her side and gave it a slight squeeze as if to say, drop it,

I'll tell you later. Jill got the message and changed the subject.
As they finished lunch, Frank asked where they were going.
Tony explained there was a great ranch outside of town.

Every Saturday they would train the horses. People were
welcome to visit and watch. Down the road at the base of the
mountain was a nice place to stop and have something to eat. The
view of the mountain tops was breathtaking. There was a road
that led to a scenic stop where you could see for miles. He and Jill
thought they would enjoy that. They could be back in enough time
to shower, change, and go to dinner and the café. As they were
approaching the car, Frank threw Tony the keys and said, "Why
don't you drive? You know where you're going. Jill was shocked.
Her father always drove. Tony accepted, and off they went.

While driving, Tony thought he and Frank had a good
understanding of the situation. He was starting to feel some relief
but was also getting the impression that the problem would come
from Jill's mother, not Frank. How would Frank handle that? The
ranch wasn't far. When they arrived, the ranch hands were working
with the horses. Today they were also rounding up stray calves
and getting them back to the ranch. Frank and Julia had never seen
this before and were enjoying the experience. Julia especially liked
the roping part. One of the ranch hands approached and said, I
can't help but notice how interested you are watching us rope the
calves. Have you ever handled a rope? Julia's mom said never. He
asked her if she wanted to try. She was ecstatic and said she would
love to. He got her a pair of gloves and started to show her how to
make the loop, spin the rope, and then she tried to rope a calf. She
missed every time. Everyone was laughing and having a good time.

A ranch hand said, "Let me tell you the trick. You have to throw
the rope where you think the calf is going, not where it is. By
the time the rope gets there, the calf has already moved."

The next time she threw the rope, she roped her first calf.
Everyone clapped. When she was done, the ranch hand took her
gloves and walked her back to the gate. She told Frank to give
him a nice tip. The ranch hand said, thank you ma'am, but I can't

accept that. We are here for you to have fun while we get our work done. If you enjoyed yourself, that's my tip. Julia shook his hand and thanked him. He tipped his hat and went back to work. Julia said, "I think that is the most fun I've had in years. Tony, I could see why you and Jill love it here." They went back to the car. They had some cold bottled water in the cooler, and Tony started to drive up the mountain. Frank and Jill had taken many pictures. They laughed and teased Julia all the way.

Tony hoped that would be the icebreaker. Julia could not stop talking about how much fun that was. When they got to the base of the mountain, they stop at an outside barbeque spot that had the best-tasting ribs. They all had a snack and split a rack of ribs. They were the best-tasting ribs Frank and Julia had ever tasted. You didn't get this where they lived. The country air was clean. It felt good to breathe in clean air. The countryside made you feel alive. This was nature in it's purest form. No tall buildings, traffic, or smog. It was nothing like city life. As they drove up the mountain road, they knew they were climbing because their ears were popping. They came to the scenic parking area. The view was breathtaking. Julia took many pictures. She had a very nice camera. Photography was her hobby. She also took some with her phone, so she could text them to her friends. It was a beautiful, warm, breezy day. They sat on the benches just chatting and enjoying the view.

When it was time to leave, Julia did something that surprised everyone. Before they got into the car, she gave Tony a hug. She said, "I just want to thank you for planning such a wonderful day. I never had so much good fun." Tony thanked her. Jill also gave him a hug and a kiss and thanked him. Julia looked at Jill. Jill was waiting for her to say something about the kiss. Julia, said, "Kiss him again, he deserves it." Jill did. Tony and Jill were confused. Was this temporary, or was Julia starting to accept Tony? They drove back and dropped Tony off at his dorm. Jill, her mother, and father, went back to the hotel to clean up and shower for dinner. When they dropped off Tony, they told him they would call him when they were ready. Tony told them the restaurant was only across the street from their hotel. It didn't make sense to drive back to campus just to pick him up. He asked Jill to call him about twenty minutes they would be ready, and he would meet them there, he would take the campus shuttle into town. They called Tony around six-twenty, and Tony left to meet them. He caught the campus shuttle and was there before they arrived. Frank had paid for everything so far, but dinner was on Tony. The restaurant was very nice, and to everyone's surprise, Tony had flowers for the table for Jill and Julia. Jill did not know he had planned that.

Dinner was going well. Everyone was laughing about the day's events and the fun they had. It was only a month before the school year ended, and their summer break began. Tony and Jill were commenting on how they had their classes and schedule all set for the following year. In their last year, they would be focusing mostly on their majors. Jill had clinical work she had to do as well. Tony had already done his internship. He sent a letter to the company he was with before, expressing an interest in doing a second internship during his senior year. He was waiting for a reply. They were explaining this to Jill's parents when Julia said, "When we get to the café we should talk about the summer. We will be leaving at eleven o'clock in the morning, so we don't get back to late. We have things to do when we get home" Tony was telling them he had never been to California. From what Jill had described it, it was beautiful, and the weather was great. Julia loved pictures. She had many on her cell phone. She showed Tony pictures of their house, and the golf and lake club. Tony thought to himself, this wasn't a house; it was an estate. Julia was raised in California. Frank came from Oregon. He went to law school in California and fell in love with the area. When he met Julia, they decided to stay. He took a position with a firm he was doing summer clerking for after his passing the Bar exam. That was where he met Julia. She was a real estate agent at the time and part-time wedding photographer. They hit it off, and eventually Frank decided to open his own practice. When they finished dinner, Tony paid the bill, and they walked over to the café.

They found a great spot where the seats were close, and it was in front of one of the fireplaces. It was far enough from the piano bar that they could hear the music, but not so intrusive that it was hard to have a conversation. While Frank and Julia

were talking, Tony quickly gave Jill a brief summary of his
talk with Frank. Jill was shocked. She never knew her parents
lived together for a year before they got married. He made her
promise not to say anything. Julia asked Jill if she wanted to
stay at the hotel again tonight. Jill told her not tonight. I didn't
bring enough clothes, and I want to spend some time with Tony
after. With summer coming, we have much to talk about, and
exams are starting. We will be busy. That opened the door
for the conversation to begin regarding the summer plans.

Julia asked, "So tell me. What were you two thinking about doing
over the summer? Have you discussed it since our phone call?"

Jill said, "Yes we have. Mom, that depends on
you and dad. We have a few options, but we can't
decide until we know how both of you feel."

Julia said, "I can't speak for your father, but as much
as I like Tony and have a great deal of respect for his
accomplishments, I still feel I would rather see you with
someone more established." That was all Jill needed to hear.

In a firm and semi-loud voice, Jill replied, "Who the
hell is established at our age. Were you? Tony and I
are probably more established than most of the other
students at this school. Don't you really mean someone
who has money? That's all you give a shit about."

Tony interjected and said, "Let's not argue.
It's been a great weekend so far."

Franks said, "Honey, I think we should at least hear their thoughts."

Julia replied, "Why? You don't agree?"

Frank said, "Let's not do this. Have you forgotten we came
from nothing and worked our asses off? I spent a great
deal of time talking with Tony. His head is in the right
place. It's not a bad thing for them to have to work and earn

their way. We can help them, but they will have a greater appreciation for what they achieve if they've earned it."

Julia replied, "Well then. I guess what I think doesn't matter. You have already made up your mind."

Tony interjected and said, "Mrs. Muller. No one has made up their minds. However, certain facts are not going to change. Jill and I love each other. I am the last person who wants to take her away from or gets between her and her family. I would never do that. Jill has made her choice. I support and respect that. My parents do as well. Hopefully, you can understand that. If everyone could accept that, we can come up with a plan to visit each other over the summer. Nothing about our school plans, degrees, or careers, has changed. There is no reason why we can't work towards that goal together. The fact is, how we do that will depend on how you both choose to handle this."

Julia replied, "Don't take this wrong, but why should your parents have a problem with this? After all, Jill comes from a well-off family."

Frank got perturbed by her comment and said, "Honey, that was not called for. I know you better than that."

Julia replied, "Tony. I'm sorry. That didn't come out right. Jill is my little girl. I want the best for her."

Tony said, "I understand, but isn't what's best for Jill defined by what Jill wants?"

Jill was very upset and was ready to cry. She stood up and said, "I have heard enough. Tony, please walk me back to my dorm." She looked at Julia and said, "If you can't decide to become a human being before breakfast tomorrow morning, I won't be there." Jill started to walk out.

Tony paid for the first round of drinks. He stood up and left a tip on the table. Frank said, "I will drive you both back."

Tony replied, "Mr. Muller, thank you. We will walk. I
will calm her down. I think we all need time alone to talk.
I'm sure she will call you later." He turned and left.

When he met Jill outside, she was crying. Tony held her for a
moment and said, "Stop crying. We knew this was a possibility.
I thought after the day we had, this wouldn't happen. Babe, she
may sound cruel, but she only wants what she thinks is best for
you. When it's all said and done, it's your choice. You know
that. I'm not going anywhere. If it doesn't work out, we can
stay here, find work, and get a small place together. It will be
offseason, and the apartments will be even cheaper to rent."

Jill said, "Honestly, I don't want to work it out. They need to
accept my choices." They started to walk back. Jill added, "I
have been giving this a great deal of thought. I didn't want
to say anything until I was completely sure this was what I
wanted. I can't go all summer and just see you for two weeks.
This sacrifice for love theory is bullshit. Two people who
love one another should be able to be together. I want to stay
here over the summer and get our own place. What's the
difference if we work summer jobs here, or back home?"

Tony replied, "Besides being able to save
more money, there is no difference."

Jill said, "My parents will be pissed. They will have
to get used to it. What about your parents?"

Tony said, "My parents won't have a problem with it at all. We have
to figure out a way for you to meet them. We can figure that out."

"It's settled. Next week, we will start looking."

While they were walking back, Julia tried to call Jill three
times. Each time Jill declined the calls. She was intent on
making her point. She explained to Tony, she wasn't sure he
completely understood her logic. Jill's whole life, with or without
Carl, she had to attend every affair her father had to attend.

Every speech, every affair, as well as meet his clients and their families. Jill felt she did her part. They needed her support, and she gave it. Now she needed theirs. Her phone rang again. As she went to decline the call, Tony stopped her. "Take the call," he said. "Just be honest. Don't yell, don't argue, don't cry."

Jill answered the call and put it on speaker. They stopped walking so she could talk. When she answered Julia said, "Is your phone on speaker?"

Jill replied, "Yes. I have nothing to hide from Tony. After the mean and cruel things you said tonight, you obviously don't either."

Julia said, "I hope you are both happy. Your father is not talking to me."

Jill said, "I didn't cause that, you did. Mom, I love you, but you forget so much. I was telling Tony my whole-life story. How I supported dad and his firm. I went to speeches, meeting clients, going to dinners, when I could have been with my friends. Callie, Jill's sister, and I did that because we loved you and supported you. Why can't you support me? You are not fair. I will always be your daughter. But I'm not a little girl anymore. I am a grown woman. I don't claim to have all the answers or all the experience. I do have the right to make my own choices. Reap the benefits, or pay the price for the failures."

Julia said, "You are right. I can only try to protect you, and it doesn't mean my choices are the right ones. Maybe your father is right. Maybe it is time for you to spread your wings and learn. I accept this relationship. Please, spend your last summer at home. I know after you graduate, you may not be coming home. Jill, I love you. Is it too much to ask for three months in exchange for the rest of your life?"

Jill said, "I understand. Let's talk about this at breakfast. I'm so upset right now, and I don't want to get more upset tonight. Tony and I have a lot to talk about."

Caesar Rondina

Julia said, "I understand. Just think about it. We will
meet for breakfast at nine o'clock at the same place."

Jill replied, "Okay, and mom, (she paused); I love you and dad."

Julia replied, "We love you too. Tony, thank
you. I hope you can understand."

Tony replied, Mrs. Muller, don't worry
about it. I completely understand."

Tony's phone rang. It was Rob, his roommate. Rob was wild and
crazy. He said, "DUDE, I had to call you. I'm sorry. I was a little
buzzed and opened a piece of your mail by mistake. It was from
the firm you applied to so you can do your second internship
next year. Okay. I was also nosey and read it. That's why I'm
calling. DUDE, they want you to call. They want to offer you a
summer job. I'm sorry man. I hope I'm not disturbing anything."

Tony replied, "No big deal, thanks for
calling. It came at the right time."

Jill was happy and excited for Tony. She jumped in Tony's
arms and kissed him. He asked, "You heard that?"

Jill said, "Are you kidding me, he was talking so loud I heard
every word. That's great babe. It fits right in with our plans."

Tony replied, "Yes it does. What about what your mother said?"

Jill said, "Let's explain it in the morning. It's only a little over
a two-hour drive. We could go there most weekends. During
the week, they both work, so I wouldn't be seeing them until
the evening anyway. If work schedules me for some evenings,
that's even less time I would be spending with them."

Tony said, "I know. But I think she really wants you home.
I could always come as well on the weekends. Either way,
we would have to get a car. That means more expenses,

but I will be making more money at that job than the part-time job back home. I could probably afford it."

Jill replied, "Yes, but if I don't stay with you, that's less money that you will have coming in. Together, we can easily afford it. Baby, I want to spend the night with you. Why don't you ask Rob to bunk out with one of his friends? You've done it for him."

Tony called Rob and asked. Rob said, "No worries man, give me ten minutes, and I'll be gone."

They stopped at Jill's first. She wanted to get some clothes. It was a co-ed dorm. Doing what they were doing wasn't allowed, but everyone did it. Jill would have to sneak out of the room in the morning, go one floor down to take a shower. On a Sunday morning after a Saturday night, no one would be up that early. When they got to Tony's room, they laid on the bed for a moment to relax and unwind.

Jill said, "It's going to be nice to sleep with you all night. We haven't done that since we spent the weekend in town." Tony agreed. Jill said, "I sense you're a bit stressed."

Tony replied, "Not really stressed, there was a lot of information to process tonight. We spoke, then Rob called. My brain feels like it's on a merry-go-round right now."

Jill said, "I think I can fix that."

She unbuckled his belt and slid off his pants. She took off her shirt and bra. When he went to kiss her, she said, "Just lay back and let me relax you first."

In minutes, they were both totally undressed and under the covers. The anticipation and excitement were overwhelming. Jill wanted him inside her, and that's where Tony wanted to be. He needed to feel like they were one. In body, mind, spirit, and soul. They made passionate love. Tony took his time. Moving ever so slowly so Jill could feel every part of him. As they moved through different positions, their excitement grew. For some reason, they both had great control tonight and could enjoy every minute. When they finally had their orgasm, Tony was still erect. He didn't stop. As sensitive as Jill felt, she didn't stop him because it felt so good. They continued to make love. Kissing, touching, and talking to one another until they exploded again. As they relaxed together, Jill explained she needed him so badly this night. Tony needed her as well. They were both totally relaxed now and fell asleep. In the morning when Jill awoke, Tony checked out the hallway. No one was there. Jill went to the floor below to shower, and Tony went down the hall. Tony got back to his room first and left the door unlocked so Jill could just walk in. They were all dressed and started to leave to meet Jill's parents. Tony's folded the job offer letter and put it in his pocket.

Jill's parents were there when they arrived. Julia needed her morning coffee. After they ordered, Julia said, "I'm sure you spoke last night. Your father and I did as well. What are your thoughts? I want to hear how both of you feel. The truth."

Jill said, "Yes. We talked. Before you called, we made a choice. We decided we were both going to stay in town over the summer. We could work here and get a small place together. We were going to do that in the fall anyway. The rents would be much cheaper since all the student s would be gone except for the few that were taking summer classes. Then I took your call, and Tony got a call." Julia just listened. "Tony received some great news. Babe, show my father the letter." Tony took out the letter and gave it to Jill's father. Frank read it and handed it to Julia, who also read it.

Frank said, "Tony, this is wonderful news. You must be so proud. It is well deserved." Julia agreed, and they both congratulated him.

Tony spoke up and said, "This certainly changes things. Before I went back to my dorm, Jill and I sat and talked about this. Obviously, I will be staying here for the summer and have to get my own place and a car. The bottom line is, there are two things we can do. We did not make a choice. We wanted to talk to you both first, and get your input. Julia looked at Frank, then at Jill and Tony. She said, "Now I can support you both. Do you know why?"

Tony said, "Yes I do. You feel as though Jill and
I are taking your feelings into consideration."
Frank looked at Julia. Julia said, "Go on."

Tony added, "Since you are a two-hour-plus drive away, Jill can
stay, and she can look for a job in her field of interest. This would
help us save money. We could come to the house on weekends.
Another other option is, she can come home and work there. I
could come to the house on weekends. Jill has mixed feeling about
that. She feels that during the week, you won't see her as much
since you will both be working. She doesn't know what her work
schedule will be. You might only have weekends to spend together.
Those were the two options we discussed. Either way would
work. I would now be living closer. I spoke to my parents this
morning. They understood. They told me I shouldn't pass over this
opportunity and should stay. All they asked is that I take a few days
before I start working to come home and visit. They would help me
with some money to buy a car. Regarding Jill, they felt that it was
between Jill and her parents. They would support us either way."

Julia started to speak. Frank said, "Honey, let me say something.
Tony, I agree with your parents. You can't pass up this opportunity.
When you graduate, they may offer you a full-time position,
and even help pay for your master's program. You would
probably have to commit to working there for some time."

Tony said, "Yes, they do have a program like that. That is
why I wanted to do my internship with this company."

Frank added, "If I may. Allow me to make a suggestion. You do not
need to give us an answer now. Jill and your mother were planning
to surprise you. She thinks about things more than you give her
credit for. As difficult as it is for her, she realizes this could be
your last summer living home. This would depend on where you
find a job, and how things work out with Tony. Remember, I wasn't
from California. She wants this summer with you. We talked last
night. We know we can't force that on you. We wouldn't want
to. If we did, your time together would not be quality time. Your
mother is taking the summer off so she could be with you. You

do not need to work this year. I will give you what you would have made working part-time. I don't want you to lose any money, but I want you and your mother to have this time together."

Frank added, "Tony, I believe you and my daughter are in love." With a chuckle, he said, "You and Jill look at each other the same way Jill's mother and I do. I know we are in love. To help ease your expenses, and since it's a two-hour-plus drive each way, you will need to have a reliable car. Take what your parents send you, I will put in the difference. I want you to have a fuel efficient, reliable car. I will register it under the firm's name. You will be covered by our fleet insurance. By doing it this way, you will not have any automobile expenses. I will give you a gas card to use. This should help so you would not need Jill's income. Once you both graduate, whether you are together or not, we will put the car in your name. I am only doing it this way so I can pay the insurance and expenses. Plus, it's a write-off. It will help you both until you are on your own. You are welcome to visit every weekend. We have plenty of room. I know what you both are thinking. Yes, we are okay if you share a room. Jill, we never told you, but your mother and I lived together for a year before we were married. We aren't stupid. We are sure you two have already shared intimate moments together. Besides, if you lived together this summer, you would not have separate bedrooms. Tony, I can teach you to play golf. Everyone in the business world plays golf. Some of the biggest business deals are made on a golf course. However, there is a catch. You both have to be willing to give Jill's mother this summer with her daughter. That's it. When you think about, you would be both working here as well. Your main time together would be the weekends. You can think about it and let us know."

Without hesitation, "Jill looked at Tony and asked, "In front of my parents, answer me one question. Do you truly love me?"

Tony replied, "If I need to answer that question, I guess I should just leave now."

Jill looked at her parents and said, "YES! Thank you, I love you both."

Tony looked at Frank. "Get used to it son. The women in this family rarely give you a chance to decide."

Tony laughed and said, "I'm good with that. It's not only the best option; it's the smartest. Are you both okay with Jill living with me during our last year at school?"

Julia replied, "Yes. The money we save on dorm fees we will give to you to help with your rent and food. It's not a handout. We pay for it anyway?" They all agreed, and everyone was happy. Jill's parents left feeling very comfortable. Frank told Tony once he made the final plans to call him. They would work out the finances for the car and insurance.

Tony and Jill were sad, yet excited. They were excited by the thought of living together, but sad it wouldn't be until the fall. They agreed this was a great compromise for everyone. They would have the rest of their lives together. On Monday, Tony would call the gentleman who sent him the letter. He and Jill would begin their search for an apartment. Jill was excited about that. In the fall that would be her home as well. When two worlds collide, one of three things occur. They both get destroyed, one wins, or loses, or in his case, they compromise. However, this turns out to be the easiest battle they fight.

CHAPTER FIVE

TIME FOR PLANNING

Jill's parents arrived home safely. Tony and Jill talked that night, and they both agreed this was the right decision. Tony's first class wasn't until ten a.m. He called Human Resources Directly promptly at 9 a.m. She was happy to hear from him. She explained that they had a full-time summer position open. It would also meet Tony's requirement for his second internship. His job responsibilities would include checking plans, making design models, checking building codes, reviewing documents, and work on project teams and be part of the design process. She also informed him when he started school in the fall, he could stay on part-time, as long as he could work at least 24 hours a week. This was a great opportunity and could lead to a permanent position when he graduated. The company was aware that Tony planned to continue his education and obtain his master's degree. If Tony accepted this position, he would be at the company long enough to apply for the company's employee tuition assistance program. He would have to commit to continued employment for three years after obtaining his degree. The starting pay was fair. It was double what he would be making if he was working his summer job in New Jersey. Tony expressed this was exactly what <u>he</u> was looking for and accepted the offer. They planned to meet at 4 p.m. that day to discuss it further. In two weeks final exams would be over. He thought he would need a week to settle into whatever apartment he found. Tony couldn't wait to tell Jill. They were meeting for lunch and would tell her then.

On his way to class, Tony called his mother to tell her the good news. His mother was very happy for him. They would chat later that night. When he met Jill for lunch and told her the news, she was excited for him. She explained this would work out perfectly, but she looked sad. Tony asked, "If this is working out so well, why do you look so sad?" Jill explained they were together at some point every day. In less than four weeks, she would be leaving. All that would change.

"Honey, I don't know if I can do this all summer. Promise me you will come and visit every weekend."

"I won't miss one," Tony replied.

Jill explained that she wasn't going to like this. All her mother would want to do is go to the lake club every day. I told you I don't hang out with those girls, and I don't want to deal with seeing Carl. Everyone will be asking questions."

"Babe. It's been two years. Everyone knows that you and Carl are no longer together. Once they see me coming every weekend, trust me, it won't be an issue."

Jill replied, "I know. I'm just making excuses because I don't want us to be apart."

Tony gave her a gentle hug. They each had to get to their next class. After this class, Tony ran back to his dorm and changed. He left for his meeting with the Human Resources Director. Tony's parents were sending him two thousand dollars towards his car. Tony appreciated that. He knew he would have to spend much more to purchase something reliable. Tony wasn't embarrassed by the amount his parents could afford. They were doing what they could. He had some money saved and felt he needed to contribute. When it was time, he would discuss this with Frank. There were many cars to choose from. It was also the time during the year when apartments would start advertising their vacancies since most of the students would be leaving for summer break. That night he and Jill would start looking for an apartment online. Tony did not want to wait until the last minute. He knew he needed to spend some money on clothing. He didn't need suits. Everyone went to work wearing a shirt, tie, khakis, or dockers.

The Human Resources Director met with him as soon as he arrived. She was a well-dressed middle-aged woman. She was very pleasant to speak with. She explained that everyone spoke very highly of him and the great job he did during his internship.

"Tony, as we discussed earlier today, we have an opening. The manager you worked with during your internship wanted us to offer this opportunity to you first. They did not want to lose you to another firm. I don't remember this ever happening in the time I have been here. This is a great opportunity for you." She went over every detail with him. When she was done, she asked Tony if he had any questions. He did not. She asked, "What do you think, do you still want to take the position?"

Tony thanked her for the time she spent with him and replied, "I would be honored to accept this opportunity. My exams are over in two weeks. It will take me a few days to get moved into my apartment. What start date did you have in mind."

She informed him they were thinking June 1st.

Tony replied, "That would be perfect."

They took care of all the required paperwork, and she informed Tony she would email him the details as to who and where to report within the next week. On his way back, Tony called Jill to tell her the good news. Jill seemed happy, but Tony still heard some sadness in her voice. He was also feeling sad. They had become used to being together. He knew when they started looking at cars and apartments, he would make an effort to make Jill feel part of each process.

He asked, "Could you help me pick out some clothes. You know I'm not good with that."

Jill laughed. "That's true, you're not. We'll do that this weekend. Not to change the subject, I was looking online and found two or three very cute apartments that aren't too expensive. Do you think we can look at them during the week?"

"Of course. Set it up. You know our schedules. Thank God I have you. This is going to be our place. Just because I'm moving in first, doesn't mean it's not ours. I want you to pick it out and decorate it. Whatever we don't get done now, we can finish in the fall when you move back. Babe, think about it. This is going to be our house. I'm so excited."

Jill perked up after Tony said that. Tony heard that in her voice and felt better. It would give them a goal. Something to look forward to. Jill started to tell him how she wanted to decorate the apartment. Tony really didn't care, but he made Jill feel he was interested. When Tony got back, they were going to get something to eat and would talk more. When Tony returned, they were starving. At the entrance to the campus was a bar and grill fast-food restaurant that had seating. The food was good, and not expensive. They catered to the college students. They decided to go there.

After they ordered and sat down. Jill asked, "Babe, can we have one last weekend in town before I have to leave?"

"I wouldn't have it any other way, "Tony said. We already decided we would do that. Think for a moment. Most of the students will be gone by then. If we're lucky and find a place, we would have some time there before you had to leave and stay there through our senior year. The sooner we get it, the longer we will have. Your mom and dad will be picking you up on a Wednesday morning. They can pick you up there, and see the apartment at the same time. I am going to try to get a cheap flight home late Wednesday night and return Saturday night. It's always cheaper to fly at night. I could visit my family for a few days and start work on Monday.

"Good point. I never thought of that. I will call these places tomorrow. By that time, we will only have one exam left. We could relax and have some time together to get the house in order." Jill was getting excited. They met up with Rob and Jodie and were telling them everything they had planned.

Rob said, "I wish you both the best. You know me. I'm the playboy type. I'm not ready to settle down. I'm going to enjoy my summer and senior year."

"Don't listen to him," Jodie said. "He's not even that good looking." They all laughed. They knew they would miss one over the summer. Jodie added, "This will be great. I'll get to visit all the time. I just hope I don't get some bitch as a roommate."

It was a long day. Everyone had to study. On Tuesday when Jill got back to her dorm, there was an envelope for her from her parents. When Jill's mother was in town, she had noticed a kitchen store and a linen outlet store. In the envelope was a fake check for one thousand dollars with a note that read.

Honey,

When we were there, I couldn't help but notice a kitchen outlet store and linen outlet store in town. I put one thousand dollars into your checking account. You and Tony will need some things for the apartment. When you find a place, get what you need. This should be more than enough, but if not, let me know. We love you,

Mom and Dad

Jill called Tony right away and told him. She said, "We are going to have so much fun buying what we need. I can't wait." Tony replied, "Are we still going to the library tonight to study?"

Jill replied, "Yes."

"I'll be over in about thirty minutes. When I get there, we will call your parents and thank them. That was very thoughtful of them."

When Tony arrived, the first thing they did was call Jill's parents to thank them. Julia explained to Jill that she loved her and wanted to support her. If this is what she wanted, she wanted to help. "Honey, I understand this is hard for you. I appreciate that you want us to spend time together this summer. Like Tony parents, your grandparents couldn't help your father and me as much as they would have liked to. We can help you, and want to." Jill thanked her mother and told her she would see her in three weeks. Tony and Jill had much to do over the next three weeks. Jill explained to Tony she had spoken to two of three landlords. One was already taken. She made arrangements for them to see both apartments tomorrow. They were close together. One appointment was at four o'clock, and the other at five. One was in an apartment building, and the other was on the first floor of a house. They both had two bedrooms. However, the one on the first floor of the house was larger. They liked the idea of a house better. They would have more privacy. Neither allowed pets, but Jill and Tony didn't have pets. The rents were reasonable, but the house was a little higher. The only problem they found was the rent would go up when school started. Tony thought they might be able to deal with either landlord to adjust the rent payments. He preferred the rent remain the same the entire year. It was easier for them to create a budget that way.

Their school had an excellent postgraduate program. They planned to stay on and complete their masters. They could take it part-time or full-time. Even online. They went to the cafeteria for dinner and talked about all the options. No matter which apartment they took, they needed to buy dishes and other items. Both apartments were furnished and came with appliances. After buying sheets, silverware, pots and pans, and other items, they would probably spend the full thousand dollars. On Wednesday, they would shop for a car. Everything seemed to be falling into place. There was much to do and not much time to get it done.

Both apartments would be available at the end of the following week. Tony and Jill would be able to live together for a week and a half before she had to go home. In one respect, they were very lucky. Their last exam was in two days. Their grades were excellent. They had enough credits to move on into their senior year. They wanted to score well. They needed to keep a high average and class number ranking. Tony finished first in his class each year. Jill finished first in her second year. She probably would have finished top of her class in her freshman year if not for her breakup with Carl. She wasn't focused as a freshman. She finished third in her class that year. She wanted to finish first again this year. After they ate, they went to the library to study. They took occasional breaks to make of list of the things they would need to buy. Tony's parents deposited the money for his car into his account. Tomorrow night they would see the apartments. Tony would have a better idea of what he needed to do after they picked one. After they looked at cars on Wednesday, they would call Jill's father.

When they left the library, Jill called her mother to tell her all the news. Julia said, "Honey, if you want, I can come up one day and help you both settle in, but that might be something you may want to do yourselves."

Jill said, "Mom, I would love that, but it would mean almost five hours of driving in one day for you. That's a lot. You could stay over, or maybe it's best we do that before I move in when school starts in the fall. We aren't going to do much right now until I am living there."

Julia replied, "That makes more sense. I'm happy to see you so excited. Thank you for calling and sharing this with me." After walking Jill back to her dorm, Tony went back to get some sleep.

*****

The following day was apartment hunting day. After their last class, they met up and started into town. Their first appointment was at the apartment building. When they arrived, they met the superintendent. She was very nice. The rules were strict, but that didn't bother them. They were not troublemakers. The apartment was beautiful and very modern. Whoever had rented it before kept it very clean. The furniture was just over a year old and was in like new condition. The rooms were a little small, and the kitchen was an efficiency kitchen with a small table. It was big enough for what they needed. The building also had a parking lot. They explained their situation to the superintendent. It would just be Tony for now.

Jill would be moving in when school started in the fall. She was fine with that. However, she would not negotiate on the rent. On September 1st, the rent would go up. She explained it was less now due to the offseason, and many of the students were leaving to go home for the summer. She knew she would have no problem renting it in the fall. Tony tried to explain if they split the difference now, she would still be getting the same amount of money at the end. For some reason, she didn't understand the concept. They thanked her for her time and told her they would get back to her. They still had one more place to look at.

Jill though in one respect, it might be easier to have a cheaper rent now, until she moved in. Jill also commented, remember, in the fall, my parents will be covering most of the rent and some of the food. They arrived at the second apartment, which was on the first floor of a house. The house was a slightly older looking from the outside but in great shape. The first floor was much larger than the apartment. There were two parking spaces on the side of the house for tenants, and there was street parking. They only needed one space. Everything in town was near the apartment. The rooms were much larger, but not as modernized. It was completely furnished and had all the appliances. The furniture was also newer. An older Italian couple owned it. Their children used to live there until they each got married and bought their own homes. They were very nice and loved that Tony was Italian. This apartment was more expensive, but it offered more rooms and was larger. It also had a backyard with trees, which offered great shade. It had a grill and deck. It was a better choice. The landlord had a company that took care of the grounds. The deal was the same. A lower rent now, and if they stayed, the rent would go up in September. Every place rented like that. Tony and Jill stepped outside to talk. This was the place they both wanted, but the rent was a bit of an issue. Tony said, "Let's talk to them."

When they went back inside, Tony said, "Honestly, we love this apartment and want it. We are just starting out and are good people. We will take care of your things. We have looked at cheaper rents, but we really like yours. Is there anything we can do to lower the rent a little? We will be here for at least a full year."

The wife asked, "What other prices have you gotten?"

Tony told them the other rent prices."

The husband and wife went into the other room for a moment to talk. When they came back the wife said, "Tony, let me be honest with you. We have shown this place to three other people who were willing to pay for what we wanted. We didn't accept them because we had a funny feeling about them. My husband and I like you and Jill. We like that your parents are supporting and helping you. We can't match that other price. However, if you are willing to take the apartment for a year, and give us the security deposit today, we will split the difference in the rent as compared to the other apartment you are looking at."

Tony looked at Jill and could see the excitement in her eyes. He knew she wanted this apartment. He asked, "Honey, what do you think?"

"I think we should take it."

They shook hands. Tony said, "If Jill wants it, we will take it, and wrote them a check for the security deposit."

They had the lease ready, and Tony and Jill signed it. Since it was only two weeks before they could move in, the landlords gave them the keys and said, "You are both so sweet, you can start moving in whenever you want."

Jill gave them both a hug and a kiss. She was very happy. She called her mother before they left to tell her everything. Julia spoke to the wife and thanked them. She also gave them their home number if they ever needed to call. Julia added, "Tony and Jill are very responsible adults. Thank you for helping them."

Tony also called his mother who also spoke with the wife. They spoke in Italian. Tony understood only bits and pieces of the conversation, but it all sounded good. Jill and Tony thanked them and went back to campus for dinner. Shortly after, Frank called Tony. He told him he heard they had found a place and congratulated them. He also added that Jill's mom said they were going to look at cars tomorrow. Frank informed him if he found one he wanted, call him. He would take it from there.

Tony explained that his parents sent him two-thousand dollars towards a car. He also wanted to contribute something in. Frank replied, "That wasn't the deal. I'll take care of the balance. Just pick out something good on fuel and reliable. I will mail you a gas card tomorrow. Tony, you will be driving for five hours every weekend. You need something newer that reliable. Call me if you need any advice when you find something."

Tony thanked him, and he and Jill sat under their favorite tree on the bench and relaxed. As much fun as this was, it was stressful in a good way. Everything was happening so fast. Jill had taken pictures of all the rooms and sent them to both sets of parents in a text message.

Jill said, "Babe. We have the keys to our house. Why don't we move our things off campus when we get the car and just start staying there until I leave? What do you think?"

Tony said, "Did you even have to ask? That was what I thought we would do. We could be together for almost two weeks before you go home."

Jill was so happy she was crying. If they found a nice car tomorrow, they could start moving their things in on Thursday or Friday. They called it an early night. They were both tired. Their last exam was the following morning. They had an early exam at eight a.m. They would be done around ten, and go straight to looking at cars. They were thinking of a smaller SUV. This would give them the room they needed if they traveled. There were many fuel-efficient SUVs on the market. They walked to a couple of dealerships and looked at newer vehicles that were fuel efficient. The smaller cars didn't have much trunk space. About three hours had passed. They weren't having much luck. They went to one other dealer. They had a nice deal on a hybrid SUV. It was a bit more money than Tony wanted to spend, but it was only two years old and still had the remainder of the factory warranty on it. It only had 15,000 miles on it. An extended warranty could also be purchased. They both drove it and loved it. It got almost forty-two miles to the gallon.

They had taken pictures of the cars they were considering. The salesman was very nice. Jill suggested they call her father.

Tony called Frank and explained the situation and sent him the pictures of the three vehicles they had it narrowed down to. Tony didn't offer a preference. He didn't feel that was right since he wasn't putting any money in. Frank told him he thought the SUV was the best deal. He asked, "How do you feel about it?"

Tony replied, "Honestly sir; that is the car we both liked. We both drove them all. It does cost more, that is my only concern. I can still put money in since this one is more than I planned on spending. I think you are right. This is the best choice."

Frank said, "Nonsense. You may need it. Can I talk to the salesman please?" Tony handed the salesman the phone.

They were on the phone for some time. Jill and Tony were out sitting in the SUV. The salesman kept walking into and out of another office. Finally, after almost an hour, the salesman came out and handed Tony the phone. Tony put the phone on speaker so Jill could hear the conversation.

Frank said, "We finally came to a deal. You are all set. I also bought the extended warranty since you will be doing some traveling. I gave him all the information. My bank is wiring them the money, and the insurance company will be faxing them the insurance card. You can have the car on Thursday afternoon."

Jill didn't give Tony a chance to say a word. She thanked her father and told him she loved him. Tony thanked him and assured him they would not disappoint them. It was time for dinner. Jill and Tony hadn't had lunch, so they were hungry. They decided to grab a bite to eat in town. While they were eating, Jill was saying how she could not believe all of this was coming together so fast, and they had gotten quite lucky. Tony agreed.

Jill said, "Babe, I don't want to go home. I want to stay with you."

Tony replied, "Hey. You're the one who jumped right up and said yes when your dad made his offer. I also want you to stay. This is killing me, but we both know this is the right way to do this. I am going to miss you so much, but we will be together every weekend. I really want to make a good impression on this job. It could mean a lot towards our future after we graduate."

Jill knew he was right. It would only be for three months. Tony wanted to work as many hours as he could. He might even get a part-time job two evenings during the week. He wanted to save enough money to get an engagement ring for Jill on Christmas. He knew they wouldn't get married until they were completely done with school, but he wanted to take this next step. Jill was telling Tony she needed to talk to her mother. Just before she met Tony, she was trying to set up a part-time job with a psychologist during the summer. That would give her some clinical hours she needed. One of the offices she applied to called her because they had an opening. She wanted to see how her mother felt about it. Tony reminded her that her mother took the summer off to spend with her. Jill knew that, but this was a great opportunity. It was only part-time, two days a week. She was planning on talking to her mother that night. Tony explained it can't hurt to mention it. Understand, if she says no, that's the way it has to be. You will have plenty of opportunities in the fall, especially if you finish first in your class. Jill agreed. She felt with that additional experience, she could get a good internship position locally in her senior year, and she hoped they would offer her a job so she could do her residency after she graduated. If Tony did well with this firm, she needed to find a local job as well.

Tony knew she was right. Jill said, "I really like it here. I would stay here after we graduate."

"That depends upon many things. First, we have to go where we can both get jobs. I wouldn't mind living here after we graduate."

Jill replied, "You're right. We have to consider our parents as well. This is closer to my parents, but further from yours. We could move in somewhere in the middle."

Tony replied, "We can do whatever we want. I think we shouldn't worry about that until we graduate, and find out if we both have jobs here. That will be the determining factor. I'm more worried about when we have children one day." Jill agreed. It didn't make sense putting the cart before the horse.

They finished eating and started walking back to campus. If everything went well, exams would be completed, they could pick up the car, and start moving some things into the apartment. The weekend would be shopping. Tony was an easy person to shop for. He didn't need that many clothes. Jill knew how to mix and match quite well. As for the apartment, they were only getting the basics. They could get more when Jill moved in. The boxed dish sets and cutlery were fine. The store had nice deals on pot and pan sets. Tony would probably not be cooking much, plus they had the microwave. When they got back, they hung around Jill's room for a while. She was telling Jodie everything. She also told Jodie she was moving out probably on Friday night to stay at their new house. Jodie said, "Great. I have nothing planned, as long as you guys give me a ride back; I'll help you load and unload the car."

Tony said, "Rob will probably help as well. When we're done, we can hang out and order pizza."

Tony and Jill didn't have much. Only clothes and school supplies. The apartment had a queen-size bed in the main bedroom, and two twin beds in the second bedroom. The third bedroom could be used for their study and computer room. They hadn't made plans for the other rooms. They would wait until Jill moved in. They really wouldn't use it. They both agreed that this was their house. Not a hotel room for their friends to bring someone to have sex with. This wasn't a motel room. Tony and Jill always wondered why Rob and Jodie never hooked up. They liked each other, and they suspected they may have even slept with one another once. They blew it off as knowing that Rob and Jodie weren't looking to be committed to anyone. They wanted to be free to have fun. Tony and Jill accepted this. It wasn't their business, and they were all good friends.

After their exams on Thursday, they had a bite to eat and wnt to the dealership. Tony had the utilities going under his name on Friday. He called the landlord to let them know. Tony felt that was fair since he would be moving in. They appreciated that and thanked him. Jill and Tony spent the afternoon getting their things boxed up. The clothes on hangers they left that way. It would be easier to just hang them back up in the new closet. They did a last load of laundry at the dorm. Their house had a washer and dryer in the basement that both tenants shared. Tony and Jill met the people who lived upstairs. They were a young married couple and very nice. They didn't have any children. They were excited to have Tony and Jill coming in. The previous tenants were much older. They each picked two laundry days. The other three days were open for whoever needed to use them. It was a good system. When that was completed, they would be living together for twelve days before Jill's parents would be picking her up. Tony offered to drive her home, but Jill's parents wanted to see the apartment. Jill wasn't bringing many things home. Most of what she had she wanted to keep at the apartment in case something changed, or she came to visit. She had more than enough clothes at her parents to wear. Tony booked the flight to go home to see his family. Jill would be leaving at one in the afternoon. Tony's flight was at ten that same night. He would return that following Saturday, and be home about two a.m.

They certainly did a great job of planning. However, Tony was worried that after living together, it would be much harder for Jill to leave. He knew it would be hard for him to see her go. He wasn't looking forward to that part. He was excited about seeing his family and coming back to start his new job. Hopefully, the summer would pass quickly. That night they were talking about the weekends. Tony would leave after work on a Friday, and leave late Sunday afternoon. That would give them two nights and almost two full days together. Neither Tony nor Jill were worried. They trusted each other. Jill went a long time without dating before Tony came along. Jill knew that Tony hadn't dated either. Tony couldn't help but wonder. He would be working. Jill would be with her mother at the clubs and events. Was all of this just her mother's way of getting Jill back home and try to get her interested in someone else? Tony didn't realize he was sitting so quietly. As if daydreaming. Jill shook him and said, "Honey, are you alright? You haven't said a word and your starring at the floor."

Tony replied, "I'm fine."

"I know you better than that. Tell me, what's on your mind? Are you having a change of heart?"

Tony replied, "God no. I am just going to miss you so much." He told Jill what was on his mind.

Jill replied, "Babe. I've already thought about that possibility. I didn't want to tell you because I didn't want you to worry. No one can take me from you. I spoke with my father the other day and even mentioned it to him. He promised me he would never allow my mother to do that. I don't think she will. I did tell my father that the first sign I noticed of that, I would leave and come back here."

Tony replied, "I know. It's probably my mind getting carried away."

"Stop," Jill said. "It's going to be hard enough to be apart. I don't want to worry about you worrying. Especially when there is no need to. I love you. That will NOT change."

Thursday afternoon they had picked up the car. It wasn't ready until later than expected. When they picked it up, it was perfect. The dealership had it all detailed and checked. It was a nice deep wine color with a slightly metallic finish. It had a rich appearance. Tony had a hood protector installed which he paid for. He didn't want the sand and any rocks chipping the front of the hood with all the highway driving he would be doing. Exams were done. It was only a matter of waiting for the posted results and class ratings. They had both passed all their exams so far and received in the high 90 percentile range. It was late in the afternoon. They went to Jills first and loaded up the SUV with all her things. Jodie helped. When they arrived at their apartment, Jodie fell in love with their place. Tony left for his dorm, and Jill and Jodie stayed behind to put her things away. Around six-thirty, Tony arrived at his dorm. Rob knew he was on the way, and a couple of the other guys helped Rob get everything outside. All they had to do was load it into the SUV. When they got back to the apartment, the girls were done. Everyone helped to get Tony's things in. They unpacked everything and put them away. They took out all the boxes except for a couple that Jill would need for the things she was taking home. Tony would put the empties in the dumpster on campus when he and Jill brought Jodie and Rob back later that night.

When they were done, they ordered pizza. They stopped at the store to get some plastic utensils, paper cups and plates they would use until they went shopping over the weekend. While sitting, Jill looked at Tony and said, "Babe, we're home." The girls even had the bed made. Other decorating items such as plants, knick-knacks or other things, wouldn't be done until Jill moved in permanently in the fall. Jill had some collectibles at home she wanted to bring back with her. They planned on Jill returning a week or two sooner than usual. They could finish up the apartment before school started. Jill would pack some things, and when Tony visited, he would bring something back each week. He would store them in the spare room until Jill moved in. This would make it much easier when Jill came back. For a moment they forgot this was only temporary. In twelve days, Jill would be leaving. They all had a great time talking about how they couldn't wait until the fall to return and hang out together. It was around ten o'clock when Jodie and Rob decided to go back. They put the empty boxes in the car. Tony and Jill gave Rob and Jodie a ride back to campus and threw out the boxes. When Tony and Jill returned, Tony unlocked the door. When Jill started to walk in, he stopped her. She asked, "What's wrong?"

Tony said, "Nothing." He picked her up and carried her across the doorway, saying, "I know we're not married, but this is our first house."

Jill replied, "You will have to do this again one day you know. At least, that's what I'm hoping for."

Tony replied, "No need to hope. It's a fact."

Jill didn't know Tony was planning on working a part-time evening job two or three days a week to save for a ring. He did want to tell Jill his plans, at least not the ring part. When they sat down, he told Jill he was thinking about working a part-time job. He explained he wasn't going to be going out, so why not work and save some money. Jill explained that she didn't want him working so hard. Her father would be giving her the money she would have made if she worked. They would be adding that to a savings account. Tony explained that it was fine. It would give him something to do. He told Jill he wasn't going to be looking for anything strenuous. Just something to pass the time until the weekends. He wouldn't do anything to jeopardize his day position at the firm. In his mind, he knew if all went well, he could save enough money to buy her an engagement ring for Christmas. They talked about the Christmas holiday. How would they do that? They wanted to be together for the holidays but also knew their families would want to see them. They decided when the time came, they would have three weeks off. They would do Christmas at one of their parent's house, and New Years at the other. They were tired. However, this was their first night in their new house. It would not go by without a celebration.

CHAPTER SIX

ALL GOOD THINGS COME TO AN END

Tonight, Jill planned something a bit different for Tony. When she walked out of the bedroom, she had nothing on. She slowly walked to his side of the bed, stopped, and asked, "Do you like what you see?" Tony pulled off his covers and asked, "Do you like what you see?" Jill slipped under the covers. They held each other for a moment. Tony had a candle lit in the room, This added a romantic touch. They started to kiss and caress one another as their excitement built. This was the first time they were making love in their new home. They wanted it to be special. Tony was always gentle. Jill liked a light caressing touch. It stimulated her. Tony knew her well. Jill also knew what Tony liked. They spend some time focusing on each other, and their individual areas of excitement. They spoke romantically to one another, always letting each other know how they felt, and how the other was making them feel. This also heightened the moment for each of them. As Tony orally caressed Jill's breast, her excitement began to grow. When he caressed her breast with his hand, she lurched back and said, "Easy babe. They are a little sore. I must be getting my period soon."

Tony replied, "I'm sorry. What terrible timing when we finally have some quality time alone."

"This is our special week. If it comes, after a couple of days, it won't bother me if it doesn't bother you. I don't want to lose one minute of the time we have together."

Knowing this, Tony was very careful not to hurt her and focused on other areas on her body. Jill was slender and toned. She had fair skin that was smooth as silk. Her light brown hair draped just past her shoulders. She took very good care of herself. Tony would place his fingertips over her body and feel how soft her skin felt. They each had only one sexual partner before they met. Learning each other did not take long. Their connection was not only emotional. It was also physical. Orally, they both learned how to please one another. Jill could control Tony's every sensation. Jill knew how to take him right to his peak, and gently bring him down until she was ready to take him. Tony knew Jill in the same way. They shared that connection. They were both open, honest, verbally pleasing, and it provided results. When they enjoyed mutual oral sex, it could last a half-hour or more before they would either have an orgasm together or proceed to penetration. Many times they mixed it up, going back and forth between the two and enjoying different positions. They didn't rush, always taking their time. Yes, there were times they would enjoy a quick lustful moment. They just flowed with the moment, and at times, enjoying each other more than once. This night, they would do it all. They teased and played with one another to see how far they could go. When they reached a point where neither could take the anticipation any longer and could not hold back, they would let themselves go. They loved it when they had their orgasm together. This night was not the night for a quick lustful moment. They were all in.

Tony never ignored Jill after making love. He would hold her tenderly, so she knew how much he loved her. Many times after relaxing, they would make love again. At times, they talked until they fell asleep in each other's arms. When they were living in their dorms, it was not easy to find moments of privacy. They took them when they could. For the next twelve days, that would be different. After making love, they were joking about how uncomfortable it would be the first couple of weekends they shared a room at Jill's parents. They knew they would adjust. They knew Jill's parents might also feel uncomfortable. Out of respect, they decided when it was time for bed, they would make sure Jill's parents were okay with them sharing a room. After the first couple of weekends, things would fall into place. Jill did not lie to her parents. They knew she and Tony were living together at the apartment for the next twelve days before she had to leave. Jill's parents appreciated the honesty. Jill hoped to make her parents, and them, feel more comfortable. Jill shared everything she was doing with the apartment with her mom and sent her pictures. They wanted her parents to know they were not just two college kids looking to play house. They were serious about their relationship and long-term plans. This was not a fling. It was all or nothing.

In the morning, they started their day early. They went to breakfast and bought some groceries for the house. They could eat in the school cafeteria until school officially ended. Later in the day, they went clothes shopping for Tony. Jill was a bit of a pain in this department. Tony wasn't the best clothes shopper and would buy anything. Jill wanted to but him clothing he could mix and match. It would save money, and he would always look professional. As a woman, Jill used that trick for many years. They dropped off what they bought at the apartment, and went to the kitchen outlet. Jill had one thousand dollars to spend. She was a thrifty shopper and a bargain hunter. Since they were buying so much, the store gave them an additional discount. Between the kitchen outlet and linen store, Jill spent a little over six hundred dollars. Their TV's were small. Fine for the spare rooms, but not for the family room. With the extra money, they bought a larger television for the family room. By the time the day was over, they had spent just under the full amount of money her parents had given her. They had a great deal to show for it. They had a good start. When they returned home, they cleaned everything and Jill set up the kitchen the way she wanted it. They took a ride to the student center to hang out with Jodie and Rob. It was a long day, and they accomplished a great deal. The next eleven days would be theirs.

On Sunday, Jill called her mom and told her everything they bought and had accomplished. Tony was not going to get a house phone. Using his cell phone was fine. Jill gave her parents the new address and Tony thanked them. The gas card arrived in the mail the previous day. Tony explained he would only charge gas on the weekend when he visited. He appreciated the card and did not want to abuse it. Frank told him not to worry about it. Tony explained that now that they had a car, they planned to visit some weekends, depending on their school and work schedules. Frank and Julia were very happy to hear that.

After Jill finished her conversation, she said to Tony,
"I will miss you so much during the week. I am happy
this all worked out. Babe, we have our own place."

Tony was also excited. He knew it wouldn't be easy for him.
He didn't know if he would have to work an occasional Saturday.
After working full-time all week, along with a part-time job,
then driving to Jill's every weekend, he would be tired. He
reflected on his years growing up. He now understood how his
father must have felt working many hours each week. He had to
do this to buy Jill an engagement ring for Christmas. This was
important to him. He was in love with Jill. He felt he needed to
show her and her family how serious and committed they were.
On Tuesday, the remainder of their exam grades were posted.
They both finished first in their class. They immediately told their
families who were proud of them. It showed everyone that their
new relationship had not distracted them from what they needed
to do. If Tony graduated first in his class, it would guarantee him
a permanent offering at the firm. If Jill did as well, that would
guarantee her getting a job to do her internship after graduation.
This was necessary before her degree would be confirmed, and she
could obtain her license. What she was doing during school were
clinical rotations. Jill was undecided if she wanted to specialize
in family counseling or child psychology. She could go do both.
That meant she would have to take additional courses in her senior
year. She was prepared for this, and that was her plan. All her
electives were completed, and most of her major courses were
also completed. She had time in her class schedule. Much of her
senior year would be spent doing clinical time at private practices,
clinics, and hospitals throughout the area. This would be excellent
exposure for her. In a way, not dating for two years worked out
for her. She carried a heavy class load during those two years.

At first, the days seemed to pass normally. Tony and Jill did
many things together, and they enjoyed each other physically as
often as they could. Jill's breasts were still sore, but she didn't get
her period. She didn't think she could be pregnant, but she bought
a test kit. It showed negative. She didn't want to worry Tony. They
were only sore when she and Tony had sex, and he touched her.

She thought it would pass. With all this new sexual activity, she though her body just needed to adjust. As the days got closer to her leaving, the time seemed to pass more quickly. It was only three days before her parents were coming to get her. Tony would have driven her home, but he needed to catch his flight that night to return home and visit with his family. As they talked about it, Jill wished she could go. She asked Tony if he thought her parents could get her Sunday afternoon. Maybe they could get a last-minute deal on a ticket. She would be able to meet Tony's family. Tony told her she better talk to her parents first. He wanted her to come but didn't want her parents to think they were playing games with what they had agreed upon. He knew Jill would not meet his family until New Years. It was Monday, and Jill called her mother.

Jill said, "Mom, I'm not trying to change our plans, but and dad have met Tony. I have only spoken to his parents by phone. I was thinking. If Tony and I can find a last minute cheap flight for me, would you be upset or against picking up on Sunday afternoon rather than Wednesday? It's only a few days. If not, I would not meet Tony's parents until the end of the year. How do you think they will feel? They haven't been involved in this like you have."

Julia replied, "Hold on. Let me get your father." Frank came in, and Julia switched to speakerphone. Jill explained her idea.

Jill was shocked when her father commented, "I think that's a great idea. We do need to consider Tony's parents as well. If you find a cheap flight, I'll help you." Julia also agreed. It was only four days later.

Jill and Tony thanked them for understanding. He called his mother to give her the good news. Tony's mom was very happy and looking forward to actually meeting Jill. They called the airline and were fortunate. Since the departure and arrival times were late at night, they still had seats available. The tickets were a little cheaper since it was so close to leaving. Jill booked herself on the same flight as Tony. They had to go online tomorrow to select their seating. Jill called her parents and told them she got on the same flights. It was all set. They would be flying back late

Saturday night and should be home by two a.m. They could come
to pick her up anytime they wanted on Sunday. They agreed to
pick her up at noon. Frank asked how she paid for the ticket and
what it cost. She told him she paid with her debit card and told
him the price. Frank told her he would transfer half of it into her
account. Jill thanked him and told him that wasn't necessary. This
was her responsibility. Frank agreed and told Jill that is why he
was only replacing half the amount. Jill's parents were looking
forward to seeing her and the new apartment on Sunday. Jill and
Tony were very happy they had the extra few days together, and
Jill would be meeting Tony's family. His younger brother and
sister would be home from college as well. Jill would get to meet
everyone. The weather looked nice for the weekend. Tony's mom
planned on a yard picnic for Saturday. Jill would soon learn how
Italians ate. They had a couple of days before they were leaving.
Jill wanted to make sure the apartment looked great for when her
parents arrived. She asked Tony if they could afford to go and buy
a couple of inexpensive pictures. What they had from their dorm
rooms were okay, but Jill wanted a couple of pictures tailored to
a home environment. They didn't have a fireplace, but there was
a mantle on one wall. Jill had put some small Knick- Knacks and
candles she had on the mantle, and their families pictures. The
second bedroom was not set up yet. With what they had, the rest
of the apartment looked very nice. When they returned home,
they hung the two pictures they bought. It made a difference in
the feel of the living room. The dining room had Tony's desk
and computer in it. They weren't sure if they were going to save
money and buy a dining room table, or use it as an office/computer/
study area. They had plenty of time to decide. Not knowing what
would happen after graduation, they didn't want to waste money.

They were both like two kids who had just had their first
lollipop. They could not get enough of each other, emotionally, as
well as physically. Jill's breasts were still a little being sore when
Tony caressed them. She was surprised. She hadn't get her period
yet. She bought another pregnancy test at the pharmacy. It still
showed negative. They were sexually active, which Jill hadn't been
for years. She thought that must be the reason. She wasn't worried
about it, and she didn't want Tony to worry. She felt herself and

didn't feel any lumps. They never bothered her any other time. Jill wasn't small breasted, but not too large either. They were perfectly proportioned for her body. She could wear anything and not feel uncomfortable. Her clothes looked and fitted her well. They were fortunate their flight was non-stop. It would take a little over three hours. Tony had a car rental all set up at the airport. They would be getting in the middle of the night. They planned to take a quick nap on the plane, and crash on the couch when they arrived. They didn't want the entire family waiting up for them, although, Tony knew his mother. She would go to bed a little earlier and be awake when they arrived. Tony's father took that Thursday and Friday off from work. Tony rented a car. He wanted to take a few hours and show Jill around. Tony's father offered to pick him up at the airport. Tony knew they only had one car. It would be hard for him to get around if they needed to use the car. His family didn't live that far from the airport. It was easier this way.

*****

It was time. It was Wednesday, and they had to head for the airport. They each had one carry on so they would not have to pay a luggage fee. They were on their way. They were fortunate that they had seats next to one another both ways. The flights were not completely full. As much as flying that late can be difficult, it was easier and cheaper. The airports were not as busy. Therefore, the security lines were not as long. Their flight took off time, and their arrival time was on schedule. The weather was good. They expected a smooth flight. They both fell asleep during the flight. They awoke an hour before landing. They landed on time and didn't have to wait in the baggage area. They picked up the rental car and headed to Tony's. Jill was hungry and wanted to stop at the diner outside of the airport. Tony said, "Trust me. My mom will have food waiting for us." About 35 minutes later, they arrived at Tony's. The living room light was on. Tony knew his mom and dad would be up. He didn't call the house because he didn't want to wake anyone up. After he parked, they went in. He had a key to the house but would not need it. As soon as they started up the front steps, his mother and father opened the door and met them on the porch. Tony's mother gave him a big hug and a kiss. She looked at Jill and said, "This is our new angel." She also gave Jill a big hug and kiss. She stepped back, looked at Jill, and said, "My God; you are so beautiful. I am happy to finally meet you in person." Tony's father also gave them both a hug and welcomed them. Tony introduced them. Tony's mother's name was Carmela, and his father was Vincent. Everyone called him Vince.

Jill replied, "Mr. and Mrs. Ricci, it's my pleasure to finally meet you. Tony's mother replied, "Honey, none of this Mr. and Mrs. Ricci in this house. You call us mom and dad."

Jill replied, "Okay mom. I feel like I have known you forever."

Carmela said, "Come in. You both must be starving. I have some homemade ravioli on the stove for you."

Tony looked at Jill and said, "I told you."

Everyone sat around the table. One by one Tony's brothers and sisters got up. In about 20 minutes, the whole family was awake and eating ravioli at the table at three o'clock in the morning.

Jill asked, "Mom, is it always like this here?"

Carmela replied, "Always. Not counting when their friends are here. Then there is more."

Jill said, "How nice to be from a large family. I only have a twin sister. We get along great, but it's not like this."

Carmela said, "Tomorrow you can meet Tony's grandparents. They live downstairs."

Jill replied, "I can't wait. Tony has told me so much about all of you. She sent her cell phone around so everyone could see pictures of their apartment.

Tony's brothers and sister liked their apartment and commented that they had a second bedroom. Maybe one day they could visit. Jill explained, anytime. That is why we wanted two bedrooms. I have to warn you. I don't cook like your mother. Carmela told her not to worry. Over time, she would teach her. Everyone loved Jill, and she got along with everyone.

Jill said, "That would be great. We can start this weekend, and I will help you cook."

Carmela looked at Tony in a way that an Italian mother does saying, "Tony, I like this one."

Tony's two brothers stepped up and said, "T," that's what they called Tony, while you were at school, we did part of the basement over. You haven't been here in a while. We fixed up half of the basement with some used couches and things. We put a rug down and a TV. That's where we hang out. It's great when our friends stop by.

Tony said, "That's awesome. I always wanted to do that, but you guys were too young. Not anymore I guess. You'll have to show me tomorrow."

We decided since the girl's rooms are in grandma's house, we are going to crash downstairs while you are here. You and Jill can use our room."

Tony said, "You don't have to do that, we can stay downstairs."

They replied, "No way. That's where we hang out when our friends are over, and sometimes we are up late. You guys take our room."

Jill and Tony thanked them. Carmela wanted to know how the summer plan was going. Jill explained what they were doing. Tony's mother thought that was a great compromise. Jill said, "Mom, I'm going to miss him so much during the week."

Carmela said, "Baby girl, you love my son. I can see it all over your face. Listen to me. You both have the rest of your lives together. Let him work and make money over the summer while you spend time with your mother. Vince works very hard. Every time he even touched me, I got pregnant. He never let me work. We get along fine. It took us longer than most to save money, but we managed. Raising five kids wasn't bad. They shared clothes, so we didn't need much. I missed his father because he worked overtime whenever it was offered to him, we survived. You will learn that it's nice to have your quality time apart from one another. It makes your time together more special. Right now it's new. You're trying to wear it out. I wasn't born yesterday you know. Vince and I did the same thing. You will be fine. Trust me. I know my son."

Jill leaned over and kissed her on the cheek and said, "I love you ma."

Carmela said, Then give me a hug, In this house, one goes with the other."

Tony's brothers and sisters already went back to bed. Tony, Jill, and his parents cleaned up. Jill and Tony went to the boy's room, and Carmela and Vince went to bed. Tony and Jill fell right to sleep. Jill awoke before Tony to the sound of people in the kitchen. Carmela and Tony's sisters were making breakfast. Jill walked in and said, "What can I do to help?"

Carmela replied, "You are family now, but still a guest. We do this every day."

Jill replied, "Well. I can't be family and a guest, so I'll take family and peel the potatoes."

Carmela was impressed. When Tony woke up, he walked into the kitchen and saw Jill peeling the potatoes. He was in shock, "Ma, you're putting her to work already."

Carmela replied, "Dio Mio, which in English means, oh my God. Are you kidding me, I couldn't stop her? She's a keeper, Anthony."

Tony smiled. Jill's mother and sisters were teaching Jill how to make home fries. Carmela told Jill she had made a recipe book and she gave a copy to each of her daughters. She told Jill she would make another copy and send it to their house. Jill thought that was great and thanked her. During the day, Tony planned on showing Jill around. They would be back long before dinner to help. On Friday, they would spend the day as a family, and Tony was going to buy the pizza for dinner. Saturday was their picnic, and Saturday night they would leave. Thursday was a fun day. Jill saw the neighborhood, where Tony worked, went to school, and met some of his high school friends. They returned home early enough to help with dinner. Tonight they would have eggplant parmesan. Jill had never had. She was having so much fun dipping the sliced eggplant in the egg and flower.

In Italian, Carmela said to Vince, "Impara presto," which means, she's a quick learner."

Tony said, "No secrets in Italian ma."

Carmela said, "I'm sorry. I forget." Tony's grandparents came up and met Jill. His grandmother put each of her hands on both sides of Jill's cheeks and kissed her and said, "Inglese, lei e' un angleo Anthony." Which means, she is an angel Anthony. Tony kissed his grandparents. The whole family was together. They were baking the eggplants, making the vegetables and mashed potatoes. Jill sliced two loaves of Italian bread. Tony's oldest sister showed her how to put olive oil in a small dish, and add fresh-ground pepper for dipping the bread. Jill tried a piece and loved it. She told Tony, "This is all so new to me. I love every minute of it. I am so glad I could come." Around seven o'clock, Jill's phone rang. It was her mother. Jill called them in the morning to let them know they got there safely. Julia asked her how things were going. Jill was very excited. She was telling Julia how she was learning to cook Italian. Julia told her that is great. Julia thought over the summer you could teach me. Julia asked Jill if she could speak with Tony's mother. Jill handed Carmela the phone. Julia wanted to thank her for having her daughter stay with them. She was happy that Jill came up with the idea. Carmela told her she raised a beautiful, respectful, and helpful daughter. They spoke for a few minutes. Julia told her at some point, it would be nice if they could all meet one another. It seemed as if both their children were quite serious.

Carmela agreed and thought that was a great idea. Julia told her they would talk more about that. Carmela gave Jill back the phone.

Jill said, "Mom, thank you so much for letting me do this and understanding. I just know you would love Tony's parents, and they would love you. Julia said I'm sure we will. When you are home, we can talk about us all getting together one day. Julia told her to enjoy herself, and they would see her Sunday.

Friday was a girl's day. During the day, all the girls would spend it together and talk. The boys could do whatever they wanted. Carmela told Vince to take the recipe book to the office store and get it copied for Jill. She didn't want it to get lost in the mail. In fact, she said, "Make three copies. One for Jill, one for Julia, and one to have as a spare." Vince told her he would drop it off in the morning and pick them up later. The boys were going to help Vince finish the new deck in the yard. After the fresh wood dried, his brothers could stain it. The girls made snacks and lunch for the men throughout the day. About five o'clock, they ordered the pizza that would be delivered. Jill never had real Italian pizza. She was in for a surprise. Tony ordered a variety of pies. Mushroom, bacon, sausage, and plain cheese, and a white clam pizza with mozzarella. When Jill tasted her first piece, she was in heaven. She had one of each type. She couldn't believe how good it was.

Carmela said, "Honey in my book there is a recipe for homemade pizza. Try making it one day. It's easy."

After seeing all the different kitchen supplies that Carmela had, Jill said to Tony, "I can see we still have a lot to buy."

Tony replied, "We'll get there."

Jill said something that shocked everyone. After she said it, even she couldn't believe what she had said. She replied to Tony, "I want our kids to know how to cook like this."

Everyone just stopped and looked at Jill. Carmela said, "Don't be embarrassed. We want grandkids, but don't rush."

Tony just looked at Jill and smiled. She was red
from blushing. Carmela said, "With both of your
looks, you will make beautiful babies."

Jill said, "I'm sure, but we will be making our family."

Everyone smiled. Jill was having an awesome time. Now more than
ever, she didn't want to leave. Tomorrow would be their last day
at Tony's. Sunday afternoon, Jill would be gone. After dinner, she
thanked Carmela for thinking of her mother and making a copy
of her book for her. Later that night Vince sat out back having a
cigar. The boys joined him. Tony's sister's were watching TV, and
Carmela was alone on the front porch. Jill walked out and sat next
to her on the chair. Jill explained how much fun she was having
and thanked her for everything and started to cry. Carmela put her
arm around Jill and put her head on her shoulders. Jill just cried.

Carmela said, "Honey, I understand. When I was dating
Tony's father, he was drafted. After basic training, he
had to leave. After that, I didn't see him for a year and a
half when he was sent overseas. I was worried sick."

Jill asked, "How did you do it. I only have to wait five days."

Carmela asked, "Are you Catholic?"

Jill responded, "Yes."

"Do you believe in God?"

"Yes."

Carmela said, "Say a prayer with me." They both said a prayer
together. When they were done, Carmela said, "Listen closely.
Trust what I am telling you. Every time this bothers you when
you are not together. Say a prayer to God. He will give you
the strength you need to get you through those times."

Jill put both her arms around Carmela and gave her a hug and
said, "Mom. I love you so much. How did you get so smart?"

Carmela laughed. "I had a mother who taught me,
just as you will teach your children. Have faith honey.
That is the answer to your heart's questions."

Jill and Carmela sat for a bit talking and enjoyed the beautiful
night. Later that evening when everyone went to bed, Jill was
telling Tony how close she felt to his mother. Tony said, "She
is an amazing woman. I don't know how she does it. Do you
see why I had to help when I got older?" Jill told Tony she
understood before, but not like she does now. Jill could see
there was a great deal of love in their house growing up, but
somehow this was different. It felt more personal. She loved it.

Jill asked, "Did you get mad when I made the
remark about our children? It just came out."

"Mad? Are you kidding? I've told you I want to
marry you and have children one day. I'm not
ashamed of that. Why would I get mad?"

Jill replied, "I know we've talked about it, but not to our parents."

Tony said, "You probably made my mother the happiest
woman in the world. Honey, Italian families are very close.
Close in a different way than most others. It's not just a family
or heritage bond; it's also a deep spiritual bond as well."

Jill said, "I understand. I was sitting on the porch with
your mother, and I started to cry. Happy and sad tears.
Happy because I had this opportunity, and sad because it
was soon ending. We said a prayer together. That helped
so much. I know we can make the summer now."

Tony was smart. He didn't ask any questions. This was a
moment she shared with his mother. That needed to stay
between them. His only response was, "I'm glad you are happy.
That makes me happy." They fell asleep after making love.

Saturday came, and it was a wonderful day. They cooked
and ate food all day. Playing games and laughing. There

was so much food left over, they ate the leftovers for dinner. Tony and Jill knew they would nap on the flight back. As they were packing their carry on, Carmela knocked at the door. Jill opened it. Carmela asked if she could come in.

When she entered the room, she said, "Anyone with eyes can see how much you love each other. As a mother, I could not have hoped for a nicer woman for you."

She handed them each a laminated card. On one side was a picture. Saint Valentine. On the other side was a prayer. The prayer that Jill and Carmela said on the porch that night.

Carmela said, "Over time, St. Valentine was thought to be associated with finding love. The Church states he is the patron saint for those who have already found their soul mate. It is to him and God you pray to when you need help, strength, and guidance during the next few months and the rest of your lives. Put these somewhere safe. Keep them with you always. Knowing that each of you always has it with you. When you look at it, you will feel as if you are together. My mother gave me these when your father was overseas during the war. I would have never made it without them. Take them with you. I have more, and remember what I said."

They thanked her, and all three of them took each other into each other's arms and held each other for a moment. They just had said their goodbyes. They said goodbye to the rest of the family. They all stood on the porch waving as Jill and Tony drove away.

They didn't get two blocks when Jill said, "I miss them already. Wouldn't it be nice if everyone lived on the same street?"

Tony laughed and said, "Let's not get carried away. This is the best part about visiting. However, when we have children, I'm sure it will be difficult for my family since we live so far away."

Shortly after, they arrived at the airport. They turned in the car and boarded their flight. In fourteen hours, Jill would be gone. They slept about half the flight. When they landed, they got their car from long-term parking and went home. This would be the last night they slept in their bed together for almost three months. It was a very loving and tender night. Jill would not let go of Tony. They awoke around nine a.m. and went for breakfast. They got back to the apartment around eleven. Jill unpacked and straightened up a bit. Her parents would be there shortly. Her parents weren't very religious. They believed in God, but in a more practical sense. She explained to Tony that she was not planning on telling her parents about the moment she shared with Tony's mother or the cards she gave them. She felt that was between them. Their personal moment. Jill's phone rang. It was her mother telling her they would be there in about twenty minutes. As sad as Jill was to leave, she would be happy to see her parents again, and they would see the apartment.

Jill looked at Tony and said, "I'm just saying we do have time for a quickie you know."

Tony, taking advantage of this moment, explained he was thinking the same thing but wasn't sure if Jill was in the right frame of mind."

"When it comes to making love to you, I'm always in the right frame of mind."

Right there on the couch, they made love. As little time as it took, it had as much meaning as any other time they had made love. About three minutes after they got dressed, the doorbell rang. They looked at one another and laughed. Jill opened the door, and there was Julia. She was holding a beautiful bouquet of flowers for the house, and Frank had three bags of things they knew from a past conversation they hadn't bought yet. They were both so thankful. They showed Frank and Julia the house. They all sat down for a moment and talked on the couch. Frank and Julia loved the apartment. They could not believe how big it was. Tony and Jill telling them about Tony's family and their visit. Jill told them all about his brothers and sisters. She handed Julia the recipe book Tony's mother had copied for her. Julia thought that was so thoughtful and looked forward to trying some of them out with Jill. It was about two in the afternoon. Frank explained, as hard as he knew this was, they needed to start back. Tony shook Franks' hand and thanked him for everything. Julia gave Tony a big hug and a kiss.

Julia said, "We will see you next weekend right?"

"Yes. I wouldn't miss it for anything."

Frank took Jill's small bag. Julia said, "Honey, let's wait in the car and give them a minute alone."

Jill and Tony just stood looking at one another as the tears rolled down their faces. Not a word was said. No words were needed.

Jill said, "All good things come to an end."

Tony replied, "No. All good things have a beginning. This is our new beginning."

He walked her to the car. They exchanged a passionate hug and kiss. Jill got into the car, and Tony watched as they drove off. He thought to himself, all the years he spent alone; he never felt as alone as he did right now. Julia called him about five minutes later.

"Tony, please talk with my daughter. I have never seen her so sad. She won't stop crying."

When Jill got on the phone, Tony said, "Do you have your card with you."

Crying and between the tears, she replied, "Yes."

"Take it out and say the prayer with me."

Together they said the prayer. This made Jill feel better. He could hear Julia ask, "What was that all about honey?"

Jill said, "I'll tell you when I hang up."

Tony asked, "I thought you weren't going to tell your mother?"

Jill replied, "At first I wasn't. No secrets. She should know. She may be hearing it again."

They exchanged I love you, and Jill told Tony she would call him when she was settled. Tony turned and walked into the apartment. It seemed empty without Jill. Feeling totally alone. He sat down and cried.

CHAPTER SEVEN
A NEW LIFE BEGINS

The next day was Tony's first day at work. After work, he would look online for a part-time job. The college students were mostly gone, there might be open positions. Tony wanted to go to bed early. He was tired from all the traveling. He got himself settled and picked out what he was going to wear on his first day. Jill had given him some suggestions on how to mix and match what they bought. He was feeling lost without her. He knew she was back home by now. He wanted to call her but didn't want to seem pushy. She told him she would call after she was settled. He stretched out on the bed and put on the television. He fell asleep until the ringing of his phone awoke him. It was his mother asking how he was doing. Tony told her saying goodbye was difficult. During his drive home, Jill's mother called. Jill was very upset and asked me to talk with her to calm her down. Tony said, "Mom, she was crying so much it was hard for me to keep it together. We said the prayer you gave us. After that, she was much better. She is going to call me after she gets settled in. Hopefully, once she is home and sees her sister, she will be fine." They talked for a short time, and he felt better after their conversation. As he was dozing off, his phone rang again. This time it was Jill. He tried to sound like himself. It was difficult. Tony was sure she sensed the sadness he was feeling. Jill explained to how much she did not want to be home and missed him. She explained that her parents and sister were very understanding. Jill asked if he was ready for his first day at work. He told her he was all set.

Jill laughed and said, "Don't worry, we'll be talking every night. I'll tell you what to wear."

Jill told Tony she didn't nap on the drive home. She was to upset. However, her parents were very comforting and talked with her all the way home. Jill told him they were serious about making arrangements in the future to meet his family. They were thinking over the holiday break, everyone could get together. Tony explained he would need to have advanced notice because his parents needed to fly, and that would be expensive since the entire family would be coming. Jill told him tomorrow she was going to go around with her mother and say hi to her friends, or she just might take the car. I wouldn't take long. She had no intentions of hanging out with them. They were still single and looking to party all summer. That wasn't what Jill wanted to do. She told Tony she asked her mom if she minded if she tried to get a couple of days a week internship time with one of the local counseling practices. Just two days. That would help her tremendously in her senior year. Jill was shocked when her mother said she didn't mind. Jill was also exhausted. They said goodnight and would talk tomorrow. Jill reminded him not to feel funny about calling and bothering them. She told him to call anytime. Jill did not want to be the only one calling. There was no reason Tony couldn't call. Tony knew this was important to Jill. He told her he would.

They both went to sleep. Tony was up early to shower. He got dressed and left to go to his first day at his new job. When he arrived at work, all those he previously worked during his internship were happy to see him. They were all glad he received the offer and accepted it. It was much different now. He wasn't an intern. He was an employee. He met with his boss who explained his responsibilities. He was a great guy. He was never pushy as long as everyone got their job done. Since Tony had worked in all the areas he had responsibilities, it would not be difficult to make the transition. Tony was a go-getter. It wouldn't take long before he would be looking for extra projects to be a part of. He had his own desk and computer. He was in a cubicle in the larger office area. He also had his own phone. Except for building the scaled models, most all of his work was done through the computer. Part of his job was reviewing designs for accuracy and making suggestions. They had weekly project meetings with the individual teams they were a part of. As long as things were on schedule, overtime was not necessary. However, if they got behind, or completion dates were changed, the company expected that each team gets the job done. Tony was hourly so he wouldn't mind the overtime. Most of his first days would consist of getting settled in. There were many people he hadn't met.

*****

Meanwhile, Jill was out with her mother. They did some shopping and stopped by the lake club where Jill saw most of her friends. Her mom went off in one direction, and Jill in another. Julia noticed that Carl was there as well. When she saw him going over to Jill, she walked over to be with there. Carl was already talking with Jill. He was telling her he was sorry that he bothered her. He still wanted to try again. As Julia approached Jill, she could hear Jill telling Carl it would never work. She wasn't interested and was seeing someone else. She was explaining that they had an apartment together, and she would be moving back in with him in the fall when school started. Carl did not know Julia was standing only one or two steps behind him when he said, "I don't care about him. I only care about us. Dump him. You're probably only with him because you are rebounding from me."

Jill replied, "There is no us, and there will never be an us. I love him. Not because of you, because of him. He is more of a man then you ever were. I am here spending what will most likely be my last summer here with my family. Tony and I will decide where we are going after we graduate. We still have our masters to complete. Carl, I will ask you only once. Please do not hassle me all summer, or I will have to tell my father."

Carl got angry and replied, "Still a daddy's girl I see?"

Julia stepped up and said, "Listen to me, Carl. Tony is a wonderful man with a fantastic future. My daughter loves him, and we want to enjoy this last summer together as a family. If you don't back off immediately, this will be a problem. I will be informing your mother about this. Get over yourself. You are not all that you think you are, and certainly not good enough for my daughter. Am I making myself clear?"

Carl apologized and walked away. Jill thanked her mother for stepping in but told her she could handle it. Julia replied, "I don't want you to have to handle anything. You have a new life and new goals. Carl is no longer part of that. To tell you the truth, your father really likes Tony. You are good for each other. I will deal with Carl. I want you to enjoy yourself. I was looking at Tony's mother's recipe book. Later in the week, why don't we make lasagna and surprise Tony when he gets here Friday night?"

Jill gave her a hug. "That's a great idea. Thank you." The rest of the day went well. Tony surprised Jill and called her for a minute on his lunch hour after he ate with some of his co-workers. He told her how much he liked the job and the people. Things were going well for his first day. Jill was happy about that. Jill explained that she hadn't been for a physical or her gynecologist since last summer. She thought she would schedule those over the summer because when she moved back in the fall, she would have to look for new doctors. Tony said I need to do that as well. They couldn't talk long because Tony had to get back to work. They would talk later that night. When Tony got home from his first day, he made some dinner. Something simple. He was trying to save money and wasn't the best cook. They bought TV dinners and other frozen foods that could be quickly microwaved. That would make it easier for him.

He looked online and found a couple of part-time jobs he thought would be good for him. He was considering many things. One job was delivering pizza, and they supplied the car. It was minimum wage plus tips, but no stress. He would get home earlier at night. Another was a job stocking shelves at the local supermarket, but some overnights and weekends were required. That wouldn't work. The pizza delivery had no overnights, but some weekends were also required. That wouldn't work either. All he was looking for was something for a Tuesday and Thursday evening. He found an opening at one of the convenience stores. It was evenings, six to eleven. That would be perfect for him. Not only did he apply online; he walked there and applied in person as well.

The manager was still there and met with him. They connected right away. He offered Tony the position with one stipulation. If he needed him for an occasional Wednesday to fill in, he would be required to do that. Tony agreed. He was all set and had a part-time job. He would come in this Wednesday and Thursday, and next Monday to learn the ropes. If all went well, he would be on his own the following Tuesday and start his regular schedule. The pay was fair for a part-time job. It was about the same as he was making working his job in the summer in New Jersey.

Tony's days were very busy. In a way, he was lucky. It didn't leave him much time to think. With the addition of his part-time job, that would help as well. Tony was used to working a lot. This wouldn't be a new rodeo for him. The summers were hot. The air conditioning would feel good. They had window units in the apartment, and each room had a ceiling fan. The first week went well. Jill and Tony talked each day during his lunch break and every night. It really wasn't that bad. At least for Tony. Jill, on the other hand, had much more free time on her hands. It would take her more time to adjust. She did get an internship position with one of the family counseling services in town. She worked two days a week from nine a.m. until two p.m. That worked out well for Jill and her mother. Friday came, and Tony had taken his overnight bag with him to work. He left for Jill's right after work. He was hungry and picked up a sandwich for the ride. When he arrived, Jill was very excited to see him. It took him about two hours and forty-five minutes to arrive and hit no traffic. He was wondering how her father did it in two hours. When Tony arrived, he met Jill's sister Callie. They were twins, so she was just as beautiful as she was. You could not tell them apart except for their different hairstyles. Although they were twins, their personalities were different. He could tell that Jill's sister liked the lifestyle that Jill didn't seem to be impressed with.

Frank asked him how the drive was. Tony replied, "How fast do you drive?"

"Between seventy and eighty, but mostly eighty, why?"

Tony replied, "I don't know how you do it in two hours. I was doing the same speed, there was no traffic, and it took me forty-five minutes longer."

"I really never timed it. You are probably right."

Tony didn't care. He just wanted to be certain there wasn't a shorter way. Sometimes the GPS systems in cars don't always take you the quickest way. When they went over the route, the way Tony came was the quickest. Julia had saved him a plate of leftovers from dinner. Tony was still hungry. On Saturday, Jill planned on him meeting her friends. Part of her was hoping Carl was at the lake. Not because she cared, because she didn't want him to think she wasn't telling him the truth. They stayed at the house and later went to bed. It felt great to be sleeping in the same bed together, but it did feel a little awkward. They checked with Jill's parents to be sure they were okay with them sharing a room. There were no issues. They knew they would get used to it. Jill wanted to know what time on Sunday he planned to leave. Since the drive was longer than her father said, he wanted to be back to the apartment around ten. He would probably leave between seven and eight in the evening. Jill was happy. She thought he would want to leave earlier. As awkward as it felt being in Jil's house, they made fantastic love. They were careful to be quiet, so they thought.

On Saturday morning they left for the lake. Everyone was there. Yes, even Carl. Over the past few months of being with Jill, Tony had learned to dress more with the times. This made him quite handsome. He lost that nerdy look. All of Jill's girlfriends loved him and were happy for them. Jill helped him to become more outgoing. Although, he had a great personality. He was only shy when it came to asking someone out. Her friends told her she was very lucky. Tony looked a bit geeky growing up. He was Italian and had a temper if someone pushed him too far. He didn't take crap from anyone. However, for him to get to that point, he needed to be pushed. Jill introduced him to everyone except Carl.

When Carl walked over, Jill and Tony were with all Jill's friends.
He walked over to Tony who was sitting down and asked,
"Are you my replacement? The gumba from New Jersey?"

Tony stood up and held out his hand to shake Carl's. Carl
didn't take it. Tony put his down and said to Jill, "This must
be the asshole that hurt you before you met me." Looking
at Carl, he said, "So, you are Carl from California?"

Carl just stared at him. Tony said, "I am not looking
for trouble. I will be here every weekend with Jill.
However, if you want trouble, I'll give you all you can
handle. Now or later, it makes no difference to me."

They both just stared at one another for a moment, Carl replied,
"No trouble man, nice to meet you and held out his hand." Tony
shook his hand and sat down. Carl walked away. He was all talk.

Jill said, "What was that all about? I've never seen you like that."

"Just because I'm shy, doesn't mean I can't handle myself. I grew
up in the streets of Jersey. In my neighborhood, you either took
care of yourself, or you got the shit kicked out of you every day."

Jill laughed and said, "Good to know." Everyone went back to
having a good time. It was about three o'clock, and Jill suggested
they leave. She and her mother had a surprise for him at home.
He told Jill her friends were nice, but he could see how she wasn't
like them. Jill explained they were nice, but very upper class. That
wasn't Jill's style. Tony thought California was beautiful. Nothing
like where he came from. Jill told him it wasn't L.A. or San Diego,
but it was nice. One day they would have to go there. She had
only been there when she went with her parents for an event when
she was younger. Her mother was from this area. This was where
she wanted to stay. Her father had no other close family, and his
parents had passed away. It was easier for him to relocate. Jill's
grandparents and family lived relatively close. When they got back,
it was about four o'clock. It was hot that day. Tony wanted to take

a quick shower. When they walked into the house, Tony could smell the Italian cooking. He asked, "What did you guys do?"

Jill said, "You'll see."

When they sat down to eat, Julia put out the lasagna, Italian bread with olive oil and fresh ground pepper. Tony was completely surprised. When he tasted it, he said, "This tastes just like my mothers. Thank you so much. What a nice surprise" On the way back from the lake they stopped at a roadside stand. Tony brought back flowers for the table.

Julia commented, "Frank, take a lesson from Tony. You never bring me flowers for the table."

Frank replied, "Tony if you keep this up, I'm not going to let you come on weekends just to make me look bad."

Everyone laughed and enjoyed a great dinner. Frank said, "If you want, maybe next weekend we can all spend the day at the golf club. I can teach Tony how to play golf. We will only play nine holes. That doesn't take as long. We have clubs there that Tony can use. If he likes it, we can get him his own clubs."

Everyone thought that would be fun. After dinner, everyone helped clean up and went to sit on the front porch. The air was dry, and at night when the sun went down, it cooled off nicely. They had a nice time talking about the day and laughing. When they went to bed, Jill and Tony made love. Jill's breasts were still sore when Tony touched them. They both felt them and could not feel anything. They didn't bother her as much during the week. She still thought it was the sexual part. She had an appointment with her gynecologist the following week and would ask.

On Sunday, they didn't have anything crazy planned. They just hung out by the pool at home. Tony wouldn't be leaving early, but also not late. It was his first weekend there. They wanted to see how it went and not push the activities. It was a great day. Frank went to play Golf in the morning. Jill's sister was out for the day.

Julia, Jill, and Tony had some nice quality time. He was telling
everyone how much he loved the job, and everything was going
well. They told Tony about some of their plans during the summer.
They had a few day trips planned, and a couple of overnight
trips planned as well. Later that day Tony and Jill were talking.
Although they miss each other, it wasn't as bad as they thought it
would be. The weekend really made the difference. It was time for
Tony to leave, and Julia gave him two large containers for food to
bring back with him. If they kept it all there, everyone would gain
weight. Frank and Jill's sister were back before dinner. Everyone
was there to say good-bye. This time there was no crying. Tony
and Jill had their private moment to say good-bye. They knew
they would be together next week. After about a half an hour,
Jill called Tony and talked with him for much of his ride back.

When Tony got back to the apartment, he felt pretty good.
He wasn't as tired as he feared he would be. This seemed to be a
good summer plan. He and Jill had said their goodnights before
they hung up. Tony went right to sleep. Tomorrow would be a long
workday because he had orientation at his part-time job as well. He
fell right to sleep. The following week went well. They spoke every
day at lunchtime, and at night. They seemed to be settling into
a routine. Carl hadn't said a word to Jill, and she and Julia were
having a nice time. Jill went to the doctor on Wednesday for her
physical and blood work, and the gynecologist on Thursday. Her
OBGYN doctor thought she might have felt what could a small cyst
in each breast. She told Jill these were benign in most cases and
can be removed if necessary. She scheduled her for a mammogram
for the following week just to be sure. Jill felt better knowing it
was nothing and could be easily fixed. She let Tony know. He
thought that was good news. The test next week would verify it.

That weekend Tony was back. They had a nice Friday
evening, and once again Julia saved him a dinner plate. Saturday
everyone went to the golf club, and Frank and Tony played nine
holes. Frank was surprised at how well Tony did. Tony enjoyed
golf. He found it relaxing. Frank told him when you play with
clients, you only have to remember to let them win more times
then you do, especially if you were trying to make a deal that

day. It was another great weekend. Jill and Tony were falling into this routine nicely. They made loved three times, but each time, Tony did not caress Jill's breast. He did not want to cause her any discomfort. She felt bad about that but was also happy. Her breasts were becoming more tender. On Tuesday, she would have the mammogram. Julia and Frank knew of this but didn't seem concerned based on what her doctor had told her. Other than Julia's mom, Jill's grandmother, there no other history of breast cancer in their family. On Tuesday, Jill went for her test. She didn't like it. Not too many women do, and it was painful.

It was Wednesday when Jill got the call. Her doctor wanted to meet with her. She could bring her mother. What did this mean Jill thought? Julia told her not to worry. Many times they don't like to go over results over the phone, especially if they want to refer to an x-ray or something. Deep down, Julia was worried. They had an appointment first thing Thursday morning. Frank took the morning off so they could all go together. Jill didn't tell Tony. She didn't want him to worry until she knew what this was all about. The rest of the day Jill was quite. Julia could see the worry on Jill's face. She needed to hide hers to be strong for her daughter. She knew if everything were fine, the doctor would have given her the results by phone. Many years ago, Julia had a similar scare. It turned out that she had cystic breasts. The larger ones causing her discomfort were removed. This relieved her pain. She needed minor reconstructive surgery to even out her breasts. She went for yearly mammograms to monitor the remaining cysts. It had been almost fifteen years now, and they never changed. Julia was fortunate that when tested, they were benign cysts. At the time, the doctor explained that many women had these and don't know it because they are so small. They don't cause any symptoms. Small cysts grow on many organs throughout the body as people age. That was a good sign. Julia sat with Jill and told her of her experience and telling her to try not to worry. She explained that Jill's blood work was normal.

*****

It was Thursday morning, and they all went to the doctor. Due to the medical privacy HIPPA laws, and Jill wasn't a minor, she had to sign a consent form to share her medical information with her family. She also added Tony's name. They all met with the doctor. She was very nice and soft-spoken. She had a comforting tone to her voice. She started by telling Jill to listen to everything she had to say. When she was done, they could discuss the options. She explained to Jill she had cystic breasts. She had many tiny cysts in each breast, but two larger ones. One in each breast. They were in a rare place for these to develop, which was why they could not be felt upon exam. The smaller ones were of normal size and shape and were probably benign. However, the larger ones were of a different shape, and possibly texture. Those were the ones she was concerned about. Although they could also be benign, the only way to know would be to biopsy them both and send them to the lab. They would also biopsy one of the smaller ones in each breast and send them along as well. She explained while this needed to be done, they also needed to be thorough and check both types. Surprisingly, Jill didn't cry. Deep down, she knew something wasn't right.

Jill asked, "Does this mean I have breast cancer?"

The doctor replied, "I am not going to say yes or no. We won't know until the results came back, which would take about a week to get the pathology report. However, the two larger ones will need to be removed. This would leave you with two spaces in your breasts. That might make you feel self-conscious. With reconstructive surgery, you would never know they were there. However, let's cross each bridge as we come to it."

The doctor wanted to do the biopsy as soon as possible. It was Thursday, and they scheduled her for that afternoon. Even though Jill didn't cry, she was very upset. She asked her mother should she tell Tony. Her father answered and said, "You have to. Don't worry, he is strong, and loves you."

Jill replied, "And what if I have breast cancer and have to need both of my breast removed. Will he still want me?"

Julia said, "Honey, if, and I mean if, that were the case, the way the procedures have been perfected, they do the reconstruction at the same time. However, don't put the cart before the horse."

"I know, I will tell Tony tonight when we talk. I want to do whatever needs to be done as soon as possible. I want to try to start school on time." When they got home, Jill went to her room and cried alone.

After dinner, Tony called. Jill explained what happened, and she had the biopsies that afternoon. Tony knew he needed to reassure her. He told her not to worry, no matter what happened, he would be there forever. Tony told her she should have called. He would have driven up. Jill snapped and said, "You have only been there a week, it was only a biopsy, not surgery."

Jill was not herself. They started to argue, which is something they never had done. Jill hung up on him. Tony knew calling her right back would only make it worse. He called Julia. Julia tried to explain how upset Jill was. She agreed that he didn't need to drive up. Julia would keep him informed. Julia told him to save his time off. He may need that time off later. After about ten minutes had passed, Tony called back Jill. She started in on him again until he yelled, "WOULD YOU PLEASE STOP AND LISTEN! I get it. Next time just tell me." Jill agreed and apologized for snapping at him. She was clearly upset. Tony asked if she understood no matter what, he was always going to be there. Jill understood, but couldn't help but wonder if things were not good, would he really stay, or was he just saying that? Tony wanted to change the subject. They talked about the things they would be doing over the weekend. He explained that he was excited. In two weeks, it would be the fourth of July weekend, and the fourth fell on a Monday. He was off. They would have an extra day together. Jill hadn't realized that and was also excited. They went to sleep. Between work, and the drive, Fridays were a long day for Tony.

He left for Jill's right from work. When he arrived, Julia had a dinner plate waiting for him. Tony appreciated that but said, "If you keep doing this, you are going to spoil me."

"I can't take all the credit. Your sweetheart makes
sure there is enough and makes your plate."

Tony thanked them both. Jill was very quiet. It was obvious
she had a lot on her mind. When Tony finished, he got up
to clean his dish. Julia took it from him. She would take
care of it. She looked at Tony then over towards Jill. Tony
got the message. He took Jill by the hand and said, "Let's
go for a walk." Tony and Jill headed out the door. As they
were walking, Tony said, "Talk to me, babe. I know you are
upset and rightfully so. Tell me what you are thinking."

"I don't want to lose you. What if I have breast cancer and they
want to remove my breasts? You aren't going to want me."

Tony said, "Are you crazy? First, they would do reconstructive
surgery. Secondly, I thought you gave me more credit than
that. No matter what it is or isn't, as long as they can make
you better, that's what I care about. Not your breasts, you.
I will never leave you no matter what. I love you,"

They stopped, and Jill looked at him and asked,
"Are you sure? I would understand."

"I am totally sure. You must believe that.
Can I tell you something?"

Jill replied, "You can tell me anything."

"My mother had breast cancer. She had a double mastectomy.
My father is still there. I'll bet you couldn't even tell."

Jill replied, "Shit, you never told me that, and I couldn't
tell. I mean she had cleavage and everything."

Tony laughed, "Yes she does. When they were both removed,
they performed the reconstruction at the same time."

Jill said, "Oh my God. I would have never guessed."

Tony replied, "So don't worry. I'm not going
anywhere. Let's not worry about it until we know
what it is. Just trust me. I will be here for you."

They held each other for a moment and kissed. Julia was
watching from the window. When she saw this, she knew Tony
had calmed her down. When they got back to the house, Jill was
in better spirits. Everyone stayed in and chatted the rest of the
time. Tomorrow will be nine holes of golf. When Jill and Tony
got into bed, Jill asked, "Do you want to make love to me?"

Tony responded, "Yes, but tonight, I just want to hold you."

Jill said, "Me too."

Before they fell asleep, Tony said, "Babe, I waited
my whole life to find you. Remember that."

The following morning everyone got up. Jill was in better
spirits. Today they had a nice picnic planned. It was a cloudy day,
and everyone hoped it didn't rain. In the town was a beautiful
park with many flowers. Many people would go there and have
a picnic. As they were driving into town, it started to rain. They
decided they would go to the golf club. They had tables that
were covered so they could eat and not get wet. They all thought
that was better than being stuck in the house all day. That night,
Jill and Tony were going to a movie. It was a great day and
night. There was no further talk about Jill's possible problems.
After the movies, they stopped at the ice cream shop in town
an brought home some freshly made homemade ice cream. Jill
called when they were on the way back and asked her mother to
put on coffee. When they returned, everyone was surprised that
Tony and Jill brought back ice cream. They all had coffee and
ice cream while listening to Jill talk about the movie. They all
laughed and enjoyed themselves. That night Jill and Tony made
love. He didn't want to ignore her breasts. However, Tony was
afraid it might bother Jill if he did. He was sure to be gentle.

Sunday was a nice day. They hung out by the pool, got some sun, and dove in when they got hot. As with all the Sundays, the time came when Tony had to leave. This time, Jill was very emotional about Tony leaving. Tony explained that maybe he should stay. Jill wouldn't have it. Not to cause an argument, he agreed. Ten minutes after she watched Tony drive away, she called him. All she wanted to talk about was the things they were going to do to the apartment in the fall when she moved back. She talked to Tony the entire way home. Tony enjoyed that. It made the time pass quicker. By the time he gets home, he was usually tired. He would get his clothes ready for Monday and go straight to bed.

It was Monday and Tony was not himself at work. His boss asked him if anything was wrong. Tony explained what was going on. His boss told him he could take whatever time off he might need. Tony explained his girl would not let him. This job was a great opportunity for him and their future. Tony's boss had him come into his office. He explained that the people at this firm have been here for years. They were like a working family. We get the job done, help each other, and pitch in when necessary. He further said, "Didn't you wonder why you were performing extra work last week?"

Tony replied, "I thought we were just busy."

His boss replied, "We were, but also Tim was out with the flu. Everyone pitched in to cover his work. That's what we do. If anything comes from this, which I hope it doesn't, tell me. You can take time off to be with her. It will not affect your future with the firm. You are young, bright, and exactly the type of person we are looking for to be a part of our family, our future, and growth. Don't worry about that." Tony thanked him in went back to work. The results would be back in a few days, and they would know. He spoke to Jill at lunch. She laughed and said, "My mother is so cute. She has really gotten to like you a lot. And my dad adores you. She was asking me what we wanted to make for you for dinner this Saturday." Tony explained how good that was. He also explained the conversation he had with his boss, and what his boss said. He told Jill if she needed any other procedures, he would be there. No arguments. They agreed.

Tony said, "Put your mother on the phone with you for a minute." When Julia got on, Tony let them know he told his mother what is going on. She works in a support group with other women. They help women experiencing these things to understand and get through the emotional healing process, which more often than not, is harder than the physical recovery. He let them know his mother did not want to make Jill feel pressured by her calling. She asked Tony to tell Jill to call her anytime day or night if she needed to talk to someone. Tony explained he had to go, and asked Jill to explain the rest to Julia. Jill explained what happened to Tony's mother and said she would have never guessed if Tony hadn't told her. Julia told her that is very nice of her to make that offer. She told Jill she wouldn't get mad and would understand if she wanted to call her. Later that evening Tony called. They talked for a while, and they both went to sleep. The rest of the week was routine. On Friday Tony made the drive to Jill's. Jill and her mom had a fun week together. They took a couple of day trips just to get away. They were now a month into the summer break. It was the fourth of July weekend. Jill and Tony would have that extra day together. They were all going to the fireworks and a party at the golf club. Tony and Frank would get another nine holes in. It was only Tony's second time at the game but took to it like he had been playing golf for years.

Frank said, "Maybe we need to buy you your own set of clubs."

"When I could afford them, I will."

Frank said, "Tony. I don't have any sons. Jill's mother always had fun buying things for the girls. Let me do this for you. Let me have some enjoyment."

Tony agreed. He knew Frank could easily afford it, but that wasn't the only reason. He remembered growing up. Every time his mother bought something for his sisters, his father took the boys to the supporting goods store to buy something for them.

He understood how Frank felt and appreciated it. There was a good shop with fair prices at the club. Frank and Tony went to the shop, and together they picked out a full set of golf clubs and a nice bag. Frank added Tony's name to his membership as a family member. This gave Tony's full club privileges should her ever want to go there and use the course. They spent the rest of the day with the family enjoying the picnic at the club. Tony met many influential people. Everyone liked Tony. He knew when to listen, and when to speak. He could talk about any subject. Frank was introducing him as his future son-in-law. Jill and Julia were in shock as to how attached Frank was getting to Tony.

Julia said to Jill, "I think your father found the son we never had."

"Mom, why didn't you and dad try for a boy?"

Julia replied, "After giving birth to you and your sister, I had some complications. To correct them, meant I could not have any more children. So your father has just adopted a son."

Later, Jill told this to Tony. He understood. Tony was well-liked at the picnic. After telling people who he worked for, many people gave him their business cards. They informed him if he was ever planning on moving to California they could help him. Jill and Tony saw this as a great opportunity down the road. It was a great day. They had a band for dancing at night. Tony said to Jill, "I could get used to this lifestyle." Jill punched him in the arm. She lived it growing up, and couldn't stand it. So many people were phonies. It was all about the money. That night everyone seemed to forget their troubles. Everything seemed normal. Tony and Jill made passionate love as if nothing else was on their minds. At that moment, nothing was.

*****

On Tuesday the doctor called. The results came back from the lab. She wanted to meet with Jill. They made an appointment for Thursday morning. Jill called Tony to let him know. Tony didn't even ask to go. He knew Jill would not want him to take the day off from work. He told her not to worry and let him know what the results were. Tony went to see his boss and explained that on Thursday Jill was getting the results. His boss didn't wait for Tony to ask. His said, "Take the day off, and Friday if you need it." Tony said, "Thank you, I will be here Friday." Tony called Julia and let her know what was going on. He explained if he told Jill he was coming, she would get mad because he took the day off. He asked if he could come down Wednesday after work and go with them to the appointment in the morning. Julia told him she thought that was a good idea and thanked him. No one would tell Jill. It would be a surprise. Tony had accumulated enough sick time to be paid for the day. When he spoke to Jill later that night, he told her he had a meeting after work on Wednesday and would call her as soon as he was out. They didn't talk much about the appointment. Jill was nervous. He could hear it in her voice. They spoke on Wednesday during his lunch break, and Jill was out by the pool with Julia. Tony felt funny that he wasn't honest with Jill by telling her he was coming. Before they hung up, he said, "I will talk to you tonight, I love you," He didn't feel as if he were lying to her since they would be talking, but it would only be in person.

When Tony left work, he drove straight to Jill's. He made the drive in record time. When he walked in, Jill was in shock. At first, she was angry. In no time she hugged him and thanked him for coming. "Did you really think I wouldn't be here for this?" Everyone had dinner together and spent a quiet night at home. In the morning, they left for the appointment. Everyone could sense how anxious Jill was. When the doctor came in, she sat behind her desk. Jill introduced her to Tony, and the doctor thanked him for coming.

Her doctor said, "Jill, I have your results. They are mixed, so hear me out first. The smaller cysts are benign. Nothing to worry about, they just need to be monitored. As for the two larger ones, they are cancerous. However, they are at the earliest stage, which is very good."

As must as Jill was upset, she also felt some relief. Julia asked, "What are the option's doctor?"

Her doctor replied, "There are three options. First, do chemo and radiation. See if we can kill it and shrink the tumors. I don't recommend that because we really never know if we got every cell. Second, we surgically remove them and do some chemo just as a precaution. However, it will leave her breasts with open space, meaning, they would not look even or the same as they do now. That is easy to fix, and we can do breast reconstruction at the same time. The third option is not to take any chances. Remove both breasts and do reconstruction surgery at the same time. That is the safest way to go. This way we know we removed it all. As I said, you are lucky because it's in it's earliest stage."

Jill started to cry. She asked, "What is the best choice?"

The doctor replied, "Emotionally, they are all difficult, but we can help with that. Medically, I would recommend the last option. In your case, it's simply internal tissue removal. This is what we have started to recommend. At this stage, it almost guarantees all the bad cells are removed. The surgeon may recommend one round of chemo as a precaution. That will depend on what they find. With the other options, the surgeon will check the tissue margins. Meaning, the tissue around the tumors after they are removed. If the margins are clear, then the chemo is just a precaution because it is always possible a cell is missed. All it takes is for one cell still to be present for the tumor to regrow. However, the good news is, the type you have is very slow growing. If you choose that option, we would have to watch you very carefully for at least five years."

Jill asked, "What about school?"

The doctor replied, "You probably would start a month late. Many times your professors would let you take the work home if it were for that short of time. I have had many girls in the same situation. For that to happen, we would have to get you into surgery right away."

Julia asked, "Do you do the surgery?"

The doctor said, "No. The doctor in our practice is considered one of the best in the country. I wouldn't send you to anyone else."

Tony said. "May I ask a question?"

The doctor said, "Of course."

Tony asked, "My mother had a double mastectomy seven years ago. With regards to the smaller cysts, if Jill chooses to just remove the larger tumors, what are the chances that a smaller cyst can become cancerous?"

The doctor replied, "Although rare, there is always a chance that a benign cyst can change."

Julia said, "Honey, we shouldn't rush, but I think if you are that concerned about school, the sooner we make a decision, the better."

Her doctor said, "Wait here. The surgeon is in the office today. Let me see if he has a moment to stop in."

When she returned, she walked in with an older stately gentleman. He was also soft-spoken. He pulled up a chair and sat down next to Jill and held her hand as he introduced himself. He said, "Hi Jill, and am doctor Reiss. Call me Jim. Everyone does. So I hear you have a decision to make. Karen, your doctor, filled me in yesterday. Allow me to say that both procedures are moderately uncomfortable, but we can control that. You are a very lucky girl. You are healthy, your asthma causes no concerns. Your tumors are at such an early stage, it is the best time to manage them. I know you're worried about how you will look. You will look as beautiful and natural as you do now. The hardest choice to have to make is how big you want me to make you." Everyone laughed. He said, "I'm only joking, but I can do what you want. I have a great team."

Julia asked, how soon would you want to do any procedure?"

Jim replied, "One of my patients is only one year older than you. She caught a bad cold, and we had to cancel for Monday because. I can get you in her spot if you decide today."

Jill asked, "Jim. What is your opinion?"

He answered, "Truthfully. You are young. If you were my wife, I would say remove them. Why live with the worry the rest of your life and constant check-ups. It has no effect on childbearing. Honestly, it's more emotional than physical."

Tony said, "Jim, Jill will be my wife one day. I could not care less if her breasts are fake or real. I love her. I do not want her to live her life worrying. If my mother could do it, anyone can. Babe, I say remove them."

Julia was in shock and started to cry and gave Tony a big hug. Frank just put his hand on his shoulder and gave it a squeeze. Jim said, "You have a good man there Jill. Don't let him go. Let me add one thing. With the surgical techniques and implants available today, they will look and feel completely natural." We would only be removing the internal tissue. If all the margins are good, all of your other physical features would be unchanged. It does take a little time for the sensitivity to return. He stood up and asked, "Does anyone have any questions for me, I have to get back to a patient?" There were no more questions. He said, "Thank you, everyone. Karen, let me know." He left the room. Everyone sat quietly for a moment. Jill said, "Let's remove them. I don't want to live in fear for the rest of my life. If Tony doesn't care, neither do I." She looked and Tony and asked, "Are you sure?"

"I'm convinced. I told you once and never want to tell you again. I am not going anywhere."

Jill replied, "How big do you want them?"

Tony laughed and said, "I don't care, just don't get ridiculous."

Jill said, "I love you mom and dad, but I don't want to live in fear. I should remove them."

Everyone agreed a double mastectomy was the safest choice. Her doctor put her on Monday's schedule and set Jill up for her pre-op physical and blood work.

CHAPTER EIGHT
WHEN LIFE GETS DIFFICULT

Tony decided he was taking time off from work, this time, there would be no argument. Jill's doctor informed them that the first day, Jill would be out of it. She said, "Tony if time off is an issue, take Tuesday and Wednesday. Jill won't even know who is there until late Monday night."

Tony replied, "I can be up by eight o'clock Monday night and will stay until Wednesday night. When I get there, can I stay in her room overnight?"

The doctor replied, "Since you come in from out of town, I will give the okay if you don't mind sleeping in a recliner."

Tony said, "I'll sleep on the floor. Her parents will be there all day. This will allow them to go home for a while."

The doctor replied, "That's a good idea."

That was the plan. When they got back to the house, Tony called his mother and told her. His mother said, "I was afraid that would be the case. Honey, she is doing the right thing. Can I talk to her mother?"

When Julia got on the phone, Carmela said, "Hi Julia. I am so sorry to hear this news. I want to help. I'm sure Tony told you I had the same thing done seven years ago."

Julia replied, "Yes."

"If you say no I will understand. Jill will be in pain, but the pain medications will take the edge off. What will be worse, is her emotional state. When she first looks at herself, she will be devastated. The bruising and the swelling will look terrible to her."

Julia replied, "Yes, the doctor explained that."

"I know. They explained it to me as well, but when I first looked, I was completely devastated. I wouldn't let my husband near me for almost a month. I felt robbed. I can help her. I would like to come and stay with you for a week when she comes home. I've been there. I know you are her mother, but if you have never experienced this, between both of us, we can save her a great deal of emotional grief. When the bandages come off, together, we can get her through this."

Julia started to cry and thanked her for caring for her daughter. Julia said, "Please, do not take this wrong, but the round-trip flight will be expensive. Please, I would love to have you, but allow us to pay for your ticket."

Carmela said, "We will find a way."

"No. I insist. That is the only way I will do this."

Carmela agreed and asked if she could speak to Jill. When Jill got on the phone, Carmela said, "Honey, I love you like you were my own. I just talked to your mother. You know I have been through this. I am coming to stay with you when you get home for a week. Together, we all will help you."

Jill started to cry and thanked her. Carmela was honest with Jill. She told her that her parents were paying for the ticket. They would not let her pay. Jill thanked her mother and father. Julia said, "She loves you very much."

Tony replied, "That is the way my mother is. She does love Jill very much, as do I."

Tony remembered what her mother went through. He hoped his mother could help. He knew this was going to be a very difficult time for Jill. He had to be strong, no matter how bad it got. Until they got her hormones regulated, she would be all over the place. He hoped they could survive this. Jill was stubborn, but he knew his mother would not take her crap. That's what

Jill would need. This was a great deal to go through and try to get back to school, along with wanting to move back into the apartment. Later that evening Tony had to get back. He told Jill he wanted to call his mother and thank her as soon as they were off the phone. He gave her a hug and a kiss and said, "Don't worry. I'll be back tomorrow night." When he left, he called his father first. He asked his father how he managed. His father told him he would have to be strong. This would not be easy.

His father added, "I love your mother. That is what got me through. Call me anytime you need to talk."

Tony replied, "Thank you. I will. Let me speak with mom."

Carmela tried to reassure him. She told him this would be difficult for Jill and for you. Even when she is healed, she might be distant for a while. Don't think she doesn't love you. It is a hard thing to accept at first. They talked for a while, and then he called Jill. They spoke the rest of Tony's drive home. Jill was worried that Tony wouldn't wait or accept her afterward. She asked him if he could go that long without sex? Tony laughed and replied, "Are you kidding me? I watched you for two years without having sex with you. This will be a walk in the park. By the way, we have great sex, but that's not what our relationship is based on, so forget what you are thinking. We'll be fine. Right now let's get you well so you can move back in with me on time. I'm tired of sleeping alone."

Jill replied, "I will. Trust me."

Tony was exhausted. When he went to work the next day, he told his boss. His boss said, "Nonsense, take the three days. It's not a problem."

Tony replied, "Thank you. However, that would only upset Jill. I don't want her to be upset. The two days will be fine."

His boss replied, "Okay. I understand. If you need more time, just call me."

Tony thanked him again and explained his mother was also flying out to be with her. He would be back to work on Thursday. Tony's boss really liked him. He was doing an excellent job. Taking on more tasks, and was highly motivated. He planned on keeping Tony on part-time when he returned to school, and if all went well, offer him a permanent position after graduation. Later that day he called Tony into his office and told him all of this. He explained he was letting him know his thoughts because he didn't want him to worry about his job. When Jill was on her feet and back in town, he wanted to take them to dinner. Tony was completing surprised and excited. He couldn't wait to tell Jill. This news would certainly make her worry less. After work, Tony left for Jill's. He wanted her to enjoy this weekend. When he arrived, his dinner plate wasn't ready. The entire family waited for him to arrive to eat dinner together. Tony said, "That's it. I am now officially spoiled." While they all ate, he told Jill about the conversation he had with his boss. He was excited to know he had a job after graduation.

Frank interjected, "Congratulations Tony. You deserve it. However, you may find you have more than one offer coming your way."

Tony, looking confused, asked, "What do you mean."

Frank said, "I'm not trying to keep my daughter close, just understand this is about your choice. When and if the time comes, I will support any decision you both make. Do you remember Paul, the grey-haired gentleman we played nine holes with at the picnic?"

Tony replied, "Yes. He was very nice and talked to me all day."

Frank said, "Well, he happens to own the largest architectural design company on the West Coast. He was very impressed by you. He called me to ask all about you. Of course, I told him everything I knew. He also asked if I thought you considered moving to the West Coast after graduation? I told him that would be up to you. He will be watching you over the next year. I have seen him do many things for his employees. Just keep it in mind."

"If that time comes, that will depend on where Jill can find work. As for me, I love it here. I would move. It's only a plane ride home to visit my family from either place. Jill being happy and finding work is what's important to me." They had plans of going to the lake tomorrow and a movie Saturday night. Sunday they would spend with the family. Jill asked that no one is told of this. "No one needs to know. I'm not around them that much. This is very private and personal. I want to keep it that way please."

Friday and Saturday night Jill and Tony made love to one another like they never had. It was so passionate, loving, and caring. Sunday morning Jill made her first joke. She said, "I hope you enjoyed them. It's the last time you will see these." They both laughed.

Tony asked, "Did you decided on a size?"

Jill said, "You are such a pervert. Of course, I did."

"Well? Are you going to keep it a secret and make me wait?"

Jill replied, "I will tell you because they won't be as big as when you see them swollen. I am only going one cup size larger. I'm a "B" cup now and going to a "C" cup. I don't want to look out of proportion."

Tony replied, "Good choice."

Jill said, "The surgeon told me if everything looked good, he might be able to keep some of my original parts, if not he could rebuild them. You know what I mean right? I might lose a little sensitivity or none at all, depending on what he found. He told me how lucky I was because the cancer was at such an early stage. If I had waited, the surgery would have to be a completely different procedure."

Tony said, "You see; that's why you met me. So you could find out your boobs were sore."

"Oh really?" She gave him a little shove.

They had a great day with the family, and it was time for Tony to leave. He told Jill he would be there Monday night and would be staying over in her room. Julia told her that she would call Tony throughout the day and let him know what was going on.

Jill asked, "Can I call you before I go in?

Tony replied, "Of course you can. I want you to."

*****

It was Monday morning. Jill had to be at the hospital early. She was the first case. She was registered and taken to the surgical waiting area. Her vitals were taken, and her intervenous line was placed. She was very nervous. She asked the nurse if she could call her boyfriend quickly. The nurse handed her a phone, and Jill called Tony. Julia and Frank were with her. They could stay until Jill was taken to the operating room. The surgery would take many hours. When Tony answered, he tried not to sound worried and in good spirits about the procedure. He heard the fear in Jill's voice. He told her to try to relax. Once in the operating room, she would be sleeping in minutes. When she awoke, the procedure would be done. He would be there after work. He was leaving at three instead of four-thirty to beat the traffic. Jill said, "I can't wait to see you. I love you. I have to go, one of the doctors came in." Tony told her not to worry. He also loved her more than anything in the world and to concentrate on all the great things they would have together once she felt better.

The anesthesiologist came in to talk to Jill and introduce the nurse who would be caring for her. They were very nice. They told her they would be coming for her in about fifteen minutes. Shortly after that, her surgeon came in. He was smiling and joking, trying to make Jill feel more relaxed. He asked how she was holding up. She told him she was sacred. He told her not to worry. She had the best team in the country taking care of her. He sat next to her and held her hand. "Jill, you made the right choice. After you heal, you can live a worry-free life, finish school, get married, have children, travel the world, or do whatever you want. The next two to three weeks would be the hardest. Together, we will get you through it." Jokingly he added, "I just have one challenge here. I don't think I can make you more beautiful than you already are. You'll be fine." Before he left the room, he told Jill's parents he would be out to see them as soon as Jill was in recovery. Everyone thanked him. He got up and left the room. Jill really liked him. He was the type of man who just by talking to him, made you feel comfortable. He was very reassuring. They knew the basic surgery could take two to three hours, and the reconstruction part would make that longer. Possibly another two hours. There are many approaches to the type of surgery Jill was having. Jill opted to have the procedure that gave the most natural results. She did not want to look like she had two bowling balls on her chest. The transport team came to get her. It was time. Her parents went to the cafeteria to have breakfast. They had some time to wait. They sat and chatted, and Julia called Tony to tell him Jill was taken to the operating room. Julia could hear the frog in his throat as he was trying to hold back his tears at work. Julia told him not to worry. She would be fine.

It was hard for Tony to concentrate at work, but he got his job done that day as if nothing was going on. It was eight-thirty when Julia called him. He tried to figure out the timing, thinking Jill might be done by two-thirty. He thought between recovery and her getting up to ICU, he might be there when she woke up. Julia and Frank went to the waiting area and sat. It was a waiting game. Carmela called to see how they were holding up. She and Julia talked for a while. Carmela could tell she needed the support. Carmela impressed how important it was for her to stay strong and support Jill. Carmela explained they shouldn't worry. At first, Jill will be in and out due to the pain meds at first. Don't be concerned if she seems in and out for a few hours. She will need the rest. Carmela told her she did research on her doctor. He was top in his field. She couldn't be in better hands. She asked Julia to call her when Jill was in recovery. Carmela was flying out following Sunday and would be there for a week.

The plan was to completely remove the breast tissue. The skin, nipple, and areola would be preserved. Because this discovered in such an early stage, the surgeon did not feel a radial procedure was necessary. Jill would probably be in the hospital for two or three days. She would go home and have a follow-up visit in a week. Normal activities could resume between two and six weeks or more as tolerated. Everyone was more concerned about the emotional recovery component rather than the physical one. That is where Carmela and Tony would come in. Tony needed to show Jill that this did not matter to him. She would need to wear loose-fitting clothes. The family met with the doctors counseling team while Jill was in surgery. They explained how important it was to let Jill express her feeling. She would probably have mood swings. All of this was normal. Let her vent, but always point out the positive aspects of the decision she made. One of the counselors explained they had spoken to Tony and explained he was very supportive. This procedure did not and would affect his feeling towards Jill. He was fully prepared to handle this and support Jill. They explained that Jill was very lucky. Most men have a difficult time with this. Tony did not. They explained that this form of acceptance by her partner would greatly help her emotional recovery.

Tony called during his lunch hour. Before that, a nurse came out to tell them everything was going well. Jill still had an hour or so before they would be done. She would spend an hour in recovery before they could come and see her. Julia explained this to Tony. Tony was happy to hear things were going well. Tony asked to speak to Frank. He asked Tony how he was holding up, Tony asked him the same. They were both doing as expected.

Tony said, "Mr. Muller. In my entire life, I have never asked for anything. This is very difficult for me. You know I am working two jobs over the summer. I am doing this because I am saving to buy Jill and engagement ring for Christmas."

"Jill's mother and I thought that was your plan."

Tony said, "We are not setting a date. It's a show of our commitment. We have school to finish, jobs to secure, and our masters to obtain. We wouldn't get married until we had secure jobs and were settled, or even after we got our masters."

Frank replied, "Son if you waited until you were settled, that is long enough. Many married couples are married while studying for their masters. If you are asking for our blessing, you have it."

Tony replied, "Yes. I am asking for that, but also one other thing. I know what type of ring Jill wants. I was a bit a detective when we would walk through jewelry stores. I will have the money saved by Christmas, but not by the time she moves in. I would like to give it to her sooner. When she moves in to be precise. Maybe at a family dinner before she leaves to come back to school. I think this is important for her to know that this procedure does not affect what we have. If I did it now, she would think it was out of sympathy, and that is not the case. She should be feeling better by the time she comes back. I think that would be the right time." Tony did not know that Julia's ear was by Frank's phone.

Julia interjected and said, "I think that is a good idea, providing this is really what you both want."

"It is."

Frank asked, "What else was there."

Tony said, "I will be a little short. I do not think I can buy it that soon, and I don't really have any established credit yet. Would you loan me the difference with the stipulation that I pay you back monthly? You would be paid back by the time I would have saved the money at Christmas time? I know you will say that's not necessary, but Mr. Muller, for me it is. That is the only way I could take it."

Frank replied, "I understand and agree. That is not a problem. Let me know when the time comes."

Tony thanked him and had to get back to work. He needed to be strong. Whenever Jill was having an emotionally difficult time, he could not do this to make her feel better. She would always wonder if it was because of her surgery. He had to wait until she was healed. She had to know that her surgery didn't bother him. This would be a great surprise when she was ready to move back in.

Three o'clock came, and Tony thanked his boss. He told him he hadn't heard if Jill was in recovery, and would see him on Thursday. His told him if he needed more time, to call. Tony told him he would, but should be returning on Thursday. Tony's part-time employer was also very understanding. One of the other employees was doing Tony's Tuesday evening shift. Tony would repay the favor if he needed a day off. Tony left work and started the drive to the hospital. He was a little concerned. He thought Jill should be in recovery by now. About three-thirty the doctor came out to see Julia and Frank, He said the surgery went well. Jill should be very happy with the outcome. He explained she will have bruising and swelling. That will all go away. His nurse would set Jill up with her follow up appointment and post-operative care instructions. He explained there was one minor complication. During the surgery, her asthma acted up. Probably from the movement of all the nerves. It was very easy to get under control. When you see her, she will have the breathing tube still in. We are keeping it there for a couple of hours until we are sure her inflammation is gone. Nothing to worry about. The nurse will be out to get you shortly. They thanked him, and Frank called Tony, and Julia called Carmela. Jill's sister was already with them at the hospital.

Another half an hour passed and the nurse came out to get the family. She introduced herself and apologized for the delay. She explained they needed to get Jill settled. If all were fine, the breathing tube would come out in about another hour. When they went in, except for the breathing tube, Jill looked good. Her color was good, and she was asleep. They would not start to wake her until the breathing tube was removed. Julia sat in the chair by the bed and held her hand. As much as everyone wanted to cry, and would be tears of joy, they didn't. They did not want to run the risk of Jill opening her eyes and seeing them cry. She would not understand why. By this time, Tony would be there within the next hour or so. Julia called Tony to let them know they were with Jill, and she looked good. They explained the tube in case it was still in when he got there. Jill was sedated. She did not make a single movement. Tony asked Julia to put her phone by Jill's ear. She did and also listened.

Tony said, "Babe, it's me. It's over. Your mother said you look great. I'm on my way and will be there within an hour. I love you with all my heart."

While Julia was looking at Jill, she could swear Jill tried to smile. Julia left the room and started to cry telling Tony what she had seen. Tony said I will be there soon. The nurse ran over to Julia to make sure everything was okay. When Julia told her what happened, the nurse said, she is sedated, but we never know what a patient can hear and understand. They must really love one another. Julia said they do. The nurse gave her a hug and said, "Let me know when he gets to here. I will have the cafeteria send him something to eat. He has had a long day and a long drive. He will be hungry." Julia thanked her and went back into the room. Tony arrived about forty-five minutes later. Jill's nurse introduced herself and explained she knew he was staying the night. She would be Jill's nurse until seven in the morning. She asked if he wanted something to eat. Tony said, yes, I could use something, anything. The nurse told him she would have something brought up. Tony walked into the room, said hello to everyone, and immediately went over to Jill. With tears in his eyes, he bent over and kissed her on the cheek and told her he was here. He was holding her hand. Everyone saw this. She was still sedated and squeezed his hand. She knew.

Shortly after, the doctor walked in and asked everyone to wait in the waiting room. They were going to remove the breathing tube and wake Jill up. He explained she would still be mildly sedated. Don't be surprised if she is in and out and groggy. The nurse would come for them when they were done. The cafeteria sent up a cheeseburger and ginger ale. Tony felt funny eating since he thought the family hadn't eaten. They asked the nurse how long it would be and if they had time to go get a quick bite to eat in the cafeteria. The nurse told them to go. By the time they got back, they would be done, and they could visit with Jill. She also said I can't let you all stay long. Tony is spending the night. Jill will need her rest. I will let you all stay for another hour. Go home and get some rest. You need it as well. You can come back tomorrow. Jill will probably be moved to another room in the morning. If all goes well, she will need to stay one more day before she could go home.

They all went to the cafeteria for a quick bite to eat. When they returned, they could see Jill. She was awake. The nurse explained she was still groggy. When her doctor walked in, everyone could see Jill was in pain. He told her everything went perfectly. He told Jill he made her a triple "E" by mistake. Jill tried to laugh, but it hurt too much. He told her if it hurts to laugh, don't laugh. He explained that everything went well and remember, she would have swelling and bruising. Not to judge his work until that was gone. He explained to the family in the morning, Jill would be moved to her room in the step-down unit for a day. They would start to get her up and moving around. He would be back to see her tomorrow. Her surgeon held Jill's hand and said, "You did really good young lady. I'm proud of you." Jill smiled and thanked him. She probably wouldn't remember the conversation. As soon as he let her hand go, she reached for Tony's. Tony held her hand and never let go. About an hour later, the nurse came in and said, "It's time." Jill needs to rest. You can't come before ten o'clock tomorrow. Before you come tomorrow, call the floor first. Jill will probably be in her new room by then. We will let you know the room number. Have a nice evening. I will take good care of her. Everyone gave her a kiss.

Julia said to Tony, "Take care of my baby girl."

Tony gave her a hug and said, "Don't worry mom. I will be here."

Julia said, "Mom? It's about time. Honey, get some sleep when she does. You look exhausted."

"I'll be fine, thanks."

Frank gave him a hug as well, and Jill's sister hugged him saying, "I love you. I hope to get as lucky as Jill did the day she found you."

Everyone left, and it was only Tony and Jill. Jill's nurse came in and said, "It's time for Jill's pain medicine. She will sleep for a while. I will turn the light off and get you a blanket. You should sleep when she does." Every time the nurse came in to do vitals and check on Jill, they were both asleep and holding hands. Tony never let go of Jill's hand. The nurse took a picture of their hands with her cell phone. It looked so beautiful. When Tony woke up, she would text it to him as a memory.

CHAPTER NINE
THE DAYS THAT FOLLOWED

The night was uneventful. Jill awoke a few times. Once she saw Tony was there and holding her hand, she would fall back to sleep. She was in pain, but the medications kept it tolerable. She was complaining of chest pressure. The nurse explained that it was normal, due to the amount of swelling. It would decrease as the swelling went down. Tony could not use his phone in her room. He would send a quick text with an update to Julia and his mother. At eleven, Jill was sleeping. He walked into the waiting room to call Jill's family and his mother to give them an update. He didn't want them to worry. They needed a good nights sleep. Julia wanted to be the one to stay, but she knew how important it was to Jill that Tony be there. In the morning, they started to cut back on her pain medications so Jill would be more awake. Her night nurse came in to wish her well and let her know she would be moved into her new room soon. Jill and Tony thanked her. Breakfast came up, and the nurse arranged for two to be delivered to Jill's room. Her surgeon stopped in and told her she was doing very well. She would be going to her new room shortly. He explained to Jill the nurses would be changing bandages before she left. He also added that the sooner she sees herself, the better.

He said, "The swelling and bruises will upset you. That is normal, but it's very important that you see yourself as it improves. Jill, you need to trust me. You will look perfectly normal when you are totally healed and have no more discomfort. Looking at yourself for the first time is the most important part of your emotional recovery, physically, you will recover perfectly. He gave Tony a look as if to say, make her do it. He told her this was an important step before he could discharge her. Later that morning her nurse came in to change the bandages. She asked Jill if she wanted a mirror to see what a great job her surgeon did. Jill replied, "I'm not ready." Tony tried to talk her into it and asked if he could stay. Jill got upset and said, "NO!" Tony didn't want to push it and left the room. When the nurse came out, she told Tony to talk to her. This was very important. She told Tony, she looked great. I have seen far worse after this type of surgery. Growing up, Jill always healed quickly. During the day, they had Jill up and walking around. Tony would take her for walks around the floor. It was tiring for Jill, but she needed to get her strength back. This would help the healing process.

After the nurse left, Tony spoke with Jill. He told her he understood her fear. The nurse told him she looked better than most she had seen after this procedure. It's only swelling and bruising. Everything else is there. The doctor wants you to see yourself. Watching yourself improve is important. I would like to stay. I can understand if you aren't ready for me to see you. It doesn't bother me. I was an EMT and have seen far worse. Please try when they change the dressing again. You need to get used to me. I'm not going anywhere and will be your husband one day. We will see far worse things about each other as we get older. Who knows, you might have to change my diapers one day.

Jill tried to laugh, but it hurt too much. "We'll see."

At ten o'clock her family arrived. Tony said, "Babe, do you mind if I take a walk to stretch while you visit with your family. I'm feeling like a cup of coffee. Jill told him to go and asked if he could bring her back one. Tony asked if anyone one else wanted one. Julia did as well. Tony said he would be right back and gave Jill a kiss. Carmela called Jill's room to see how she was doing. She told Carmela and her parents she didn't want to see herself when the nurse came to changes her dressings. Tony wanted to stay, but she wouldn't let him. Carmela explained how important this is. She said, "Honey, it's important. As you see yourself heal, you will realize that this was all worth it. I know it's hard. It was hard for me as well, but I did it. You have to as well. Trust me on this. It's only swelling and bruising. But don't get used to the size, they will shrink to what you wanted after the swelling goes down. Again, Jill tried to laugh, but it hurt too much.

Jill said, "I know. I'll do it. I know I have to."

Tony came back with the coffees. Soon it was lunchtime. Everyone went to the cafeteria to have some lunch while Jill ate. After they ate, they went back to Jill's room. She was due for her pain medications, but the nurse wanted her to take another walk first. Everyone took a walk around the floor. They went around twice, and Jill did very well. She had a private room. When she got back, she sat up in the recliner for a while. The nurse gave her the pain medication. When she felt tired, she got into bed and took a nap. Everyone else chatted. Jill's sister was working. Tomorrow was Wednesday and Tony would have to leave. His mother would be there on Sunday. He was picking her up at the airport so he would see her before he had to leave. When Jill woke up, she started talking about starting school. It was only six weeks away. Based on what the doctor said, if she did everything she was told to do, at most, she might only miss one or two weeks of classes. Tony explained that wouldn't be a problem. He could bring her work home to her.

"We'll see. I might want to stay in the dorm for my last year."

Julia looked at Tony and said, "Maybe this is just a mood swing." Tony didn't reply. Later that afternoon Tony saw her doctor. He went out of the room to talk to him privately. He told him about the comment Jill made. He said, "Son, that is normal. You have to be strong. She is feeling uncomfortable right now with you seeing her. She doesn't know how you will react. She is looking to avoid that. Let me see what I can do when I come back."

He told the nurse not to change her dressings. He would come back early and do it when he returned. The rest of the day was uneventful. Everyone let Jill vent. At four-thirty, her surgeon came in with a tray with fresh dressings on it.

Jill asked, "It'sn't my nurse going to do that?"

The doctor replied, "No. I thought we would do it together."

"No offense, but I'd rather have the nurse do it."

141

Her doctor replied, "Really? Jill, I am a soft-spoken man. However, as a doctor, your doctor, I can also be firm. No one in this room has seen you as I have. I will be changing your dressings. I can't release you tomorrow unless I examine you. This is not an option." He asked Frank to leave the room and told Julia and Tony to stay.

Jill asked, "What is going on."

He replied, "I need to show your mother and Tony how to do this."

Jill replied, "My mother okay, Tony, NO!"

Her doctor said, "Well from what I understand you and Tony will be moving in together in six weeks? He needs to know what to watch for."

Jill replied, "I'm not sure about that yet. I might go back to my dorm."

The doctor replied, "I see. You are running from the man who loves you. How nice. The man who slept in your room all night, after working all day, and driving here for over two hours to be with you. The same man who I watched support you when you made this decision and told you he didn't care. It was you he loved. Young lady, let me tell you something. When you came from recovery to your room, no one could get a response from you. You heard his voice on the phone and smiled. When everyone in your family held your hand, it was only his hand you squeezed. You know; you have your own skin and external anatomy. Frankly, I worked my ass off to save that for you. The only thing different is what's under the skin. What you or no one else can see. Is this really what you want to do to the man you claim you love? The truth is, you can drive him away, or embrace the love he has for you. That's your choice. I will tell you this from experience. There are very few men who do what he has done. We are all going to leave you alone for ten minutes. You think about it, and when I come back in, you let me know, and I will respect your wishes." Everyone left the room.

They were outside the door and could hear Jill crying. Julia and Tony wanted to walk in. The doctor would not let them. He explained this was the break down she needs. Let her get it out. She needs to move forward. I have had to do this many times. Trust me. She is strong. Before the ten minutes passed, Jill yelled out to the doctor to come back in. When he walked in Jill said, "Thank you. Please ask Tony and my mother to come in."

When Tony walked in with Julia, Jill held out her hand. Tony took it, and Jill said, "I love you so much. I'm sorry I hurt you."

"Sorry for what? IS there something I am not aware of ?"

The doctor said, "Let's get started." He handed Jill a mirror and explained we would do this together. He unbuttoned her top. Her breasts were exposed except where the dressings were. The doctor removed the dressing and said, "You are healing beautifully." He showed Julia and Tony how to change them, and they stepped back. He then asked Jill if she was ready to take a look. Jill told him, no, but she knew that wasn't an option. She took a minute and lifted the mirror. She said, "They don't look as bad as I thought. I still have my own parts. Are they going to stay this big?"

The doctor laughed and replied, "I told you I saved them, and no. They won't stay this big. They will go down to the size you requested when all the swelling goes down."

Jill gave him a hug and a kiss and thanked him. Before he left, he told her he would be back in the morning to go over everything she had to do and discharge her. He explained if she did everything he said, and took care of the incisions as directed when she looked at herself, she would never know she had this done. He told her he would see her in the morning. Jill asked her mother what she thought. Julia said they look a hell of a lot better than mine did. Frank was in the room now. Jill looked at Tony. Tony said, "What? What did I do wrong?"

"Nothing silly, you did everything right. What do you think?"

Tony said, "I think they are beautiful. I think you
are beautiful. I told you I love you. If you never had
them, I would still love you. But they are nice."

Jill said, "I know. To me, it's important."

"I know it is. I love them. They look totally awesome
and completely natural. I was expecting to see two
bowling balls. Honestly, besides the larger cup size,
they look exactly like they did, but fuller."

Jill laughed and said, "I told him I didn't want bowling balls. So
does this mean I can move back into the apartment in the fall?"

"Babe. That's not an apartment. It's our home. We
picked it out together. You don't have to ask me if
you can still move into our home. It's ours."

Jill reached her arms out to give Tony a hug and kiss and
whispered I love you in his ear. Meanwhile, Frank was
just standing there and said, "Well. Everyone has seen
these things. I'm your father, do I get to see them?"

Jill said, "Absolutely not!"

Frank laughed and said, "You know I'm only kidding."

Before the doctor, left he waved to Tony to come outside. When
Tony walked out, he thanked the doctor. The doctor told him the
hardest part was over. He told Tony to check her often. The more
she let him see her, the easier it would become. Eventually, things
would get back to normal. It takes time. Be gentle, but firm. When
you two start to become intimate, you don't need to worry about
anything breaking. She should have her full sensation back in a few
weeks. Gauge what you do by her level of comfort. Understand,
this isn't over. She may still experience mood swings. When
she is like that, you can't back off too much. You'll know when
you need to draw the line. Tony thanked him for his advice. He
gave Tony his card and said, "Call me anytime if you have any
questions. I'll be seeing her until she goes back to school. By then,

she should be all set. I'll want to follow up with her in six months."
Tony went back in. They went for another walk. When Jill saw
her nurse, her nurse gave Jill the thumbs up, and Jill smiled.

Visiting hours were over, and Jill's parents were leaving.
Tony was staying the night again. They watch some television
and Jill looked at Tony and asked, "Did you really like them?"

"Yes, the doctor said it would only take in a few weeks for
your sensitivity to return to normal. Can I see them again?"

The doctor conveniently left the mirror with Jill.
Jill said, "Can we look at them together?"

"I was hoping we could."

Jill opened her top. Together they looked at her breasts. Tony
told her how beautiful they were. Jill agreed, once you looked
past the swelling and bruising, they were perfect. It was painful,
but the pain meds took the edge off. Tomorrow when Jill was
released, they would start to wean her off of them. She was
now using cold compresses to help with the pain and swelling.
No more than ten minutes on, and at least thirty minutes
before she applied them again. After the nurse gave Jill her
pain medicine, she dozed off. This was Tony's cue to sleep.

In the morning, Julia and Frank came up. Her doctor had
called to let them know he was releasing Jill. When the doctor
came in with the dressing tray, Jill told him Tony and her mother
would change them while he watched. Frank stepped outside.
It went well. Frank came back in. Her doctor said, "There is
no reason for you to be here anymore. I'm going to let you go
home. The nurse will go over all your home-care instructions.
Follow them to the letter. I will see you in my office in one
week. After that, I will see you again in two weeks. If things
look good, I will see you before you go back to school. Our last
follow-up will be six months after that." He wished Jill well
and told her to call the office with any questions. When he left,
her gynecologist Karen stopped in. She happened to be in the

hospital checking on a patient and wanted to see Jill. She asked everyone to step out of the room for a moment. She examined Jill.

She said, "I can't believe what a great job he does." Jill agreed. Karen said, "Honey, I want you to go to a couple of meetings with a support group of young woman who has gone through the same procedure." Jill thought that was a good idea. Karen gave her the information. Karen also said, "If you ever need to talk, call me, but from the support I hear you have, I think you will be fine."

Karen left. Everyone came back to the room. The nurse came in and went over the care instructions in detail. She also gave her a prescription for a special antibiotic cream, and a lesser dose of pain medication, as well as two reusable ice packs. The nurse made sure that everyone understood the instructions. That was it. Jill was on her way home. One or two times while Tony was sleeping, Jill called Carmela talk. She was a great help to Jill. Jill was looking forward to seeing her on Sunday. It was also a hard two days for Tony. Sleeping on and off, and not very long, when they got to Jill's, he crashed for about two hours. Later that night he had to drive back, and return for the weekend. The remainder of the day everyone relaxed. Tony and Jill took a couple of walks. Frank went out to pick up her medications while Julia prepared dinner. When Jill's sister got home, she went into Jill's room. She wanted to see them. Jill showed her. After dinner, Tony would start back. While they were eating, Jill's sister said, they looked awesome. She wanted to do that. She was naturally smaller breasted than Jill before her surgery. Everyone laughed at her. She was wilder and crazier then Jill. When dinner was over, it was time for Tony to head back. Jill didn't want him to go. He told her boss said he could take more time if he needed to.

"I'll if you want me to."

Jill replied, "No. You need to get back to work. They have been very kind by letting you take this much time off and pay you. I will see you in two days. Jill sat on the porch as Tony drove off.

Julia came out to sit with Jill. They talked for some time. Jill asked, "Mom. Do you really think Tony is okay with this? I would let him go rather than hurt him. I don't want him to feel obligated to stay with me."

"Honey, no man does what he is doing out of obligation, or if they don't want to. Get those thoughts right out of your mind. I just had cysts removed, and your father was terrible. Don't tell him I said that. Tony is fine with this."

Jill said, "I hope so. I'm going to go call him now."

Jill left and called Tony. She couldn't help herself. She had to ask Tony the same questions. Tony replied, "Babe. I get it. I understand your concerns. Ask me as often as you like. My answer will never change. I love you now more than ever. We have handled many things together in a short time, and here we are. Still together. We have always been honest with each other. That will never change. If I had any concerns, which I do not. I would tell you. I would never lie to you. I love you, and can't wait until you move back to our house. We still have much to do."

Jill replied, "I know. We will get it all done. I can't wait either. I have to call the school when it gets closer when I have a better idea of how I'm feeling. I need to find out what arrangements I may have to make if I start my classes one or two weeks late."

"Yes. You do. Don't worry. If you have to start late, I will get work back and forth to school." They just chatted about things in general. Tony expressed how he liked talking to her on the drive back. When he got home, he went straight to sleep. Even though he had to work his full-time and part-time job, tomorrow, would seem like a break for him. He spoke to Jill at lunch as he always did. She seemed to be fine. She was still quite sore, but that would get better with time. When he got home from his part-time job, he called. This time Jill seemed depressed. Once again, she was questioning if he was really okay with this and was he sure he wanted her to move in. Julia had sent him a text earlier letting him know Jill was having a difficult time emotionally that night. He expected this. Even though the doctor told him to expect this, being a man, he was a more logical thinker than Jill. He was having a hard time understanding this constant shift. He reassured Jill and let her vent. After they hung up, he called his mother to discuss this. He explained that he didn't understand this. To him, it was quite simple. You had an issue. You fixed it. Nothing has changed, move on.

Carmela tried to explain the hormone changes her body was going through that were also attributed to her mood swings. She also attempted to explain that a part of Jill does not feel whole anymore. Part of her was taken away. No matter how good they look or feel, to her, they are different. She feels as if she lost something. A part of her. Carmela explained it took her a long time to understand and accept this herself. She told Tony he had to understand. Reassure her, and give her time and space when she needs it. She also told him not to try to reason it out with her. She can't see that right now. She said, "Honey, it's a process. One that will require a great deal of compassion and understanding on your part. Can you do this?"

"I can. It will be hard. I can see that. I'll do it." Tony explained his thought about getting engaged when Jill moved back it rather than wait until Christmas.

Carmela replied, "Only if Jill is in a better state of mind. It can go two ways. First, she might think you are doing this out of pity, or it could be the thing that shows her how committed you are. That will depend on how much better emotionally she is. I will be there all next week. We will be having many conversations. I will help her."

It was late. Tomorrow would be a long day between work and driving. Tony told his mother he would see her at the airport. He hoped that Jill was up for taking the ride with him. Both of Tony's employers were happy that everything went well. Tony stayed up in bed for a moment wondering how long this would go on. Earlier, his mother told him it is different for each woman. Some have no issues with it at all, and for others, it can take months or even years. Some never get over it. There are many determining factors. In Jill's case, she was young and had a great support system. She needed time to realize that. Tony was so tired, he fell asleep thinking.

The following day he realized it was only five weeks until Jill moved back in. Since he was going to see her every week, when would he have time to get her a ring? He didn't know any jewelers where he could get any deals. Maybe this was something that he and Frank could do where he lived. He thought he would discuss that with Frank this weekend. David spoke to Jill at lunch, and she sounded much better today. Tony didn't know what to trust. He could get there later, and find a completely different person. It was a tiring and stressful week for everyone. No matter what, he knew he had to be strong. After work, he started his drive to Jill's. He had much on his mind. How should he act? It was hard for Tony to be himself because he never knew how he would find Jill. He had to think about every word he said before he spoke it. Anything could trigger a mood swing. The doctors did say it would take about a week and a half for the medications she was prescribed to take effect. Some were temporary, and another she may have to take for the rest of her life. This was all dependent on how she mentally and physically adjusted.

Tony tried desperately to stop thinking about all of this. It only made it harder for him and made him more conscious of everything he did or said. He and Jill were very physical. One never waited for the other to kiss, or hold hands. It wasn't important who initiated the romance. It came naturally. It hadn't even a week since the surgery. He knew he had to give this time. For Tony, it was difficult. After the two of them being so open with one another, how do you hold back? He finally got it out of his mind. He knew he had to be himself all the time. If Jill didn't respond or snapped at him, he would just understand and not worry about it. The doctors said the emotional healing takes longer than the physical healing. He needed to remember this. It only seemed like yesterday he was with a girl who was ready to forget her family to be with him. Now, he didn't know from one hour to the next whether she would be with him. What a roller-coaster ride this was. He listened to some music to relax. Jill always called at some point during the drive. Today she didn't. Was this a sign of what was about to come?

Tony arrived at Jill's and walked in like he always did. Jill normally would run up to him, jump in his arms, and give him a hug and kiss. Not today. Jill was just sitting on the couch with her sister. She turned, looked at Tony and said, "Hi. Mom left a plate for you on the stove." She turned and went back to watch the television. Tony went into the kitchen to say hi to Jill's parents. Julia told him it was a rough day. Have patience.

Julia said, "Let me warn you. Try not to feel bad, but Jill said earlier she didn't want to sleep in bed with you over the weekend."

Tony replied with a sad look, "I understand. I guess I expected that. I'll sleep on the couch."

Julia replied, "Nonsense. We have a smaller room. I just have to get some things off the bed."

Tony insisted that she not do that. He said, "I'd rather sleep on the couch. If Jill wakes up and wants to talk, she may find it easier if I'm on the couch."

Julia looked at Frank, who gave her a nod as if to say; I agree. While Tony ate, he explained his ring dilemma to Frank. He asked if over the next two weekends they could look locally. Tony knew exactly what Jill liked and wanted.

Frank asked, "I don't mind, but are you sure you still want to do this now?"

Tony replied, "I don't want to change anything. I'm afraid if I do, in my own mind, I'll be giving up. I think it's important for me to proceed as if this will all get resolved."

Frank replied, "If that's how you feel, sure; we can do that."

Tony explained he would try to get the balance on credit, but with no credit history, that might be difficult. If Frank put in the rest, he reminded him he would make payments to him until Christmas when all of the money would have been saved. Frank explained he didn't have to strap himself.

Tony insisted and said, "I have to do this my way." Frank understood. He was taking responsibility. That was good.

Frank replied, "Another option is, if they don't give you credit, I will co-sign for you. This way, you can start to build credit." Tony agreed to that. It was an excellent idea he hadn't thought of. Tony went into the living room and sat next to Jill. He gave her a kiss on the cheek, and she slid a little further away from him. Tony didn't say a word. In the presence of her sister, Jill said, "So we don't have to discuss this later, I don't feel comfortable sleeping in bed with you tonight."

Tony had to fight saying the words, *'maybe I should just leave.'* He bit his tongue and replied, "No problem. I understand."

Jill replied, "No. You don't." Tony kept ignoring her comments. Every time he tried to have a conversation with Jill, she would say, "I'm trying to watch this show."

Julia and Frank noticed this. Frank said to Tony, "Tony since Jill is busy watching this show, can you help me move something in the garage?"

Tony replied, "Sure." He got up and left. Jill didn't look at him or say a word. When they got into the garage, Frank said, "Are you okay? I know this must be difficult."

Tony said, "No, I'm not okay, but I can handle it. Thanks." They went to sit on the porch. After about a half an hour passed, Jill walked out to the porch, gave Tony a kiss and asked, "Are you going to come and sit with me?"

Tony felt like a ping-pong ball. Take a hit and go one way, take another hit and go the other. When they sat down, Jill leaned up against him and said, "I'm such a bitch. I'm sorry. I can't seem to control it. If you want to take a break from coming, I'll understand."

"No way. I'm not taking a break from coming, and I don't want to. What are we going to do? After you

come back to our house, is one of us going to move
out every time there is an obstacle to overcome?"

Jill replied, "No. Of course not."

"Stop worrying. This will all pass. Are you going to take a ride
with me to pick up my mother at the airport on Sunday?"

Jill said, "Of course. I can't wait to see her. I
know she will help me through this."

Tony, not wanting to comment on that part replied,
"Thank you. I would like the company."

During the past couple of days, Tony and Julia had been talking to
Carmela so she would know how Jill was doing and what to expect.
Carmela didn't seem concerned and explained this was normal.
The majority of women who have this procedure go through this.
I did. She explained she drove her husband crazy. He was a saint.
He never said a word. Her experience is what made her want to
take a counseling class and help other women going through this.

The rest of the night was uneventful. Everyone went to bed.
Tony slept on the couch. Julia gave him a pillow and blanket.
She couldn't talk him into sleeping in the other bedroom. On
Saturday, he and Jill went for a walk and had a picnic in the yard.
Tony didn't feel the closeness between them like they normally
had. They were together, but he gave her a lot of space. Everyone
hung out eating popcorn and appetizers while watching movies on
Saturday night. Everyone went to bed, and Tony got comfortable
on the couch and fell asleep. About two in the morning, Tony woke
up and found Jill just standing there in her nightgown starring
at him. He asked if everything was okay. She started to cry and
said this is so unfair. She missed him so much and asked him to
come to bed with her. He got up, and they went to her room.

When they got in bed, Jill said, "I wish I were up to making love
to you. I want you so bad. If you want I could take care of you."

"It's good to hear you say that. I want you just as much, and maybe more. I can't believe I am saying this, but no. You don't have to take care of me. I want to wait until we are able to do this together."

Jill cuddled up to him and said, "I love you. I would like that. You know you didn't ask to see them. They are starting to look much better."

"I wanted to, but I don't want to make you uncomfortable and think that's all I care about. I don't. I care about you."

Jill asked, "Do you want to see them?"

"Of course, but only if you want me to."

Jill said, "Of course I do. You are stuck with them for the rest of your life."

Tony replied, "I don't look at it that way."

Jill unbutton her top. Tony smiled. He wanted to make Jill feel good about herself, but he was also honest. He said, "God babe, they look great!" I love them. They look perfect. My God, they are awesome!"

Jill smiled and gave him a passionate kiss and said, "I'm glad you like them. That's important to me."

Tony replied, "I know. How do you like them?"

"Honestly, at first I hated them. Now that the bruising is much better, and the swelling is almost gone, I really like them. It was hard for me to visualize them before, and they feel so natural." She took Tony's hand and placed it on one breast. She said, "Just don't squeeze hard."

Tony felt them. Both her nipples reacted to his touch. He said, "Well then, it seems like everything is working fine."

"Oh yes. A little more of the sensitivity comes back each day. God, your touch feels so good. It's getting me so excited. Maybe you're right. We should wait until they are healed more. I don't want to pay for it tomorrow. Are you sure you don't want me to take care of you?"

Tony laughed and said, "No, I'm not sure, but I am sure I want to wait for you."

Jill cuddled up to Tony, and they fell asleep. In the morning, Frank and Julia were awake before Tony and Jill. They noticed Tony wasn't on the couch. They certainly were not going to walk in Jill's room, but to them, this was a good sign. Carmela's flight arrived at one o'clock. Julia made a nice Italian dinner. Tony and Jill left for the airport to pick her up. Her flight arrived on time. When she got off the plane, they both gave her a kiss and Jill thanked her for coming. Tony said, "Why don't you two talk and I'll get your bags."

"That's a good idea. I have two. You know the ones. I've had them for years."

Tony thought it would be good if they had a few minutes to talk. Before he left for the baggage area, he said, "Why don't you two wait outside. I'll get the bags and the car, and pick you up out front." When Tony arrived, they were both sitting on the bench, waiting and talking. He made sure it took him about twenty minutes. Everyone got in the car, and they started for Jill's. Tony asked if anyone needed anything. He called the house and asked Julia if she needed anything. Everyone was all set. He let them know they were on the way back. Julia had the other room cleaned and ready for Carmela. It wasn't a long drive back.

When they arrived, Tony put his mother's bags in the room she would be sleeping in. Julia had coffee and some snacks on the table. They all chatted for a bit as Julia was starting to prepare dinner. They normally ate a little earlier on Sunday because Tony needed to head back. Next Saturday, they would bring Carmela to the airport. They had some things planned

for the week to show Carmela around. She and Jill would have
plenty of time to talk. Dinner was great. It was about seven
thirty by the time they finished with dessert. Since Saturday
night, Jill seemed to be herself. Tony was getting ready to
leave and kissed everyone good-bye. Jill walked him out.

Jill said, "God I don't want you to leave, but
I am happy your mother is here."

Tony replied, "Both of those things are nice to hear. I wish I
didn't have to leave either. Why don't you guys chat? You don't
have to call me. I'll be fine. I'll call you when I get home."

They kissed and exchanged a light hug, and Jill watched
Tony drive away. Jill walked in with watery eyes.
Julia asked, "Honey, is everything alright?"

Jill replied, "Yes. I miss him already. I've been such a
bitch. This is so hard on him. I have to fix myself."

Carmela replied, "Sweetie, he can take it.
This will get better. Trust me."

They all talked for about an hour. Jill excused herself and said,
"Tony told me not to call and enjoy everyone. I have to talk to
him on his way home. I do it every week. Is that alright?"

Julia and Carmela said, "Go, call him."

Jill went into her room and closed the door. She called Tony. He
was not shocked. Jill told him she couldn't let him drive all the way
home without talking to him. Tony told her he was glad she called.
He hoped she would. They had a nice conversation on his way
back. Jill was talking about the apartment in a positive way for the
first time. Tony was happy to hear this. When he got home, they
hung up. He was emotionally exhausted and went right o sleep.

CHAPTER TEN
THERE'S NO MATCH FOR LOVE

This summer was proving that love can transcend time and space. They were no match for true love. Next Saturday Carmela's flight would not depart until five o'clock in the afternoon. That morning would be a perfect time for Frank and Tony to steal away out and pick out a ring. Tony talked to Frank about this before he left, and he was fine with the plan. Tony was back to his normal work schedule now. Jill had her first follow-up appointment on Wednesday. He was happy that his mother would be going. He didn't need to take the day off for that. On Monday and Tuesday Jill, Julia, and Carmela took it easy. They went out a ride to show Carmela around and took walks together. They showed each other pictures of their children growing up. It was good quality time. Carmela was an intelligent woman. She didn't want to dive right in. She wanted to establish in Jill's mind, family love and togetherness. Each night after dinner, Carmela and Jill would sit and talk. Julia would join in at times. Julia wanted Jill to feel comfortable talking to Carmela. After a couple of days, she joined them each time they chatted.

Jill vented about her concerns regarding Tony accepting this, and her emotional insecurity about the surgery. In the beginning, Carmela just listened. It was important that Jill express everything she was feeling. Carmela reassured her as she felt Jill needed it. Nothing changed. Tony and Jill spoke every day while he was at lunch, and each night. Tony could tell by her voice she was becoming more relaxed. However, she still had her moments, but not as often. On Wednesday, Julia and Carmela went with Jill for her follow up appointment. Carmela met her surgeon. She told Jill, "I wish my surgeon were that nice." Carmela and Julia waited outside as her doctor and nurse examined her. When Julia and Carmela came back into the examining room, the doctor expressed how pleased he was at the rate she was healing. He also joked about the great work he did, which made everyone laugh.

He said, "Jill, let's talk about your emotional
state, and please be honest. These two young
ladies will spill the beans if you're not."

"I guess I'm getting better. I know I was mean to Tony many
times. I don't know why he even comes every weekend."

The doctor replied, "Jill, you know the answer to that, don't you?"

"Yes. I know he loves me. It's just hard sometimes. I've already
started cutting back on my pain medications. I hate the one for my
emotions. It makes me tired. I really want to come off of that."

Her doctor said, "I'm happy you are weaning off the pain
medications. We have another visit in two weeks. You will
be off them totally by then. I want to start taking the other
medication every other day until Saturday. On Sunday, switch to
taking one every two days. I will be seeing you on that Friday.
If all looks good, we will stop them. Jill, that will depend on
you and how you adjust. The medication is only to help you.
However, your brain has to do the work before we can stop
them altogether. Surgery such as this is a matter of acceptance.
Physically, you look perfect. Probably better than you did
before. All parts will function normally. It's not about you
losing something. You lost nothing. It's all in how you perceive
it. Have you gone to any of the support group meetings?"

"Yes. I've been to two. Those women are amazing. Some
of their stories are much worse than mine. I have to
tell the truth, my mother and Tony's mother have been
a great help. After dinner, we all sit for a short time
and just talk. They let me vent, and they listen."

Her doctor replied, "Well. It seems like you are in the best of
hands. I believe that once you feel up to it and get back to your
normal routine, you will be just fine." He added, "We are all
adults. I'm sure both of these ladies are aware that you and Tony
have been intimate. Medically, you can start whenever you'd like.
Let your degree of chest discomfort guide you in that area. I do

not want you to hold back. Normally, this is the hardest part of the process. I have a funny feeling Tony will make it easier for you. The longer you hold back, the harder it will be to start."

Jill replied, "I know. I am much more comfortable with Tony seeing me now. You are right. They do look great, and he tells me he loves them. Thank you."

He told her he would see her in two weeks. If she had any questions, call the office. Due to the time of her appointment, she didn't speak to Tony during lunch, and Wednesday was their afternoon project meetings. They wouldn't speak until tonight. She did send him a text that everything went well and looked good. She said she had a question to ask him later. He responded he was glad all went well and would call her as soon as he got home. They all went for lunch and ice cream. Julia called Frank to give him an update on how the appointment went. Everyone was in good spirits. Later that afternoon, Tony called Jill. However, she was napping. Carmela told him everything the doctor said. She also said that Jill was doing better. She really needed to get things out the first couple of days. Now she would need to focus on getting back to her normal routine. Tomorrow they would all put on bathing suits and sit by the pool. Earlier that day, Jill tried on her bathing suit. The top was too small. While they were out, Jill bought three new suits. Carmela explained to Tony is a one step at a time process. Jill was much farther along at this point then she was, and where she has seen others. The trick would be not to push too hard, yet be firm when needed. Jill seemed to be more receptive when she felt things were her idea. She told Tony to eat, and she would have Jill call him when she awoke.

About thirty minutes later, Jill called. She didn't know that Carmela told Tony everything. When she started to tell him what the doctor said, he just listened. Tony asked what else they did that day. Jill explained they were talking about sitting by the pool tomorrow. She told him she went into her bedroom to try on her bathing suit. The top was too small. Tony laughed. I wanted to sit with them, so I asked if we could go bathing suit shopping after lunch. I picked out three cute suits.

"That's great," Tony replied. "I can't wait to see them."

"Well, I took a selfie of me in each. Do you want me to send the pictures to you?"

Tony replied, "Of course I do, but if you want to wait and show me in person, I understand."

Jill said, "No. I'll send them now, and tell me the truth."

Tony replied, "I've never lied to you. I'm not going to start now." With that said, the pictures came through to his phone. He looked at them. Jill looked outstanding. Tony said, "Babe, I don't know what to say. If I say how good you look, you might think I thought you didn't look good before. Honestly, you look awesome. I'm getting excited just looking at them. I can't wait until you feel up to making love to me. I miss you so much."

Jill replied, "I miss you too. That is what I wanted to talk to you about. The doctor said it's up to me. Physically, there is no reason why I can't be intimate with you. He told me to judge how my chest feels as we go. Can we make love this weekend?"

"There is nothing more besides spending time with you that I would rather do. We'll take it as it comes. We will go slow and easy. I would never hurt you."

Jill said, "I know you wouldn't, and I knew you would say that. I love you so much." She added, "The way I am feeling, hopefully, I will be able to start my classes on time. It's only three and a half weeks away. I can't wait to come back to our house. Do you want me back?"

"If you could, I would come and get you right now. I cross off each day on my calendar just waiting for the day when you will be here with me in our house."

They chatted for a while longer and hung up. Tony thought she was in better spirits. Maybe wearing the bathing suit at the pool, and making love, would make her feel back to

normal; like her old self. Tony didn't want to worry about it
or get his hopes up. He would be there in two days and take
it as it came. Tony always planned on the worst, and hope
for the best. The following day he and Jill spoke during his
lunch break. Everyone was out by the pool. He thought that
was a good sign. On Friday, they were going to the lake.

Saturday night there was a dinner-dance at the golf club, and
Jill wanted to know if Tony would go. Tony told her, "Of course
I will go." It would be a great time and an excellent opportunity
for them to network with people. He told her contacts were good
to make if she found a job back home. Jill agreed. No one knew
she had this surgery. Everyone kept it a secret. She wouldn't feel
uncomfortable, as if everyone was staring at her. He wished his
mother was leaving on Sunday, so she could attend as well. They
had plenty of time to get her to the airport, get back, and make the
dinner dance on time. Everyone was so busy, the fourth of July
just came and went. The night of the fourth it rained. The dance
was postponed until this weekend. At some point, Tony and Jil had
to make plans as to what date she would be coming back. They
originally talked about her come back one or two weeks before
school started, to give her a chance to get settled. The following
week Tony's boss wanted to sit with him to go over a part-time
schedule since he already knew his class schedule was for the next
semester. Some universities had a three-semester year, and others
only had two. The university they attended had both, depending on
what your major was. Jill and Tony both had a two-semester year.

This worked out perfectly. It afforded them time to do their
required field internship during their junior and senior years. Tony
was fortunate. His summer job would count for his senior year
requirements. That afforded him the time to work his part-time
job. His class schedule was not bad. He and Jill really loaded up
their schedules in their earlier years to have an easier senior year.
On Friday, Tony left for Jill's and brought something nice to wear
to the dance. The drive wasn't bad. He was in good spirits after the
couple of nice talks he had with Jill. This time when he walked in,
Jill was in one of her bathing suits. He immediately complimented
her. She came right up to him and gave him a hug and kiss. He

thought to himself; this might turn out alright after all. Friday night was fine. When it was time to go to sleep, Tony walked into Jill's room. She didn't say anything. When they got into bed, Tony told her again how good she looked in her suit. She told him she didn't realize the difference one cup size made. She was lucky that the rest of her clothes fit her because she likes loose tops. She would probably have to give away her tighter fitting ones. Tony laughed and said, "I'll have to take your word for it. It's not as if I have a great deal of experience here. However, I will let you know."

Jill asked, "Well, do you want to find out?"

Tony didn't answer. He simply kissed her. He didn't rush. As much as he couldn't wait, and was excited, he took his time. As he removed her top, he took a brief look at her and told her how beautiful she was. He was so gentle. With only his fingertips, he ran them over her breasts. Her nipples seemed larger to him but just as sensitive as they always were. When he ran his fingers over them, Jill would take a gasping breath. She was telling him how good that felt. She couldn't believe it. She missed him so much. He cupped his hand gently around one of her breasts. He told her so sweetly how soft her skin was and how good she felt. He did make a joke and said, "You are right. One cup size makes a difference." Jill responded and said, "I told you. Make love to me. You can rub them, just go easy." Tony was very gently. He didn't want to spend much time, or not enough time. He didn't want her to be sore the next day or feel self-conscious. He gently ran his mouth over them and caressed them. Jill was becoming very excited and now was touching him. Tony was going crazy with excitement. He switched positions, and they took each other. They both enjoyed oral sex and knew exactly how to please each other. Jill did not forget a thing.

Jill finally said, "Go inside me baby, I feel like I'm going to explode." Tony got on top and held himself up with his arms so he would not be leaning on her breasts. His slow, smooth, circular motions were driving them both crazy.

Jill couldn't hold it any longer. "Are you ready?"

"Yes. I can't hold it anymore."

As he increased his rate and depth, they both shared an orgasm at the same time. It was pure ecstasy. They forgot they were at Jill's, and moaning quite loudly. Afterward, Jill cuddled up and said, "My God we were so loud. Everyone had to hear us."

"So what. It's not as if they don't know. This was a big step for us, and it was perfect. You were perfect."

On Saturday morning, Julia could not help herself. At the breakfast table, she asked, "So, did you two have a nice time last night?"

Jill blushed, and Tony replied, "Actually; we did. Thank you for asking."

Jill burst out laughing. Julia said, "I'm so sorry. I didn't mean to embarrass you. Honestly, I couldn't be happier. With a chuckle, she said, "Next time, leave the bullhorn turned off." Jill laughed.

Later that morning, Franks phone rang. He asked Tony if he wanted to take a ride with him. He needed to pick up something for tonight. Tony went along with it. Frank said they would be back shortly. They went into town and stopped at a jewelry store that was one of Frank's clients. Tony described what he was looking for. The owner went into the back and came out with a tray. Tony saw the exact size and shape that Jill wanted. It was a near-perfect cut. It was beautiful. Tony asked Frank what he thought. Frank loved it. It was a bit more than what Tony wanted to spend, but it was worth every penny. The owner gave Tony a discount which put him in the ballpark. Tony bought it. He gave a sizable down payment and applied for credit for the balance. The owner came back and informed Tony since he had no credit history, they would require a co-signer. Frank told him he would co-sign for Tony. The credit went through with no problem. The ring was already Jill's size. The jeweler wrapped it, and off they went.

On the way back to the house. Tony said, "Mr. Muller. I need to ask you a question."

Frank replied, "Go right ahead."

"In less than four weeks we go back to school. I was going to give this to Jill when I picked her up to come back to our house so she would be with her family. I feel bad that mine will not be a part of that special moment. Since Jill is doing better and my mother is here, do you think tonight at the dinner dance would be okay?"

Frank replied, "Well son. You already have our blessing. That choice is up to you. There will be many people there including all her friends. It would be a hell of a time for her to have a moment, but then, it would also be a very exciting time. Are you willing to take that risk?"

"I think I'll play it by ear. If the night is going well, I will ask the DJ to play our favorite song and ask her at the table. If she says yes, we can dance to our favorite song. Please don't say anything to anyone, even Mrs. Muller. If it's not going well, I may change my mind."

Frank replied, "I understand. Don't worry."

Frank thought about this all day and made a decision. He had enough faith in his daughter. He believed things would go well. He had a florist deliver roses to the club. He called the club and explained the situation. Tony was considering proposing tonight. If that happened, bring out the roses. If not, give them to your wife."

The club manager replied, "No problem. I will wait for your cue. I know how men can get cold feet. It took me three times to gain the courage to ask Joan."

They laughed and hung up. Tony had already checked with the airlines to see if there was a later flight or one in the morning. There was. After explaining the situation, he begged them to switch his mother's ticket. They did. When they got back, it was close to having to leave. Tony said, "Mom, I have a surprise for you. I switched your flight to tomorrow morning.

I will get up early to take you. You have been so kind, We would like you to come to the dinner dance with us."

Jill said, "Oh please Mrs. Ricci. I would love you to be there."

Carmela agreed. However, she knew her son. She didn't know what it was going on, and he always talked to her about things. Not this time. She knew he had something up his sleeve. Later they all went to the dance. Dinner was excellent, and everyone was having a good time. They danced, Tony danced with his mother, Julia, and Jill's sister. The night was about an hour from being over, and Frank was wondering if Tony got cold feet. When Tony went to the bar to get Jill a soda, Frank followed.

Frank asked, "So, are you getting cold feet, or are you going to do this.?"

"I'm scared as hell sir."

Frank said, "After all you to have been through together, scared is the last thing you should be, or do I need to get a bullhorn?"

Tony laughed and knew exactly what he meant. He said, "Please give this to Jill, tell her I stopped at the men's room. I going to make my request."

Tony went to the DJ and explained what he wanted to do. The DJ said, "I will handle it. Just be ready. I will make it special for you."

Tony went back to the table, he gave the nod. Frank, in turn, gave the nod to the manager. When the song was over, the DJ asked everyone to please take their seats and give him a moment of silence. When everyone was seated, they waited. The DJ brought an empty chair to the center of the dance floor and went back on stage. At this moment, Tony nearly shit his pants. Frank leaned over and said, "Was this your idea?"

"Hell no. He said he would play the song and make it special for me. I had no idea."

The DJ asked, "Is there a Jill Muller in the audience?" Jill raised her hand. The DJ asked her to please take a seat on the chair. When Jill sat down, he started to play the song "Stand By Me." That was their song. He then added, "Tony, it's all you now."

Tony walked out to the middle of the floor. For some reason, he forgot everyone was there. It was only him and Jill. He wasn't nervous at all. He got down on one knee. Jill's eyes started to get watery. She knew.

Tony said, "Jill. You are the love of my life. The only woman I have ever loved. You are my best friend. You make me happy, strong, and feel like no one ever has. You make every day I awake worth living. You make every night I come home something to look forward to. You live deep in my soul. Without you, I am lost." He took the ring box out of his pocket and opened it. He showed her the ring and asked, "Would you do me the honor and say yes and be my wife?"

Jill was crying. She screamed, YES! I love you so much."

The DJ said, "Let's put our hands together for the happy couple, and join them in dancing to their favorite song as a newly engaged couple. Julia danced with Frank, and Jill's sister danced with Carmela, who had taken a video of the whole thing to show her family. While dancing, Jill started to ask, "You aren't," Tony immediately interrupted her and said, "Don't you even think that for a moment. I had this planned for when you came home. I did it tonight because most of both our families are together. I wanted that for you, and for me." Jill stopped dancing and gave Tony a passionate kiss. When they got back to the table, the manager brought over the roses.

The card read:

"To the most courageous person we know. We all love you. Congratulations." Frank had the names from both families list on the card.

Jill said, "Mom you knew, Mrs. Ricci, you also knew?"
Frank replied, "No Honey. No one but Tony and I
knew. Frankly, it was getting so close to the end of
the night, I thought he developed cold feet."

Julia slapped Frank on the arm and gave him a kiss.
Carmela was crying and sent the video to everyone's
phone. At that moment, all of Jill's friends ran over to
her. They thought the diamond was beautiful. It was.

Carl walked over and said, "Congratulations. This man really
loves you. I could have never done that. Way to go." He shook
Tony's hand and walked away. Tony and Jill were now engaged.

Julia said, "Over your Christmas break, we will have to plan an
engagement party. Carmela and I will figure out a way to get
both families here. I've gone to so many engagement parties at
this club, I'm not letting these cheap bastards off the hook."

Frank walked over to tip the DJ and thanked him for the
wonderful job he did. It turned out to be a grand evening for
all. This summer Jill and Tony faced every challenge and
every obstacle. Health, distance, time, and space, being a
few. It is difficult to love and transcend through the physical
laws of nature. When you only talk on the phone or see
someone a couple of days a week, it can be very difficult
when you're younger. Luckily, Jill and Tony were strong and
believed in one another. Tony learned quickly that always
feeling tired was not just for the moment, but his lifestyle this
summer. There were only three weeks left before Jill would
move back to their apartment. Much could happen during
that time. Jill was still not totally physically or emotionally
healed. Tony did not want to get his hopes up too quickly,
just because they had a few good days. His mother would
be leaving in the morning. Although only a phone call
away, it's not the same as having that person sitting right
next to you. Tony feared this might be a setback for Jill.

That night Jill and Tony made love. There were no issues, and it seemed as normal as it always had been. Tony used that to gauge Jill's frame of mind. As much as she would be undressed in bed with a candle on, she still wasn't able to get undressed in front of him with the lights on. Tony was wondering why? There was next to no physical signs that any surgery was performed. He wondered why Jill couldn't see that. There was no reason to feel self-conscious about her body. She looked outstanding. He summed it up to the emotional component. Soon her doctor would see Jill for the last time before she went back to school. Her final appointment would be in six months, providing she didn't have any problems. If needed, he would discuss this with him at that time. The following morning Jill and Tony got up early to get Carmela to the airport. Everyone took the ride.

Before Carmela started to walk to the security line, Julia took her aside and said, "Don't worry if you can't afford to pay for everyone to come when we have the engagement party. Frank and I will help. With all you have done for our daughter, that is the least we can do."

Carmela said, "Thank you. We will work something out. The other kids are older now. I've been bugging Vinny to let me get a part-time job. I'm bored at home. When you have a date picked out, let me know. We will start saving for it. There's plenty of time."

Julia replied, "I understand. You will all stay at our house. We will make it work. Have a safe trip."

Carmela thanked her for her hospitality and reminded her to have Jill call her anytime she needed to talk. She got into the security line and everyone waiting until she went through before they left. Physically, Jill felt she should be able to start her classes on time. The walks she was taking helped to get all her strength back. She had to buy new bras. She was weaning off the after surgery bras and getting back to wearing a regular bra. Her physical recovery was going excellent. She was healing faster than most. Being in great shape before the surgery certainly helped. She was off all of the medications now.

The night before, everyone was up late. Jill and Tony relaxed for the rest of the day. Carmela called when she landed to let everyone know she had arrived safely. They had an early dinner and sat on the front porch. Callie, Jill's sister, was also very supportive and helpful during this time. She worked a lot in the summer to have more spending money when she went back to school. It was time for Tony to leave and start the drive back. Jill did not call as quickly as she normally did. Tony thought she and Julia were probably talking about the dance and the engagement. They had made it clear that they would not be setting a date until school was over, and they knew where they would be living. They could do their masters program anywhere. A great deal of time passed, and Tony was a little concerned. Finally, his phone rang about thirty minutes from home. Jill apologized. She and Julia had gotten carried away talking. She seemed in good spirits until she said.

"Tony, I know this is stupid, but now that you and your mother are gone, I feel alone."

"Babe, it's not stupid. You just had your family, my mother, and myself all together. Saturday night was your first real night around many people. That's a huge difference. You know we are only a phone call away."

"I know. But it was so nice when everyone was here with me. It must have been hard for you all summer being alone most of the time."

"Yes and No. I was with you every weekend and worked for most of the week. The truth is, it was only Monday, and Wednesday night I was alone. I did miss you all the time."

Jill replied, "I missed you too. Thank you for the wonderful surprise. I knew one day it would probably

happen, but had no clue it would be now. Are you sure
the surgery didn't have anything to do with it?"

"Not the slightest bit." Stretching the truth a bit, he added,
"Honestly, I had this planned since before your surgery. I didn't
talk to your dad about it because of all that happened."

Jill said, "Okay, you know I had to ask. We can't
be doing this for the wrong reason."

"We are doing this for one reason. And it's the right
reason. We love each other. End of story."

By this time, Tony was arriving home. Tony went inside and was
exhausted. He went right to sleep as he always did. While in bed,
before he fell asleep, he was thinking how nice it would be that
soon, he would not have to do this every weekend. It wasn't so
that it was getting old; it was just tiring. Even when they relaxed,
it wasn't the same as if they were in their own apartment. He
was happy it would soon be over. Three more weekends. Next
weekend he would start bringing some things back with him.
On the third weekend, Jill would be coming back with him.

The next week would be a difficult week for Tony. He had to
pay back the favor to his co-worker and work one of his nights.
This left him with only one night off. At the firm, they were
wrapping up a project. He needed to go in early each day to
finish the model for the presentation on Friday. He was basically
done, but the client kept making minor changes to the design.
Each time he did that, Tony had to modify the model to reflect
those changes. The model of a project was one of the most
critical parts of the project. This provided the client with an exact
replica of what the finished project would look like. Down to the
parking lots and landscaping. This was the part of most projects
that often times secured the deal. Tony was great at doing this.
This was where many of his ideas would be suggested as he
saw what was working and what wasn't. Something as simple
as the placement of a tree can block the view from an office.

Many times you don't see this until the model starts to come together. Tony was really hoping for a non-eventful week.

*****

It was Wednesday, and he was tired. The week was going well. Jill was getting out almost every day with Julia. Shopping, or going to one of the clubs. Unfortunately, Jill could not get any of her internship time done over the summer. This was not a big issue. Her class schedule was light. She would have plenty of time. Julia kept her fairly active. Jill did call Carmela once or twice to talk. She missed their conversations. Carmela was very comforting. One time, Jill had a conference call with her mother and Carmela. Jill seemed to be doing better each day. Carmela was concerned that Jill kept asking about the reason for the engagement. Did Tony make a mistake by not waiting until Christmas? It was Wednesday, and he was tired, but the week was going well. Jill was getting out almost every day with Julia. Shopping, or one of the clubs. Unfortunately, Jill could not get any of her internship time done over the summer. This was not a big issue. Her class schedule was light. She would have plenty of time. Julia kept her fairly active. Jill did call Carmela once or twice to talk. She missed their conversations. Carmela was very comforting. One time Jill, her mother, and Carmela talked. Jill was doing better each day, but Carmela's only concern was the fact that Jill kept asking about the reason for the engagement. Did Tony make a mistake by not waiting until Christmas?

It was Friday, and Tony's week went well. The presentation was a complete success, and the firm won the bid for the project. Before he left, his boss called him in his office. He asked Tony to sit down. He handed Tony an envelope. Tony wasn't sure if he was getting laid off. His boss asked him to open it. When Tony opened it, he was in shock. It was a small bonus. Not a great amount, but enough to pay off Jill's ring. He asked his boos what this was for. His boss explained that the client loved the changes he had made. That was the main reason they got the project. This is a thank you for doing a great job, especially with all he had going on.

He added, "Tony, this is a great accomplishment for you. You accomplished this with everything else going on in your life right now. This is well deserved. You should be as proud of yourself as we are of you. Tony thanked him and left. He couldn't wait to tell Jill and let Frank know he would be paying off the ring as soon as the check cleared. When he arrived at Jill's, he told Frank the good news. When he saw Jill, he hadn't noticed she wasn't wearing her ring. He was so excited, he told her all about the meeting with his boss. Frank was very proud of him. Tony was displaying a great sense of responsibility. He had a quick bite to eat and now noticed Jill wasn't wearing her ring. He asked her why she wasn't wearing it. Jill told him they should go outside and talk. When they went out to the porch and sat down. Frank and Julia had no idea this was coming. Jill had worn her ring all week and never said a word.

"I'm not wearing your ring because I don't know if this is the right thing to do. Please do not be mad. I must be sure. Please understand."

Tony lost it. He didn't yell, but this would be the first time he even slightly raised his voice and was firm with Jill. It was a cool night, and the window was open. Frank and Julia could not help but overhear the conversation.

Tony said firmly, "I want you to listen to every word I am saying before you speak. When you do, be sure of what you are saying. It will mean the difference between me staying tonight or driving back, and us never seeing each other again. Do you understand?"

Jill replied, "Yes. But don't yell at me."

"I'm not yelling. If I were, you would know the difference."

Tony went on to say, "Jill, I followed you like a puppy dog with his tail between its legs for two years because I didn't have the balls to confront you. Everything I have done, I have done for us. It is what we both wanted. I have supported every decision you have made. I have gone along with every plan we have discussed and agreed upon. I've worked all summer to a state of constant exhaustion. Do you want the truth, well I will give you the truth."

"You're yelling at me."

Tony replied, "Okay. Maybe I am. Maybe it's about time someone knocked some sense into you. You don't know jack shit about men and how we think. Honestly, that's because you spent so many years with an asshole who didn't appreciate you. You are perfect. Your body is perfect. There is nothing wrong with your breasts. I love them, and I love you. It's all in your head. You need to get it out of there. We have made love, I have seen you with no clothes on. Do you see me having a problem? I was planning on doing this at Christmas. I decided to do it early. Before we knew of your cancer. Let me tell you why. First, I love you and believe you love me. Second, a man has pride. We all know the way people think. I did not want you moving into our house, the house we picked out together, and have anyone look at you as if you were some college bitch shacking up with a guy. So I decided to ask you to marry me early. What the hell is the difference that I asked you now, or in December? Either time would be after your surgery. I will tell you what. I was going to give you the night to think about this. Honestly, this has hurt me so much, that I had to speak to you this way. I'm leaving. I don't want you to call me all week. If you do, I will not answer the phone. Get your head screwed on straight. When I come back next Friday, I expect you will be wearing your ring, or I will find it in the box on the porch. If so, I will take it and leave. That will be the end of it." At that moment, Jill started to cry.

Julia and Frank walked out to the porch. Julia in a calm voice said, "Tony, this doesn't have to go this far. Let's all go inside and talk."

Frank said, "Honey, Jill is our daughter. I love her more than life itself. However, in this case, Tony is right. Maybe this is what she needs to snap out of this. Tony is a grown man, and also has the right to feel the way he feels."

Tony thanked them for the meal. He said to Frank if this doesn't work out, I will find a way to pay you back. He asked

that no one discuss this with his mother. He was not planning
on telling her until he knew how it worked out. Tony got into his
car and drove off. He had tears in his eyes all the way home. He
didn't know if he had done the right thing, or this was a result
of the stress he had been under all week. Either way, it was
done. He had to stick to his guns. If not, he would never know
if he could trust anything Jill ever said to him. Jill tried calling
many times. She left him voice messages saying I'm wearing
my ring, please come back. Tony never answered or returned the
calls. Each time he heard a voice message he had to pull over to
clear his eyes. This was the hardest thing he had ever done and
was feeling a great deal of emotional pain and hurt. Feelings he
never felt before. He was too embarrassed to call his mother.
He wondered how many other people had seen her without her
ring. He was working himself up with all these questions.

When he walked in, he did not see Jill wearing her ring.
When he noticed she wasn't wearing it, he thought she just
washed her hands or took it off to shower. But when she said
what she did, it was like someone stuck a dagger in his heart. His
thoughts were running wild now. Julia called next. He answered
the phone. She could hear the frog in his throat and asked him
if he was driving. He told her he was. She said why don't you
pull over and calm down. He said he was fine. She asked him to
come back. Jill knew she was wrong and was wearing the ring.

Tony said, "I can't go back on what I said. If I do,
I will never know how she really feels. Can you
understand that mom? I don't want to hurt her, but this is
something I think she needs, and I need to know."

Julia laughed and said, "You called me "mom." I do
understand. As much as I love my daughter, she has to
take responsibility for what she does and says."

Tony said, "Thank you for understanding. The last thing I want
to do is hurt Jill. If she moves back without me knowing how
she really feels, it will destroy us anyway. Yes, I called you
mom. You and Mr. Muller have been like a mother and father

to me. I will always love you. I have to drive now. Take care of Jill. I will see you next Friday, and I guess we will all know."

When Tony got home, he couldn't sleep. The phone calls stopped. What did it mean? His was very upset. Every possible scenario was haunting him. He couldn't call home. He couldn't face Carmela. He finally fell asleep. Every morning for the three days, Jill sent him pictures of her wearing her ring. Everywhere she went, she took a picture and sent him a text. She tried calling three or four times, and he didn't answer her calls. She didn't leave any voice messages. She knew he would not return the calls. Jill could be just as stubborn as Tony. However, in this case, she knew she was wrong. If she was stubborn, she knew she would lose him forever.

*****

It was now Thursday evening, and Carmela called. Tony was at work and told her he would call her back when he was done at eleven. When he called, his mother asked him why he didn't call and tell her what happened. Neither Julia nor Jill called her all week. She knew something was wrong. She heard about it earlier that day after dragging it out of Julia when she called to check on Jill. Tony tried to explain that he didn't want her to worry. He told them not to call. If it didn't go well, that would be the time for him to call. In the meantime, why make anyone concerned.

He said, "Mom, I'm a grown man. Although you may or may not agree, I needed to do this."

Carmela said, "I understand honey. If you want to talk, I'm here. If not, please do not make me have to wait all weekend to find out the outcome."

Tony replied, "I won't."

Tony calmed down a great deal in six days. At first, he was hurt. That hurt turned to anger. The anger turned into acceptance. He knew whichever way it went, he needed to know to move forward.

Friday was over. Tony left work and started for Jill's. He felt anxious about not knowing what to expect. Throughout the entire drive, he kept saying to himself, "No matter has this works out, it's for the best." He didn't want to be unhappy, and he didn't want to see Jill unhappy. The hurt would eventually go away. One way or another, time cures everything. Not knowing if he would be eating when he got there, he stopped at the rest stop along the way and sat down to eat a grinder. He ate and sat to think for a while. An hour had passed which would change the time he normally arrived at Jill's. Jill and her family were worried. He wasn't answering his phone. Was he alright? Did he get into an accident, or was he not coming at all? Finally, they heard a car coming up the driveway. Tony had arrived. Julia was sitting on the couch by the window holding Jill's hand. After Tony left last Friday, she never took her ring off again. Not even to shower. What Julia didn't know was, Jill had a plan. If it worked, it would be great. If it didn't, it could backfire, and she would have to run out to the porch. She left the ring box on the porch right in front of the front door. If Tony opened it, it would work. If he just picked it up and started to leave, she would have to stop him. When Tony got out of the car. He stopped for a moment. He just looked at the house. He started up the walkway towards the porch. They heard him walked up the steps. Jill knew by this time he had seen the ring box. Would he open it, or just leave? He didn't walk in, and she didn't see him walking off the porch. She thought he must have opened it. Tony did open it. Inside the box, there was no ring. There was a note folded up. He put the box in his pocket and sat down on the porch. Jill and Julia could see him from the window. Julia not knowing what was going on whispered to Jill, "What the hell is he doing."

Jill replied, "Just watch."

Tony was pressing the note as if to feel if the ring was inside. He slowly opened the note. He held it on his lap. He was hesitating to read it. The anticipation was driving Jill crazy. She whispered, "Just read the Damn note." Julia said, "You are taking a big chance."

Tony finally lifted the note to read it. It read as follows:

My Dearest Love,

You are the light that brings sight to my soul. You are the breeze that flows gently over my skin. You are the faith when I feel I have none. You are my world, my life, and the reason I awake each and every day. My head is screwed on straight. It always has been. I have been scared. I am no longer afraid. You are my strength.

I have not taken my ring off since you left. Can you find it in your heart to forgive me? I want you and I to spend the rest of our lives together. Separated, we were like two lost souls wandering in the night, not knowing which path we are on. Together, our hearts combine as one, and our souls are like one that knows the path it is taking. I love you now and will love you forever.

I'm inside waiting for you. Get up off your ass, come in, and hold me and kiss me.

All my love,

Jill

Tony sat for a brief moment. Jill watched him wipe a tear from his cheek. When he stood to face the door, she couldn't wait. She stood and went to the door and opened it. The note fell to the ground as Tony and Jill held each other and kissed which seemed like a lifetime. They walked in, and Julia noticed the note on the ground. She got up and picked it up and closed the door. Jill and Tony walked into the kitchen. Frank walked over to Julia. He knew she would want to read the note. He wanted to stop her. He couldn't. Rather than argue, he let her read the note, which he also read. Julia had tears running down her face as she walked into the kitchen. Tony got up to say hi. When he did, she wrapped her arms around him and gave him a hug. She lifted up the note and said, "You dropped this on the porch. I'm sorry, I'm a mother, I couldn't help but read it." She handed it to Tony and sat down. Tony sat as well. Julia added, "Save that note somewhere safe. At any time during your marriage you feel troubled, take it out and read it together. Never forget why you both are together." She gave Jill a kiss and left the kitchen.

CHAPTER ELEVEN
LET'S PLAY HOUSE

The following weekend Jill would be going back with Tony. Her doctors follow up was on Tuesday. Jill learned a lot about herself this past week. She had forgotten how strong she was. She and Tony talked about this. Jill wanted him to understand what she was going through. Tony listened. However, he never apologized for last weekend. He felt he made a stand. If he apologized for hurting her, he thought that would take the meaning of what he did away. Jill never knew his limits, because they were never tested. If they were to spend the rest of their lives together, it would be important for both of them to know how far they could push one another. They didn't discuss those events. Tony understood everything Jill had told him. He explained to her what she went through was a traumatic experience, and her reactions were normal. It was now time to do what that always agreed they would do. Whenever there was an issue, once resolved, leave it in the past. Tony explained it's was time to leave this in the past.

He asked, "Do you realize that next weekend you are coming back with me to our house?

"That's all I've been thinking about. I can't wait."

Tony suggested that she use her last week home to have fun and clear her head. She needed to focus on her last year at school. Jill agreed. She explained that she felt bad she couldn't do any internship time over the summer, but with Tony going to school and working part-time at the firm, this would give her time to get that done. For the past couple of weekends, Tony was bringing her things back to the house. At most, Jill would only have one bag bring back when she moved.

Tony asked, "What do you think, are you going to try starting your classes on time?

"Yes. I am completely off the pain meds. I don't need to nap during the day. Hopefully, on Tuesday, the doctor will tell me I can completely stop that other medication that makes me feel fatigued. I have just about stopped it on my own anyway."

Tony thought that was great progress. Classes didn't start for just under three weeks. He told Jill that would give her time to get settled and back into a routine before they hit the books. Julia and Frank came into the kitchen and asked if they were still talking. Tony said, "No, that's all in the past now." Julia put on some coffee and suggested they all go into the living room. They all sat down, and they were talking about the upcoming week. Tony excused himself for a minute. He promised he would call his mom. Jill went with him. They both spoke to Carmela for a moment. She was very happy they worked this out. She explained that she had seen this before while counseling other women. She explained it was the same for her. Vince also reached a point and had to knock some sense into me to bring me back to reality. They ended their call and went back into the living room.

Julia and Jill were talking about what they wanted to do during her last week at home. Frank and Tony were talking about golf. Frank interrupted and asked, "Do you all want to go to the club tomorrow? I just want to say that Tony made an outstanding impression at the dance. The owner of the firm that is interested in Tony invited us to play 18 holes tomorrow with him and his business partner. He also wanted us all to go to dinner. I think they want time to get to know Tony better. This is a great opportunity to do some networking son. Depending on where Jill finds work, it's always nice to have other options."

Everyone thought that was a great idea. Jill added that on Sunday, she wanted to spend time alone with Tony. Julia asked, "Honey, you sound a bit confused. What's on your mind?"

Jill explained, "Nothing serious. I was telling Tony that I felt bad that I didn't have the opportunity to do my internship over the summer. I really wanted to do some time in. Who knows, maybe I would have a chance to get a job here."

Julia said, "I can understand that. Let me add a
piece of good news to this. Do you remember
Maryanne, the manager at the clinic in town?"

Jill asked, "The one that runs the marriage counseling
service and the troubled youth clinic?

"That her. Anyway, I was telling her what your studies were,
and you were going into your senior year and needed to get
some internship time. She asked me why you didn't go to see her
when you were hone all summer. Honey. You know we can trust
Maryanne. I explained the situation. She told me she wanted to
meet with you. She will be at the club tomorrow. She wants to
talk to you about doing an internship during your holiday break.
She really needs help and is looking to add more counselors. She
told me you were a hometown girl and had more experience than
most. She knows you love children. I think you would be a perfect
fit for her." Jill was very excited about this and looked at Tony.

Tony said, "Babe, don't look at me. This all works out perfectly.
I would love to do an internship here at the same time, but I will
be working part-time at the firm. They do close for one week,
and maybe I can do a week at the firm here if they let me. I
can't afford to quit the job. We will need the income, and my
schedule is easier than yours. I don't want you to work. Don't
forget, my work time counts as internship time. I think it would
be irresponsible for us not to explore every option. What do you
think? Does that make sense?" Jill, Julia, and Frank agreed.

Frank added, "Tony, I know so much is happening at once.
Sometimes opportunity only knocks once. The firm here is
much larger than the one you are working for. The opportunities
for advancement are greater. I think they may ask you to
do an internship with them over your holiday break."

Tony looked amazed. "That's great, and I want to do it, but I need
that job back at school. I can't make that kind of money working
anywhere else. I doubt they will give me the whole month off. I
know you are paying most of our expenses by not having to pay

the school for a dorm room and meal plan. I've have paid off the
other item and have saved enough money to get us through the
school year. I started paying on my school loan early as well.
We'll have to see how it plays out. I would love to do it though.
How great would that be if Jill and I could get job offers here?"

Frank asked, "I don't want to tell you what
to do, can I make a suggestion?"

"Of course," Tony replied.

"If they ask you to intern here, be honest about your situation
and plan. These are two guys who came from the bottom.
They worked hard to build the company they have today. They
are real people. They may have a solution. Just tell them the
truth. Always tell the truth. The truth is something you never
have to remember, but a lie you have to remember forever."

Tony replied, "I will."

After coffee, Jill and Tony went to Jill's room to relax and
watch a movie. They were both very excited and had much
to talk about. For now, they wanted to relax and enjoy their
time together. They would know more after tomorrow. During
the movie, Jill excused herself to use the bathroom. A few
minutes later, the door opened. Jill stood in the doorway. She
had nothing on. This was the first time she had done this
since the surgery. Jill asked, "Do you like what you see?"

"I love what I see." Tony stepped off the bed. Took off all his
clothes, and walked over to Jill. This was their time for love
and passion. They both needed this. Not only physically, but
emotionally. Jill had made a huge step forward by presenting
herself in this manner. When they spent the last eleven days
together before Jill came home for the summer, many times they
showered together. One or the other would be running around
without clothes on. Jill standing in that doorway, showed Tony she
was comfortable and back to herself. He wanted to acknowledge
that. Not verbally, but emotionally. He knew she would get the

message. And she did. After making love, they fell asleep. Tony woke up in the middle of the night, and they made love again. They were both spontaneous people. Their intimate moments were not scheduled or planned on a calendar. That was one of the things that made it special. One never turned the other away. When they awoke, they both showered. They had a long day ahead of them. They each brought a change of clothes to the club. They could shower and freshen up there before dinner.

Tony and Frank went to start their game, and Jill and Julia went to sit by the pool. They decided to get facials and a body massage. Tony met the firms business partner. It was the first time they had met. Throughout the game, they were talking about Tony's long-term goals and education. Tony explained he wanted to become part of a team at a firm that could offer growth. He explained he had no desire to be the type of employee who jumped from job to job. He was aware he would have to pay his dues no matter where he worked. However, he wanted to be part of a team, not just an employee. He was hoping to work for a company that had a tuition assistance program. He wanted to obtain his master degree and didn't want to wait. He explained that he could handle school and work full time. He had been doing this for some time now. They asked how he liked working for the firm he was with. Tony remembered what Frank said. Tell the truth. Tony explained I enjoy working for them. They have been very good to me. They even gave me a bonus for the suggestions and work I did on the model for a presentation which helped them land the project. I have learned a great deal there. Bill and Blake were the owners of the firm they were playing golf with. Bill said, "That's very good to hear. Mark, who was the owner of the firm Tony worked for, and I, are very good friends. They had finished nine holes and were taking a break.

*****

Meanwhile, Julia and Jill were having their spa time when Maryanne came in. When they were sitting in the sauna, Maryanne told Jill how nice it was to see her. They started to chat about Jill's studies. Maryanne asked her what she wanted to do after she graduated. Jill laughed and replied, "I guess the same as everyone else. Find a job."

Maryanne replied, "Good answer."

Jill explained how she loved working with troubled kids. That would be her first choice. Marriage counseling or general counseling would be her second. Maryanne asked Jill if she would be interested in doing an internship during her holiday break. Jill told her she would love to. Maryanne explained her business was growing rapidly. She now had contracts with many of the surrounding schools. In the next year, she would have to hire more counselors. She didn't want to hire people. She wanted the right people. People with a passion for what they do. Maryanne had a great reputation and did not want to jeopardize that by just hiring anyone with a degree. Jill said, "Let me be upfront. I want to settle somewhere where there is growth. Possibly an opportunity for partnership or associate position might become available one day. She explained she would be obtaining her master's degree. Maryanne told her their goals were the same. It would be a good idea to start with an internship over the holiday break and see how things went. They could talk more at that time. Jill was very excited about this opportunity. She was wondering how the day was progressing for Tony. The subject changed to girl talk.

*****

Back at the golf course, Bill said, "I have a great idea. Tony, what do you think about this? Blake and I have discussed you a few times. The reason he is playing with us today was to meet you. He is quite impressed as I was the first time we met. You have gained a great deal of experience in a short time. We can challenge you to be even better. You are exactly what we are looking for. We are growing and will need more people on board. Would you object to me calling Mark and asking him if you could intern with us over your holiday break, providing it would not jeopardize your job? Mark is no dummy.

He knows we will try to recruit you, but he is also a fair man. He would never hold you back from any opportunity."

Tony replied, "I am honored sir, and thank you for understanding my position and loyalty. I think that is a wonderful idea. It works out well with my fiance's plan to do her psychology internship here during our holiday break."

Bill said, "Let me be totally up front. We like you and want you as part of our team. After you graduate, we would offer a sign on bonus, pay for your master's program, and most likely start you a little higher than entry-level due to your experience and accomplishments. You would have to agree to stay on for five years. If your internship works out, how does that sound?"

"That sounds wonderful. I know my present firm was going to offer me a position after graduation, but to be truthful, much depends on where my fiance finds a job. If all goes well and we both receive offers here, I would gratefully accept that."

Bill replied, "I like that answer. A man's family must be important to him. I will call Mark after we finish the day and make the arrangements. He owes me a favor or two."

They got up to start the last nines holes. Frank whispered to Tony, "Remember I told you that many deals were made on a golf course?" He gave him a wink. There was no more business talk for the rest of the game. They enjoyed themselves and finished the last nine holes. Tony played a good game, but still had a lot to learn. They went back to the clubhouse and met up with the girls by the pool. The men all had something cold to drink and set a time to meet for dinner. Jill and Julia walked over to their table. They asked how their day went. Tony and Frank were both excited, they couldn't wait to tell them the news. After telling them, the girls exchanged their good news. Jill and Tony were both so happy this worked out the way it did. Frank said, of course, you are welcome to stay at the house. Jill, your mother and I talked. While you are here, you know she is planning your engagement party. We will pay to get Tony's family here.

If Carmela agrees and Vince has time off, we thought it would be nice to have Christmas and New Year's together. Frank coughed and under his coughed he mumbled, my wife could use the cooking lessons." They all heard him and laughed.

Jill's eyes were watery. She thought that was a beautiful idea. Tony thanked Frank. Frank added, "Tony, you have turned out to be like the son I never had. Not that I don't love my daughters, I love them more than life itself, but I have grown quite attached to you. Thank you for letting me be a part of this and helping. I am not trying to be your father. You already have a great man doing that for you. I will gladly accept being a good father-in-law."

Tony replied, "Mom, dad, I already look at you as my family. Thank you for everything. Jill and I will not let you down. You will be proud of us."

The rest of the day was great. They all talked about all the possibilities. They separated to get ready for dinner. Dinner was also a wonderful time. Everyone got to meet Bill and Blake's wives. It was a very relaxing evening. Tony thought to himself, these men are like real people. They weren't stuck up. They were very down to earth. At the end of the evening, Bill said, "One last thing everyone. Tony, Mark and I talked. He is fine with you doing an internship with us during your holiday break, and your job will be there when you get back. Blake and I have decided as a sign of good faith, we are going to pay you what you were making with Mark. It's not right that you should lose money. This will also get you on the payroll in the event our future plans materialize."

Thanking them both, Tony replied, "This worked out quite nicely since Jill will be doing her internship with Maryanne at the clinic. I can't thank you enough for what you are doing for us."

Everyone departed and went home. Tony and Jill called Carmela to give her all this news. Carmela was very happy for them and loved the idea of doing Christmas and New Years as a family. It would be a great time to teach Jill some Italian traditions. It also worked out well since the company Vince worked for closed that week. Everything seemed to be falling place. On Sunday, Jill and Tony spent a beautiful day together. Discussing the holiday break, and how lucky they were in so many areas.

Jill said, "Just think babe. If it wasn't for Carl being such an asshole that day, and me having an asthma attack, we might have never met. Do you think you would have ever gotten the courage to approach me?"

Tony replied, "Eventually. Everything happens for a reason."

After dinner, they sat on the porch talking about how this time next week they would be going home together. Jill couldn't wait. She and her mother had some nice things planned for the week. Jill was looking forward to their time together. This certainly turned out to be a rough summer. However, everyone survived it. That was the important part. It was time for Tony to head back. Tony reminded Jill to call her after her follow-up visit on Tuesday with her surgeon. Everyone watched as he drove away. Jill called as she normally did and they talked. She liked to keep Tony company on the drive home. The next week went fairly well. Jill's follow up went well. She was doing fine and did not have to return for six months. She was off all the meds now. She was feeling back to normal. Tony met with his boss and thanked him for letting him do the internship with Bill's firm. Mark said, "Actually Tony, I thought it was an excellent idea. Every firm operates differently. It's good that you see that, even if it means I lose you when you graduate. You always have to do what is right for you and your family. No one has the right to put pressure on you or try to hold you back."

Tony replied, "I have learned so much here. Not only about this industry, but about life. You can't imagine how much your kindness has taught me."

After work on Friday, Tony started for Jill's. This was it. Her last weekend home until the holiday break. Tony had mixed feelings. He was happy she was coming home but said she was leaving her family. He knew that was the cycle of life. One day that would happen with their children. That's how people grow.

For a while, he felt a little sad that he might end up living closer to Jill's family than his own. He knew how much Carmela wanted grandkids. Tony knew where he came from, the pay was much cheaper for his line of work because more candidates were looking for jobs. It was an employers market. He thought when they had children, they would have to find a way for his family to see them at least four times a year. He put those thoughts aside. It would be some time before they had children. They weren't even married yet, and that wouldn't happen until after graduation, and they were settled somewhere. When you drive as much as Tony did, you have time to think. Tony wondered how the world got to a point, and how disappointing it was that families had to separate because of jobs. It wasn't like years ago when he was growing up. Many of his older cousins had children and lived in other parts throughout the country for the same reason. Somehow, it just didn't seem fair. These were all thoughts to discuss at a later time. For now, getting Jill home was paramount. They had a nice weekend planned. On Saturday night they were cooking at home and would all enjoy the night together. That night they discussed the holiday break, picked a night for the engagement party, looked over the dates to get Tony's family there, and Christmas dinner. Julia and Carmela already talked about that. It would be a traditional Italian dinner. Julia had never experienced that. Carmela would email her a list of what to get at the store. Julia, Jill, and Callie would learn about Italian cooking this year. Carmela's daughters already knew how to cook. It would be a fun time.

It was Sunday, and almost time for Jill and Tony to leave. It was time to play house. They only lived together for eleven days. This would be the true test. They got along so well, they did not expect any problems. They had a unique respect for one another. There was an emotional moment when they were about to leave. This family went through hell together this summer. Tony and Jill transcended time, space, and distance. Julia and Jill were hugging each other very tight, and both had tears in their eyes.

Tony said, "Let's not forget. We will be visiting for one weekend each month. I have to get my golf game up to

par if I'm going to beat dad. We won't be strangers." That
helped to break the emotional feelings of that moment.

This was amplified by the fact that next week, Callie would also
be leaving to go back to school. Although they were twins, they
had different personalities. Jill and Julia were always closer. Cassie
was not as warm an individual as Jill. This was a house that was
filled with family for three months, and would now be an empty
nest again. Julia was not looking forward to going back to work.
However, she was happy to hear she would see Jill more often.
Before this plan was developed, Jill only came home on breaks.
They had many things to plan for, and Julia was happy about
that. On the drive back, they were like two school kids who had
just started dating. This was an exciting time for them. When
they got home, Jill got herself settled in. Nothing had changed
since she left. Jill remembered Tony telling her when she went
home for the summer, he wouldn't do anything until she moved
in. He kept his promise. Together, they would now make it their
home. When they chose this apartment, they thought this would
be where they would be living after graduation. Now, with all
these new possibilities, that might change. This changed their
plans as to how much they wanted to do there. They might only
be there until the end of the school year. They decided to wait
as see. Only do the things that needed to be done until they had
a better idea as to where their future would lead them. They sat
and relaxed and were talking about choosing a wedding date.
They decided shortly after graduation and they were settled
would be a good time. It was getting late, and they were both
tired. When they got in bed, they cuddled. They were both happy
they could be in the same bed. It was real. It finally happened.

Jill said, "It went by fast. Remember how we both felt this
day would never come? The summer would seem like
forever. I know it was hard on you making the drive every
weekend. I am glad we did it. It worked out for the best.
My mother and father have come to love you so much."

"You're right. It worked out perfectly. To do it any other way
would have been selfish. Your parents were great to us and

accepted me much better than I thought they would. I love them as well." They kissed goodnight and fell asleep.

Monday morning Tony left for work. Jill was having a cup of coffee and was thinking, as great as this was, it would now mean work. When they lived in the dorm, their meals were paid for. All they had to do was go to the cafeteria. They didn't have to cook. They certainly could not eat out for breakfast, lunch, and dinner every day. Maybe they should have paid for the meal plan? Jill called home to speak to Julia.

She asked, "Mom, what the hell am I suppose to cook every day? I never thought of this part."

Julia laughed and replied, "You are finding out that playing house is not that easy. Don't panic. Go shopping. Get breakfast cereal, bananas, oatmeal, and eggs. Breakfast is easy. Do things that are quick and simple. On the weekends, you can make a bigger breakfast. For lunch, get some bread and cold cuts, or things to make salads. There are many things you can do for dinner. Pre-made meals, go out or do take out once or twice a week. Do you have a grill?"

"Yes. There is a grill that the tenants can use in the yard."

Julia replied, "Get some steaks and boneless chicken breasts and frozen vegetable. Honey, cooking is no different than how you choose your clothes. Get the essentials, and simply mix and match."

Jill felt much better and replied, "Of course. I can do this. I want to have a nice meal ready for Tony when he comes home from work. I'll run to the store now. Thank you for the great ideas."

When they hung up, Julia started laughing. Playing house is more than playing with dolls and having sex. It's the real world. Her little girl was finding that out. Jill also had Carmela's receipt book. That would come in handy. That night Jill panned a nice meal. Tony was normally home by five. It was five-thirty, and he hadn't gotten home yet. He didn't call, and his cell phone was going straight to voicemail. Dinner was ready. There was no Tony. She thought he was in a late meeting. However, he always called when his scheduled changed before they lived together. She wondered, was he going to stop doing that now? It was six-thirty, and she was starting to really worry. She called home. She didn't want to call Carmela and make her worry. She thought that maybe Tony tried to call, and she was in a bad service area, but there were no voice messages.

Julia tried to calm her down, and Frank was also listening to the conversation. As they were talking, Jill had an incoming call. She put Julia on hold to take it. As it turned out it was the hospital. Jill started to panic and asked them to hold so she could connect her mother on the other line. When they were all connected, Jill asked what was going on. The nurse identified herself as the charge nurse in the emergency room. Tony was in an accident. Her number was in her wallet as his emergency contact. Jill asked if he was alright. The nurse told her that they could not discuss his condition over the phone without knowing who she was. She needed to come to the hospital. Julia asked if his condition was stable and what his injuries were. The nurse told her all she could say is he was sable. She left Jill her name and told her to ask for her when she arrived. Jill told her she would be right there. Jill did not want to call Carmela and get her worried until she knew more. Julia told her to stay calm. She and Frank were leaving now and would meet her at the hospital. The hospital was too long of a walk. Jill called for a cab but was told it would be at least thirty minutes. It would take her parents about two and a half hours to make the drive. Between the wait, and the drive to the hospital, Jill wouldn't get to the emergency room for an hour. She took this time to get the spare room ready so her parents could stay over if they wanted. She wrapped the food and put it in the refrigerator and went outside to wait for her ride.

It took almost an hour for her ride to arrived. By the time she got to the hospital, her parents would only be an hour away. Jill had never had to go through this before, yet go through it alone. Her mind was thinking crazy thoughts. Would he be alive by the time she got there? When Jill arrived, she went right in and asked for the nurse by name. She was very busy at the time, and Jill had to wait for her to come out, which took almost another thirty minutes. They were very busy. There were police officers all over the emergency room. Something must have happened. The ambulances just kept arriving. Jill was fighting not to lose control. No one would tell her what was going on. Jill's parents arrived just as the charge nurse was coming out to greet her.

Jill introduced herself as Tony's fiance and showed her her ID. When Tony was brought into the emergency room, he gave the hospital permission to talk to Jill, her family, or his family. She explained that Tony hadn't gotten back from his cat scan yet. She asked them to follow her to the family room, and the doctor would be in shortly to talk with them. Minutes seemed like hours. Around fifteen minutes later, a young doctor walked in an introduced himself. He apologized for all the delays. There was a major accident on the highway, and they got bombarded with many patients all at once.

He explained while Tony was driving home, he was struck broadside on the driver's side by a drunk driver who ran a stop sign. The police had him in custody. He explained he wanted to wait for the results of the x-rays and scans before he came in to speak with them. Tony was awake and was waiting for transport to bring him back down. His scans were negative. He did not have any significant head injuries. He sustained a left dislocated shoulder, a couple of broken ribs, and had many small cuts from the broken glass. A couple required stitches. They gave him some medication for the pain. When he returned, they would set the dislocated shoulder. He would be in a sling for a few days and may need some physical therapy, but should have a full recovery. He explained that he was very lucky. When the paramedics brought him in and should them the pictures of the car, they couldn't believe he was alive. He told them he was sorry, but your car is totaled. Jill asked when they could see him. The doctor said I will let you see him for a minute when he gets back. Then we will have to set his shoulder, and you could come back in. We will watch him for a while and repeat the cat scan. If there are no changes, we will release him. Everyone thanked the doctor and said they would wait. They called Carmela and let her know.

She was happy. Tony was alright and thanked Julia and Frank for driving all the way to the hospital. She told Jill she was a very strong woman and also thanked her. She asked Jill when Tony got home to have him call so she could hear his voice, and if anything changed to call her right away. Carmela added. "My God, you kids have been through so much this year. Stay strong."

Jill replied, "I know, and we will. Tony is my whole life."

Tony came back, and they all went in to see him. They were only able to stay for a moment. The doctors wanted to get his shoulder set, but at the time, the cat scan was more important. When they walked in Tony looked like hell, but was in good spirits. Maybe that was the pain medication. He would certainly be sore the next day. He was happy to see everyone and thank them. He felt bad the Frank and Julia made that drive. Frank told him not to worry about that or the car. He would take care of the car and get him a rental until the insurance companies figured this out. He also told him not to discuss this with anyone other than the police. He would have a local lawyer he knew contact him. He added, "Do what he tells you to do." Frank called his friend and asked him to represent Tony. He told Frank not to worry. He would come right down. When he got to the hospital, he had already spoken to friends he had in the department. This guy's alcohol level was two and a half times above the legal limit. He was under arrest when the hospital released him. He had insurance, but he didn't know the limits to the policy yet. He told Frank they would talk. He met with Tony after his shoulder was set and told him not to discuss anything with anyone other than the police. They would talk in a few days.

Tony was very lucky. He remained stable, and the second set of tests were normal. He was released with instructions to follow up with his doctor. Since he didn't have one, his attorney would send him to one. Frank had already called his office and arrangements for a rental car were made. On the way home, they picked it up so there would be a car at home for Jill and Tony. It was all part of the firm's insurance policy. The two insurance companies would work out the details. Tony was pretty sore as the medications were starting to wear off. They got the prescription the hospital gave him filled in the pharmacy. Tony had gotten hurt before and was not a fan of pain medications.

At home, Julia and Jill took out the dinner that Jill had prepared. There was plenty for all. Jill made extra for later in the week. She told Tony that this dinner was his first surprise, but he ended up surprising her. They all ate, and dinner was delicious. Tony would be fine to start school in two weeks, but they wanted him to take the rest of the week off from work. Tony told Jill he would take tomorrow off but go in on Wednesday. Tony insisted that Frank and Julia not drive back that late and stay the night. They had plenty of food for breakfast in the morning. They agreed. The next couple of weeks went well. Tony healed fine, and Jill was able to start classes on time. Life was finally going as planned. Tony had a great part-time schedule at the firm. He managed to move one class around to have a full day off so he could be in the office at least one full day a week. As it turned out, when Tony was in the hospital, Jill saw one of the psychologists that did a lecture for one of her class last year. She remembered Jill because they had a great discussion during the class that stuck out in her mind. She had given Jil her card and told her to call her when she was ready to do her internship, and she would have her do it with her in the hospital.

Things seemed to be falling into place. School, Tony's job, Jill was putting many hours in getting her of internship time completed at the hospital. In both the adult and children's units. It was almost Thanksgiving. Jill and Tony would spend it at Jill's parent's house. Tony's lawyer reached a settlement on the lawsuit. This was a slam-dunk case. The driver was in the wrong, he got arrested, it was not his first DUI, and his alcohol level was through the roof. His insurance company did not want this to go to court. They were eager to settle. Tony's car was replaced, and they had a nice chunk of money left over which would go into a joint bank account they set up.

*****

It was Thanksgiving. While everyone was together, they had a phone conversation with Carmela. The date was set for the engagement party at the time when Tony's family would be there for the Christmas holiday. They made all the arrangements to have Tony's family at Jill's parents. Carmela saved some money for the tickets, and Frank contributed as well. Since Tony and Jill had settled the case, they insisted on putting money in. Tony felt this was his family, and Frank had done so much already. He was happy they would all be together for the holidays and the party. Jill and Tony's grades were the highest in the class for this semester. They both made the dean's list again. During Christmas break, they would be doing their internships in California. Although Tony and Jill did not attend church every week, they did believe in God and had great faith. They believed that things were going well because they never lost their faith when things were very difficult.

When Christmas break arrived, Jill and Tony were at Jill's parents and started their internships. Less than a week later, Tony's family would arrive. Christmas would only be a few days away, and the party was the following weekend. Tony's family would stay for New Years and go back home. During this time, Jill and Tony spoke to their parents about a wedding date towards the end of June or July the following year. That felt by that time, they would know where they had jobs and would be living. In the fall, they would start their master's program. Doing it part-time would take close to two and a half to three years. They didn't want to go full-time and not work full time. They wanted to buy a house and not keep renting. Everyone thought that was workable and a solid plan.

CHAPTER TWELVE
WHEN A PLAN COMES TOGETHER

Jill's and Tony's internships were going very well. Christmas dinner was a grand success. Everyone pitched in to help. Italian tradition was the Christmas Eve fish feast, followed by the huge Christmas dinner the following day. They cooked enough to eat for the following week. Jill's parents never saw this much food at one meal, and they loved it. Frank told Carmela she should move to California. He could get her a job as head chef at the Golf club, and with Franks experience, he would have no trouble finding a job. He could actually work for Frank's firm as a property manager. Tony's brothers and sisters loved that idea. They fell in love with California. They mentioned since the kids were facing the reality of obtaining jobs offers in the area, it would be wonderful to have the entire family close. Saturday came, and their engagement party was that night. Earlier in the week Jill, Julia, and Carmela had gone shopping, and each bought a dress for the party.

All the women looked beautiful, and the men handsome. They had a wonderful turnout. Everyone they invited came. Frank and Julia never missed one when they were invited. It was payback time. For some members, they attended one for each child. Tony and Jill would do quite well. Not knowing what they needed, most gave a cash gift. This was ideal for them. With the lawsuit, what they would save on their own, and this party, anywhere they moved they would have enough for a down payment on a house. The party was a complete success, and everyone had a great time. Julia spared no expense and had the best of everything. Jill got a little tipsy. This was the first time Tony had ever seen her this way. She was not a big drinker. She was very funny. They loaded her up with coffee. Between the dancing and the coffee, she was almost sober. There was a photographer who also made

a video. Carmela ordered three copies of all the photos and
video. One for Tony and Jill, and one for each family to have.

Tony's grandparents who lived on the first floor were very old.
They did not come. Most of Tony's family were spread out, but
send a card with money in it, as did their friends. Over the years,
Carmela and Vince never missed these occasions and always sent
a card with money in it. What goes around comes around, or at
least it should. Even though Tony's family was spread out, they
were relatively close and often spoke by phone. No one felt as
if they had to keep up with the Jones. They believed it was the
thought that counted. People sent what they could afford, and that
was appreciated. Later that night when they got back to the house,
they opened their gifts. Julia and Carmela wanted to make a list
of what people gave. They would have to reciprocate to their own
families and friends when that time came. As it turned out, Jill and
Tony made far more than even their families expected. All the kids
were exhausted and went to bed. Vince asked Frank if they could
talk privately before they turned in. Frank and Vince stepped out
to the porch to have a cigar. Tony's father asked him to join them.
When they sat down, Vince explained that he wasn't the type to
beat around the bush, and wanted to get right to the point. Frank
told him he was the same way, and appreciated that quality.

Vince said, "Tony tells me he and Jill's internship is going very
well, and there is a strong chance he and Jill will be offered
jobs and may live move to this area. Frank, I may not be a fancy
businessman, but I have always worked hard. I can see the writing
on the wall. I own a three-family house which is finally paid off.
Tony's grandparents are old. They live on the first floor. We have
to take care of them. We live on the second, and I rent the third to
a young couple whose family lives right around the corner. The
neighborhood is decent, but may not stay that way. Since my house
is much bigger than my tenants families house, they have asked
me many times if I would be interested in selling it. They would
have both sets of parents live there, and they would buy it together.
My tenant's wife is pregnant. Having both their parents living in
the same house would be a great convenience. I know one-day,
Tony and Jill will have children. It will kill my wife not to be able

to see them more than three or four times a year, but I can't hold Tony back. It's his time to live, and their time to start their family when they are ready. As we get older, like you, we just want to be a part of it. I know the way my wife thinks, and my children love it here. I want what's best for my family. I don't think New Jersey is that place. I certainly cannot afford anything like this house, but I have been looking while we have been here. There are smaller homes with an in-law setup that would be perfect for my family, and Tony's grandparents. I could never make that move without having a job. Carmela has been bugging me to go to work because the kids are older now, and she is bored to death. I have worked at my company long enough that my pension is maxed out. I'm only working for the overtime now. I am very flexible. Were you serious about the things you mentioned the other day?"

Frank replied, "Regarding the chef position at the club, and the property manager position at my firm?"

"Yes. I am not asking for a hand out here …." Frank interrupted him and said, "Let's get one thing straight. I'm not offering one. I have too much respect for you to insult you that way. If we do this, trust me, you would work for your money."

Vincent replied, "I'm not afraid to work. My company switched our pension to a 401k a couple of years ago. I can take that with me."

Frank sat for a moment in silence. "I am the director of the golf club. I can't tell you how many relatives of board members work there. We take care of our own. Our families are now one family. We will help each other. Next year the head chef is retiring. In June, if my memory serves me correctly. I have needed a property manager for some time now. We manage so many properties, the one man I have can't handle it alone much longer. With all that has been going on, I just haven't gotten around to hire anyone yet. If you wanted to do this, we could make this happen, and in your timeframe. If Carmela only wants part-time, that's fine. She can still work in the catering department. The weather here is different than New Jersey. We book events twelve months a year, and the club is always booked."

Vincent looked at Tony and said, "Son, I haven't said a word of this to your mother. I wanted to talk to Frank first, and talk to you. How do you feel about this?"

"Dad. Are you kidding me, I would love it. Jill would love it. I can tell you this. I know she wants to take a job here. She has never come out and said it, but just the way she talks, I know. I can't please everyone. I can't live on two coasts at the same time. I do not want to see either side miss out on seeing their grandkids grow up. However, I know my opportunities to make better money and get ahead are not on the East Coast, or even where we live now. They are here. Jill and I would be very happy if you moved here. I know this sounds selfish, but it would certainly make it much easier for us to decide where to take jobs, and live somewhere without feeling guilty. Dad, I say do it. I've seen you work so hard your whole life, not meaning you wouldn't work hard here, but the winters are rough. You and mom deserve this, and our family deserves it. Everyone loves it here."

Frank said, "Well, it sounds to me like a decision had been made."

Vince replied, "I believe it has. I believe it has."

Frank said, "Since that's the case, and you are leaving in the morning, why don't the men of this family give the women in this family the good news, and Vince, it should come from you. After all, it is your idea."

They got up and went inside. Vince asked Julia, Jill, and Carmela to come and sit at the table and gather the kids. When they all sat down, Vince said, "Ladies, I have some news. Frank wanted this to come from me. However, I want you all to know that this is not only my decision. Frank, Tony, and I talked about this. We are all in agreement." The girls and the kids were looking at them with great curiosity.

Julia said, "Well Vince, don't keep us hanging. Tell us."

"Julia, I know everyone is tired. Frank can give you the details another time as to how this came about. The bottom line is this. Carmela, you know the house is paid for, and my pension is maxed out and in a 401k. You know we have an opportunity to sell the house. Tony and I have spoken, and it appears that he and Jill have a great opportunity to work in this area when they graduate. We both know that seeing our grandchildren regularly will be very difficult for us to adjust to. We have lived to one day have grandchildren. I know that. While I was here, I looked into housing. We have to take your parents with us. I spoke with Frank about work, which I will fill you in on later. Tony also supports this. Together we have decided this a smart decision, and the time is right for us to do this since we can get a good price for the house now. The kids love it here and have been talking to me all week to move here. You have been talking to me almost every day about going back to work. I think this is the time. What do you all think?"

Jill sprang right up, ran over to Vince and gave him a hug and said, "YES! I'm all for this."

Julia replied, "I think that's a perfect plan. I think you should do it."

Carmela was listening and sat for a moment. With tears rolling down her face. She couldn't speak. Vince reached out, held her hand, and said, "I'll take that as a yes."

Franks said, "Let's work on this and make it happen."

Tony added, "Since we are playing let's share the news, Jill and I have something to share. Jill was offered a position by Maryanne after she graduates and the firm has offered me once as well. We have decided to accept them. We still have many details to work out, but after Maryanne spoke to the psychologist where Jill is doing her internship at school, she told Jill she had to bring her on board. She was a perfect fit. I must say, this has been the best week of news I've heard in some time. Whoever expected this much could happen in one week" All the kids were excited.

There were many opportunities for them. There would be a great deal of planning to make this dream turn into a reality.

The following morning everyone was up and getting ready to leave for the airport. Before they left for the airport, Frank said, "Okay, we have a plan. Vince. Do not lose the opportunity to sell your house. Julia and I spoke last night. Sell it. Cassie goes back to school next week. We have plenty of room if you sell it and need a place to stay until you find one. Carmela can start working if she wants. You can put your things in storage until you find a place. The way the housing market is if you can sell it, do it."

Vince replied, "I will, and thank you. We will do our share. I have three unused weeks of vacation on the books. We should be able to find something during that time."

Everyone took the ride to the airport. They went in two cars. Jill and Tony were going to head home from there. They left a little earlier because Vince spotted a house online he wanted them to see. It was not that far from Franks. It needed a little work, and he could do it. It was exactly what they needed, and could afford it. There was an open house that day. They could see the house. Tony put the address it into the GPS. It was only five minutes out of the way, and they went right over. They did their walk through and loved the house. It was perfect, and exactly what they needed. Vincent explained his situation to the realtor. She gave him her card. She explained that in the price range Vincent wanted to spend, this was the best deal on the market. It needed some work. Nothing major. It had been vacant for some time. Vincent could easily handle that, and the owner was aggressively looking to sell. Vincent thought they could make a deal that would work. He would talk to his tenants tomorrow. They were really pushing him to sell his house. One of their parent's leases was almost up, and the other already had their house sold. They were pressured for time. Vincent and Carmela thought this could come together very quickly.

Carmela added, "I would love to get rid of most of our old furniture and get new things. I hate to pay to have to move that old stuff."

"We can talk about that. Let's see what kind
of deal I can make with our tenants."

Jill stepped in to say, "Don't worry mom. Between all
of us, we will make this work. Everyone has done so
much for us, we want to help where we can. Besides,
we are getting two sets of babysitters in return."

The in-law setup was perfect for Tony's grandparents. After they
were gone, it could be used for the other children as well. The
house needed new gutters, painting, and minor repairs. Tony
could help his dad on the weekends. This was sounding too
good to be true. Vince thought the three weeks vacation time he
would be cashing out was plenty of time to get the house fixed
up. He explained he would fly out and stay there for a week
and get all of the inside painting done. The following week the
movers would come. The last week they would make the drive.
His car was older. If he could sell it and got enough for the house,
they could take some clothes, fly out, and make due until the
movers arrived. He could buy another car when they arrived.

Jill said nonsense. My dad said you all can stay at their house. It
would only be for a week or so. You all can't sleep on the floor."

*****

Next week the process started. The details they would
decide on as things developed. Much would depend on how
quickly the tenants would want to close on their house.

Vincent said, "I don't want to be putting the cart before
the horse here. We will take it as it comes."

Jill and Tony saw them off at the airport and started the
rest of the drive to their house. Jill feel asleep for some of the
drive. They were up late, and up early. She still didn't have
all her stamina back. Tony was happy they were finally going
home, and his life could get back to being normal. When they
got home, they relaxed and went out to get take out. They forgot

to take the leftovers home with them. Neither of them felt like cooking. It was a good night for pizza or Chinese food. They both could tell the other was happy being in their own house.

Monday came, and the realtor called to tell Vince there was someone that might put an offer in on the house in the next day or two. She suggested he get his offer in first. The house had been sitting, and the owner might jump at it. If he did, he could put down the minimum down payment to secure the contract. Vince told her he would call her later that night. He discussed this with Carmela. Hopefully, his talk with the tenants would go well. Vincent wasted no time. He left a note on the tenant's door call him regarding the sale of the house. Later that evening, the tenants called. They decided to set up a meeting with everyone to discuss this. They decided on Tuesday, the following day. They seemed very excited, but Vince had to decide on this other house. Would he take the gamble and make an offer, or run the risk of losing it. He and Carmela spoke again and decided to take the gamble. Vince called the realtor and made a reasonable offer. Within a half an hour, she called back. The owner accepted the offer. They did not want to tell anyone yet until this was a done deal. He knew his tenants would want to close quickly.

While Tony was at work, Jill did some shopping. They would have to get used to doing some cooking. She called her mother who helped her make a grocery list. When Tony got home, Jill had the week all planned out, Tony was impressed. No matter what his parents did, they still had another six months of school to complete until they could move. Rob and Jodie called to see if they wanted to get together this week. They had something they wanted to tell them. Jill still had not told them what happened that summer. Jill looked at this as something very personal. Not something she wanted anyone to know. It wasn't necessary. They planned a get together on Friday night. Tony's part-time boss wanted him to stay on when he started school, but Tony wasn't sure and told him he would let him know. It was not a difficult job, and the extra money they could save. Jill thought if he wanted to, she would support it, but she was also doing some tutoring again, and that money was being saved. That Friday night, Tony and Jill were in for a big surprise.

On Tuesday evening, Vince met with his tenants and their families. He did not want to appear as if he was in a rush. He knew they were. He needed to get every dollar he could for the house. There wasn't a larger house in that neighborhood, and none were in as good as condition as his. When they all met, he explained that after being asked about selling the house so many times, he and Carmela had given it a great deal of thought. He explained his son and fiance were going to move to California after graduation, and it made sense for them to do the same. He decided they were going to put the house on the market. His tenants and families were quite pleased. They asked how soon the house could be available. Vince explained that was flexible, he knew of their time issues. They asked what he would be asking. He explained he hadn't decided yet, but before a realtor was involved, if they were ready, make him an offer. After some discussion, Vince was not happy with their first offer. He came back a bit on the high side because the house was in perfect condition. It had been recently sided, had new gutters, and the roof was replaced last year. The house was in turn key condition and didn't need anything. He thought they would try to get him down, but to his surprise, they explained they had been looking at houses every day for the past two weeks. Nothing compared to this house. They said they would pay his price. They would not need a mortgage since his tenants had money saved, the wife's family has money saved, and the balance of the money would come from the sale of the other house, which was only six weeks away.

Vincent explained the timing was not a problem. It would give him time to get things ready and move. They could close on the same day. They shook hands, and they gave him a deposit check. Vincent took their attorneys information and said he would have his attorney contact theirs to set up the contract. The other parties were going to set up the house inspection. This was a requirement for their insurance company. Vincent was fine with that. Everyone was happy. The following day, the attorneys called their respective clients to stop by and sign the contract. Vincent and Carmela went to his attorney's office after work to sign the contract, as did the other buyers. Vincent gave him the deposit check to be held in escrow. The house inspection was scheduled for Saturday. Vincent called the realtor from California and gave her the update. He knew the house needed some work. The realtor gave him the number for a mortgage broker. It was unlikely they would be able to close that soon since he had to obtain a mortgage. However, he was putting so much down it might go quicker.

That night Vincent called Frank and informed him of everything. Frank thought that was great. He told Vincent they could stay at their house until the closing if the timing didn't work out. Frank a mortgage broker very well and offered to put Vince in touch with him. They had done a great deal of business together. He told Vincent he would call him to see if he could move things along quicker. He asked Frank for a favor. The house inspection for his house was scheduled for next Monday. He wondered if Frank could be there for him. Frank told him that wasn't a problem. He would get the details from the realtor. He also explained he probably knew everyone involved since he had so many real estate transactions over the years. Frank said, "I will let you know how it goes. Vincent had put the deposit on the house on his credit card. It would all work out at the closing. Carmela was very excited. She told the kids to start going through their things. Anything they weren't using was going to get thrown out. They wanted to only move what they were keeping. Carmela had made some calls. The best way to go was to get one of those the pods. Load it up in New Jersy, and have it delivered to California. Once they were there, they could unload it themselves than have it removed.

Carmela asked Vince, "How does the money look? Are you going to get rid of the car here and buy one in California?" She also asked "What about furniture? What can I get rid of? Can we afford to buy some new things?

Vincent replied, "We got the new house for less than I thought, and we sold this one for full price. If all goes well and no other costs arise, yes, I will sell the car here. Yes, you can spend up to three thousand dollars on new things. However, I would not buy them here, and then we have to ship them. Wait until we move in."

Carmel replied, "That's what I was planning."

Vincent wasn't going to play around. He was going to wait until the last minute and just bring his truck to the place that advertised they would buy cars outright. Get his check, and be done with it. The following day, he set up bank accounts at a bank Frank recommended, and wired money into those accounts. He still hadn't told his work of this decision. He was planning on working until the last day. He would leave with three weeks of vacation pay that would cover them until he started working for Frank.

Meanwhile, all of this was kept a secret from Jill and Tony. Vincent wanted to wait until everything was in place. His other children were very excited and couldn't wait. He swore them to secrecy. He wanted this to be a surprise. For Tony and Jill. Life was going well for Jill and Tony. They were turning out to be good cooks and enjoyed doing together. Tony kept his part-time job as well as the one at the firm. Jill was tutoring in the evenings that Tony worked and was completing her internship time as well. Jill was completely back to herself. Their intimate moments were better than ever. On Friday night when Jodie and Rob stopped over, they hit them with some news that shocked them. These were two people that wanted nothing to do with commitment or relationships.

As it turned out, because they spent so much time together doing school, and didn't live that far apart, they also spent a great deal of time together during the summer. Two people who started as friends fell in love. This year they went into a co-ed dorm so they would be closer together. Their relationship was going well. Tony and Jill were in shocked and excited about this. This was the last thing they expected. Jodie and Rob were also shocked to find out they were engaged. Jill did not mention her health scare. She wasn't ready to be open about that yet. Jill and Tony were working very hard. After they graduated, they would have more than enough saved to buy a house. Their car was new, they had no debt, and they only spent money when they needed to. Their goal was to have a house.

Jill, Carmela, and Julia had been talking. The wedding date was set for the last weekend in June after graduation. The reception would be at the club. It would be a spectacular event. The church was beautiful. It would be a sit-down dinner with three menu choices. Hor devours and a cocktail hour with a piano player and open bar throughout. They wanted an ice sculpture carving and all the trimmings. Jill wanted a band and not a DJ for the reception. Jill was excited as all these plans were being made. Tony had asked his brother to be his best man, and Jill asked her sister to be her maid of honor. They also asked Rob and Jodie to be in the wedding party, and they gladly accepted. Since Tony and Jill would be starting their new jobs, they planned on taking their honeymoon in the fall or over the cooler months. They hadn't yet decided where they wanted to go. At this point, things could not be any better. Tony and Jill spent a good deal of time with Jodie and Rob, although they liked their private moments as well. They thought that Rob and Jodie could stay with them after school, and go home after the wedding. Jill and Tony already had their wedding party gifts picked out. The balance of the wedding party would be Tony's brothers and sisters, and Jill would ask some of her closest friends. This was a fast pace for Tony and Jill to keep up to. Most of the arrangements for the wedding Julia made with Jill's approval.

*****

Meanwhile back in New Jersy, the house inspection went perfectly. This was a locked in the deal. The house inspection in California also went well. The only issues that came up were the ones that Vince already knew about. The owner agreed to no additional down payment since it would all be paid at the closing. The broker worked very hard to get the bank to approve the mortgage. It wasn't that hard because the equity in the house was very high, and Vincent and Carmela had excellent credit. He expected a definitive answer the following week, If that came through, both houses could close at the same time. Vincent and Carmela did not have to be at the closing in New Jersey. They could sign the papers early. They would have to be at the closing in California. The money would be wired. They needed a two-hour window between the closings for all the transactions to go through.

Vincent let Frank know all the details. He and Carmela chose a moving date. Vincent was going to let the new owners move in sooner providing they had the proper insurance and had the utilities in their names. The pod was delivered, and they had started loading things a little each day, leaving only the essentials out. At this rate, the entire family would be able to fly over at the same time. I was time to tell Tony and Jill. The closing was set for the second week of March. Vince had permission from the owner to have the pod left on the property. They would arrive in California a little less than a week before the closing. Vince would have the insurance and utilities switched, and the owner told them they could start moving their things in when they arrived and start painting and fix things up. He would not let them sleep there until the closing. This worked since the pod should be there three days after they arrived, which gave them time to get the inside ready.

That evening Vince called Frank, who called Tony and placed them all on speaker. Everyone could hear one another. Vince gave Tony and Jill the good news and all the details. They would only have to stay at Jill's parent's house for about a week, and much of that time would be spent getting the new house ready. Julia and Frank offered to help in any way they could. Carmela had already contacted the school to get the children registered, and their records sent over. They would have to start school as soon as they arrived. Tony and Jill were excited. Both of their families would be living within fifteen minutes of one another. Knowing this, Jill and Tony could start looking for their house in April. Frank had many real estate connections, and Tony intended on taking advantage of them. It would be hectic, but a fun time. Tony and Jill would go there on the weekends to help. Tony and Jill had their eye on some new homes that were being built. A very nice neighborhood complex. Frank was on the board as a partner in this project. They would get a good deal on their house. Frank explained that many of the houses would be ready for occupancy, and was selling fast. Tony and Jill would have to move quickly if they wanted one. They decided that weekend, they would go to Jill's parents and look. They had more than enough for the down payment. Anything else they saved they would just add to it to have a cheaper mortgage payment. They still had to start their master's program to consider, but their employers would be helping with that cost. The complex was located about twenty minutes in a different direction. Everyone would be close, but not that close. Tony teased Frank because he would be living closer to the golf course.

That weekend Tony and Jill went back to Jill's parents. On Saturday, the realtor met them and showed them some houses. This was a unique complex. In many of these types of complexes, the houses all looked all the same. Not here. There were five different styles of homes to choose from. Jill fell in love with a contemporary colonial with crown molding. It had four bedrooms and three baths. It was 3600 sq feet and perfect for raising a family. It was a bit more than what Tony wanted to spend, but it was new. When they sat down and did the math, and figured in their discount, they knew they could afford it.

When Tony went to give them the retainer, Frank and Julia stepped in. They insisted on giving them that portion as part of their wedding gift. By the time the home was built, Tony and Jill would be finishing school and could move it. They would start moving some things and leave them at Jill's parents as the time got closer. As a wedding gift, Carmela would buy them some furniture. If they made anywhere near as much on the wedding as they did on the engagement party, they would have no financial problems. They wanted to keep whatever they made at the wedding at the start of their savings account. Tony would be starting at a higher salary range than entry level and was also receiving a sign-on bonus. They would use that to buy Jill a car. Jill would be starting at entry level salary until she was there a year and her degree was confirmed. She would get an increase then, and when she received her masters. They would be making enough money to live a comfortable life.

Next month Jill would go for her Pet scan. If all were negative, she would require one each year for five years. If they were all negative, she would only need to have them every five years. Time went by very quickly. Tony's family had moved and were all settled. Vince had a great job working for Frank. He managed five properties for him. He was excellent at this work. Vincent was a hands-on person, so everyone who worked for him loved him. Frank was very happy with his choice. Carmela started working part-time at the club. She would decide on full time after the head manager retired. The school year was nearing a close, and finals and graduation were in the next two weeks. Tony and Jill's house was complete. They were going to the final inspection over the weekend and would close that Monday. They took that day off. Over that weekend, they would meet with their new employers and finalized their starting dates. Everything went well at the closing. That weekend they picked out their furniture. Most of it would be delivered within two weeks. As it was being delivered, Julia and Carmela would talk to Jill to see where she wanted things. The rest of the decorating Jill would do when they moved in when school was over.

After exams, Tony and Jill got their final grades. They both finished first in their class. They graduated with the highest honors and received many achievement awards. Between their SUV and Rob's truck, they could get the remainder of their personal belonging loaded. The furniture had all been delivered. Rob and Jodie would spend the next three weeks at their house until after the wedding. Between all the girls, the house was completely decorated by the wedding. The house was beautiful. Jill found she had a knack for interior decorating. They had some time. They were not starting their new jobs until after the fourth of July. They only decorated the master bedroom and spare room. They left the other rooms empty anticipating children at some point. Tony and Jill set up one room as an office. They had many books, and Tony had a drafting table as well. It was a very comfortable setting. In the finished basement, Jill had an office in case she ever wanted to do counseling at home.

*****

It was their wedding day. The weather could not have been better. For both families, this would be the first child who would be getting married. The church ceremony was very touching. Tony and Jill made their own vows. Tony's read like this.

"To my bride. Jill. You have brought out the best part of me. You have intertwined your life into mine. You have filled every empty void my heart has ever had. You are not only going to become my wife, but you have also been my best friend. Your laugh, the way you cry, and your emotions, make me feel alive. Together we have survived it all. We have transcended time, space, and distance, with love so strong, that nothing could surpass it. I will forever be devoted to you."

Jill's read as follows.

"Tony. I've longed for a love that we both share. You have taught me how to be strong and overcome any obstacle. Without you, I am not complete. Without you, my heart is empty. Many nights I awake and watch you sleep. It makes me realize how lucky I am to have you. Alone, we were two people searching for something we didn't understand. Together, we ended our search and found the meaning of what we were both looking for. You are my love, my friend, my life. I breathe for you. I awake each day for you. Every thought I have revolves around you. This is what we have. This is what defines our love. I will always be yours, forever."

There wasn't a dry eye in the church. They were pronounced man and wife. As they went for pictures, their guests left for the club and cocktail hour. Everyone raved how wonderful this was set up. They were approximately two hundred and seven- five guests. The reception was wonderful. As with all weddings, at the reception, Tony and Jill were quite busy, and it went over the allotted time. After the wedding, Jodie and Rob headed home. This was not a night to be spending with the newly married couple. Tony and Jill went home. He carried her over the threshold. They never made it to the bedroom.

The next day they would spend with their family opening up their gifts envelopes. Julia was big on that list. She wanted to know if people did for her what she did for their children, and what she needed to do for those that would be getting married. The bride and groom never think of that. They just count the money. One day when their children grew up, they would see how that would change. They did better on the wedding than expected, They had a nice nest egg to start their life with, and had no bills other than their mortgage and utilities, and of course, Tony's school loan. They had already registered to start their master's program at the local college. Some of the classes would be done online. On Monday, they started work. After all both families had been through, the story had a happy ending. An ending that could have easily led to tragedy. Tony and Jill proved that true love can beat the odds when they are stacked up against you. It takes love, family support, hope, and faith in one another; and maybe in a higher power to succeed.

It was late fall, and one day Jill came out of the bathroom. She was holding something in her hand.

Tony asked, Are you alright? You look a little pale."

"I have been throwing up every morning."

Tony said, "We should get you to the doctor."

"That won't be necessary. I have something to tell you." Jill walked over to Tony and handed him what looked like a thermometer.

Jill asked, "Do you know what this is?"

"A thermometer?"

Jill laughed and said, No silly. I'm pregnant."

Tony jumped up and yelled so loud he thought the world would hear him. Jill was pregnant. They called their parents to give them the good news. Many times, life can get complicated. Could Tony and Jill find out that this was just the beginning?

Coming in 2020

My new private investigator series

FROM THE "AX" DIARIES

Trapped In Revenge

Featuring:

Blake "AX" Miller

and

Roxanne "Roxy" Carter

THE END

CREDITS

Book cover design by Jodielocks Cover Designs - https://jodielocksdesign.weebly.com/

Printed in the United States
By Bookmasters